DARKNESS RISING

ALSO BY CHRIS MULLEN

PRAISE FOR CHRIS MULLEN

"Things are heating up down on the border..."

— CRAIG JOHNSON, *NEW YORK TIMES*
BESTSELLING AUTHOR OF THE WALT
LONGMIRE MYSTERIES

"Chris Mullen crafts a twisty tale of Texas-sized intrigue and larger-than-life characters..."

— BRUCE BORGOS, AUTHOR OF *THE
BITTER PAST*

"Cass Callahan is a can't-miss character."

— JAMES WADE, TWO-TIME SPUR
AWARD-WINNING AUTHOR OF *BEASTS
OF THE EARTH*

"Chris Mullen's writing is sharp and action packed. His talent and enthusiasm are enviable."

— CHRIS ENSS, *NEW YORK TIMES*
BESTSELLING AUTHOR

"Chris Mullen crafts a gripping tale of suspense, resilience, and an unbreakable spirit set deep in the heart of Texas."

— JACK STEWART, BESTSELLING
AUTHOR OF *UNKNOWN RIDER*

DARKNESS RISING

CASS CALLAHAN
BOOK FOUR

CHRIS MULLEN

WOLFPACK
PUBLISHING
— EST 2013 —

For those who had the patience to walk through darkness with me

DARKNESS RISING

CHAPTER ONE

I whispered to the darkness, "*What are you hiding?*"
And the darkness answered in spades.

CHAPTER TWO

The crackle of snapping branches, the rush of pounding feet, the low groan of primal irritability—a raucous burst of energy masked in the night thundered aloud, and then, as abruptly as it had disturbed the night, silence fell once more. I stood up, squinting as if I could sharpen my vision to see through the blackness.

"Cass?" Raven's voice fell like gentle puffs of breath on my ears.

I ignored her as I stepped one foot in front of the other, walking into the inky cloak that surrounded us. My fingers twitched at my hips, ready to pull a weapon, but I was unarmed. A muscle memory moment at its finest.

"*¿Qué pasó?*" Chance said, joining me as I strained to locate the cause of the noise in the brush.

A twist of wind and tree limb seemed to shriek as I took another cautious step.

"You heard it, right? Or am I going bat-shit crazy?" I whispered.

"That's debatable, *mi amigo*."

I let out a sigh. "*Cabrón!*"

Stepping further, our feet crunched on a mix of dead grass and displaced gravel.

"*Órale*, now yer speakin' my language." Chance placed a palm on my shoulder, causing me to flinch. "But it's time ya lighten up. There's nothing out there. Just some animal running around. Remember why we are here, *mi amigo*. To relax."

I stopped in my tracks. The stillness of night eased back into focus. The breeze whistled through the trees, caressing my face and refreshing my fractured nerves. A hint of Desert Marigold drifted into my nose, and the soothing trickle of the Rio Grande, a mere hundred feet from our camp, was the therapeutic nudge I needed to come around.

"Yeah," I said.

"Big Bend is full of life. Let it soak in. Let that be what calms you."

I felt the squeeze of Chance's palm and turned to face him. Under a star-speckled sky where the waning crescent moon seemed to drift just above the distant rise of desert cliffs, I could see the shadowed outline of his figure, Stetson, and all, but it was his wide, Cheshire smile that illuminated the night.

I took a slight breath, preparing to answer, when a garbled lowing erupted before us, causing us both to jump. An agitated cow tore through the brush, its blackened form charging like a coal-stained locomotive. It cried as if it were Ferdinand and had been stung by a bee, and we were in the way of its escape. Chance pushed my shoulder back, and we both fell to the side yelling as the cow stampeded between us. Its hooves crushed the ground, narrowly missing my lower leg as it fled whatever invisible terror had spooked it so.

Looking back toward camp, the bumbling bob of a flashlight bounced frantically, then was still as its beam illuminated the cow. As if attempting to buck a bull rider from its back, the cow changed direction and hurried into the night. Snapping branches, rustling hooves, and pitiful lows stained the calm as the frightened cow barreled back into the brush.

Raven met us with the flashlight as Chance and I walked back to camp.

"You two are the perfect pair…" She paused, then laughed. "Of dufuses I've ever seen. The Ranger said there might be a stray cow or two that wanders over from Mexico. Count yourselves lucky if you didn't wake up the whole campground."

I looked at Raven, then noticed she had a hitchhiker tagging alongside. I knelt and looked into the dark eyes of Miguel, the little boy Raven was looking after following his surprise arrival on the CR.

"What do you think, Miguel?"

The boy buried his head behind Raven. She looked down and stroked her fingers through his hair.

"*Todo está bien*," she whispered.

I stood up, my heart rate finally beating at a normal pace.

"Give it time," she said, looking back at me.

I nodded.

"Now, how about a beer, my lovely dufuses?" she said in a loving, sarcastic tone.

"Ah, yeah!" Chance replied. "Ya read my mind."

"Cass?"

Raven's voice was soft. She reached a hand to me and touched my arm.

"Sure thing, Little Bird."

Raven turned around with Miguel still clinging to her and followed the bouncing beam of her flashlight back to camp. I heard her grumble to Miguel as she went.

"Sure wish we could have a campfire. It'd make telling stories so much more fun later, don't you think?"

Chance followed, but I held back a step. Nearby, the Rio Grande flowed lower than usual, causing its water to clash with rocks and stones that emerged along its meandering path. While it's song called to me in lulling harmony, I felt uneasy. What else lurked in the dark, in the brush, beyond the clean, green boundary waters?

"*Amigo! Un cervesa?*" Chance called out.

Setting concern aside, I reminded myself that not everything unseen was a threat and joined my family at camp.

With dripping hands, fresh from diving into the cooler, Chance handed me an ice-cold Modello Especial. We clinked cans.

"*Salud.*"

He swigged from his, and I took a long draw of mine. From lips to stomach, it felt good going down.

The four of us sat in folding chairs around the glow of an LED lantern Raven had placed between us on the ground. It was the closest we would get to enjoying the crackle and dance of fire on this camping trip. NO WOOD FIRES, the multitude of signs read throughout the park. South Brewster County, including the entirety of Big Bend National Park, was under a burn ban. The signs of drought were obvious: brown grass at our feet that looked like over-cooked, dried-up spaghetti, the depleted water level of the Rio Grande, and the tan, arid expanse as far as the eye can see when gazing into the distance from atop the Rio Grande Village Overlook. We were smack dab in the Chihuahuan Desert, and the threat of fire in the region was not a chance anyone was willing to take.

So, here we were. Away from the CR. Away from civilization, without even a blip of cellular service. The sky overhead sparkled with stars that could only be seen on the blackest of nights. Aside from our uninvited guest a few moments ago, the call of wildlife composed a melodic symphony that could calm any soul. It was just what the doctor ordered following the weeks of turmoil in which I had found myself, and yet I felt a raging storm continue to brew inside of me.

I stared into the light, then looked across at Raven. Her arms were wrapped around little Miguel as he nuzzled into her chest. His eyes slowly closed, then opened with the force of a child fighting the sandman. It would be of no use. In fact, I had wished that I were able to sleep so carelessly as Miguel. Raven shared a glance with me, smiling as if she could not have been happier. That was golden.

"Have you heard from your friend, Ray?" Chance asked.

"We talked about a week ago. He's nearly recovered and beating up the brass pretty good to get him placed back on active duty. It was a hard sell explaining his injuries, but thanks to our good friend and professional liar, FBI Agent Thomas Zuñiga, Ray's captain was briefed on his confidential involvement with an ongoing federal case. Zuñiga might as well have stuck a banana in the captain's tailpipe because when he had ended the call, he had left the captain sputtering to understand how Ray had been a part of some multi-jurisdictional task force without his knowledge."

Damn it, Ray! I allowed a smile to crack through my lips.

"They took a page straight out of Eddie Murphy's playbook."

Chance wiped his mouth with his sleeve following another sip of beer, then leaned forward to rest his elbows on his knees.

"Ya know, it's too bad he's not here. Bet there are

plenty of embarrassing Cass Callahan stories he has tucked away."

"Yeah, I bet you'd like to get an earful," I said.

Raven giggled, causing Chance and me to turn our attention to her. She dipped her chin and covered her mouth with a fist, failing to hide the growing convulsions of building laughter dying to be released.

I raised my eyebrows, curious as to what she was thinking.

"Do you have a story to share, Raven?" Chance asked with enthusiasm.

She lowered her fist, then locked eyes with me.

"Uh. I might have one or two you haven't heard yet."

"Rave," I said.

Chance leaned over and picked up the lantern, then positioned it to shine down on Raven as if she were the headliner in the middle of an interrogation room.

"Please, I think it's time we hear the truth." Chance looked over at me, showing teeth under his curling lips.

Branches cracked in the brush across from our campsite. I looked over my shoulder.

"Sounds like our friend has returned."

Chance stood up and raised the lantern above his head.

"*Vete, vaca. No hay nada aquí para ti!*"

The crackling in the darkness continued.

"I don't think that cow speaks Spanish, Chance," I said. "How's that for irony?"

"It heard me. It is like you, I think. Just bein' bullheaded."

Raven snorted, then forced herself to hold back when Miguel stirred on her lap. Drawing our attention once again, Raven drew center stage.

"Out with it, Raven," Chance insisted.

"Okay, okay."

She gave me the side-eye and mouthed "sorry."

The darkness rustled in waves, yet I dismissed the noise.

"Have you heard about the time Cass pulled over the ice cream truck?"

I huffed an exasperated sigh and downed the rest of my beer. I glared at Raven, my eyes begging her not to continue, but it was of no use. I crushed the beer can with my fist.

"You'll regret this," I said playfully.

A loud swish of displaced brush not more than twenty yards from camp tested my resolve. My eyes shifted back and forth. I folded my hands, clasping them together now that I had disposed of my beer can. *Goddamn cow!*

"Maybe, but it's a good..."

Raven froze mid-sentence, her eyes shooting past me, while her jaw dropped open. She instinctively hugged Miguel in a protective grasp.

"Cass!" she yelled.

I stood and twisted around. Chance jumped up, knocking his chair over. Miguel woke with a start, crying out in Spanish, but his words were lost on me.

Stumbling forward with staggard steps was a blackened shadow, its arms reaching out to guide the way as if running blind, and voice murmuring words I did not understand. In a swift blur of time, a man had emerged from the wilds and was heading straight for us.

CHAPTER THREE

Time accelerated and instinct took over. Stepping together in a defensive position, Chance and I created a human barricade between Raven and Miguel and the darkness that had birthed a threat from seemingly nowhere. With our bodies blocking most of the lantern light behind us, our shadows were the first to engulf the stranger. Behind us, I heard a door on the Explorer slam closed.

Good, I thought. *Raven and Miguel are safe. For now.*

Even in the most desolate of places where light was sparse and the moon was but a scratch in the sky, my vision was clear. Adjusting to the dark, my eyes had a monochromatic front-row seat as I advanced on the charging man with Chance at my side. We cut the distance between us by half with only a few cautious steps. I could hear breathing, raspy and labored. The man continued to mumble as he approached, though his words were still foreign to my ears. Whatever he was saying was choppy, forced, as if he fought what breath he had to communicate. But to whom? Himself? Us?

Chance placed his left hand across my chest, stopping

our advance, then stepped forward one step, feet angled to one side, and raised his left palm out in front of him.

"Whoa there, stranger. That's close enough," he said.

The man slowed, each step more like the thud of a child in a whirlwind temper tantrum, but he continued to draw nearer.

"¡Alto ahí!" Chance's voice boomed. "Stop right there!"

The man did not respond. Instead, he shuffled his pounding feet and raised his arms. Though dark, I could see that his movements were erratic, oddly reminding me of the mindless zombies chasing Brad Pitt in *World War Z*. A low, extinguishing moan flooded the remaining space between us, filling the dark and listless shadows with exhausted rumbles and desperate draws of breath.

"What the hell?" I said loud enough for Chance to hear.

Two more steps. One more. One arm dropped while the other reached out. Foreign spurts of airy words spilled out as the gas in his tank seemed to finally run dry.

We were never off duty, Chance and me.

At ten feet, the man's figure came into focus. I squinted, relying on the detective in me to take over. Adult male; five-foot-five, maybe six; dark hair; mix of dark and light clothes; hands free of weapons.

The man's head bobbled as he slowed further. His face was indistinguishable until a piercing stream of light shot past us, flooding the dwindling space between friend and foe.

I raised a hand to my face, but it was too late. Blinded by the sudden flash, my night vision was wrecked, but one thing burned red into my mind in a ghosting after image.

The beam wobbled as footsteps approached from behind. I shook my head to clear the fog from the shock of the unsuspected light. In that instant, the man dragged his feet, then buckled at the knees and fell face first on the ground.

The thud was distinct, like a dead-weight impact tremor on the mat after a knockout front kick to the face.

I glanced over my shoulder. The brilliant beam shot ahead. I raised my hands and waved it off.

"Cass?"

"You're blinding us, Raven."

"I was just..."

She cut herself off and angled the light at the ground instead of straight ahead.

"Stay back," I said.

The beam stopped bobbling.

Turning back around, I saw the man lying face down on the hardened earth only feet in front of us. Chance was already kneeling next to the mysterious stranger. I stepped closer and saw that his clothes were soaked through. I knelt across from Chance.

"He's out cold."

"Check him for weapons?" I asked.

"Did. Except for the pack on his back, he's clean."

"Let's get that off and roll him over."

Chance lifted the man's left arm and slid the shoulder strap free. I did the same with his right arm and pulled the backpack off him. It was heavier than I expected.

Extending the man's right arm over his head, I took the lead.

"On my count," I said. "Three, two, one."

We rolled the man over and the flashes of red in my mind were confirmed.

"Raven! Bring the light closer."

The beam bounced again as Raven jogged ahead.

"Oh. My. God," she said as the light shone upon the man on the ground.

His shirt was ripped and stained with blood from an

open wound beneath one massive slice across his chest. His hands were cut and full of thorns. His arms were raw with red trails of deep scratches that looked as if he wore his veins on the exterior of his skin. His injuries should have been the most distinguishing concern, but it was his face that drew my interest.

"You seeing this, Chance?"

"Yeah. No wonder he didn't follow my commands."

"There's only thick brush and the Rio Grande where he came from. And he's soaked."

Fresh blood trickled from the man's chest. His left eye was bruised and swelling. Wet hair stuck to his scalp along a cavernous gash along his forehead.

"Raven," I said. "Go grab the first aid kit and some towels."

The light followed as she quietly turned and headed back to camp.

"Another illegal attempt to cross the border?"

"Seems likely," Chance said.

"Kinda odd though, given his likely background."

"Nope. Just confirming that it ain't only Mexicans that are tryin' ta sneak in."

I pulled my cell phone from my pocket and pressed the flashlight icon. A small circle of white light filled the face of the man on the ground. His complexion and bone structure coupled with characteristic facial features was a dead giveaway.

"Yeah," I said. "Didn't want to believe it, but here's proof in the flesh."

I clicked off my light and pocketed my phone when Raven returned with the supplies. She handed me the first aid kit and a towel then directed the beam of the flashlight on the man. She gasped when she saw him up close, seeming to realize what Chance and I already knew.

"He's not from Mexico, right? I mean, he looks Chinese."

CHAPTER FOUR

Unconscious and barely breathing, our uninvited guest's eyelids fluttered, flashing slits of white as his eyes had rolled back into his head. I placed the towel under his neck while Chance tore away his blood and Rio Grande-soaked shirt.

We could see the injuries to his face and head as well as the scratches on his arms and the thorns that still clung to his skin. At first glance, I knew he had additional injuries to his midsection, but once Chance had finished removing the man's shirt, we saw the wreckage laced across his torso. Seeping in pulses that mirrored the shallow beat of his heart, red waves of blood flowed from an open cut that sliced his right nipple down the middle and continued across his chest in an arc that ended just below his left shoulder.

"Ain't no mesquite thorn or rocky crag that'll cut ya that clean," Chance said.

I opened the first aid kit and removed three squares of gauze, quickly placing them across the cut and pressed down.

"Raven. Go find the camp host and see if they have a

radio or a sat phone. Get a Ranger on the horn and tell them we are caring for a man with life-threatening injuries. Take the Explorer and keep Miguel close. Hurry. This guy is in bad shape and needs more help than I can give him."

"Where..." Raven paused and looked over her shoulder.

"Main campground. Loop one. The RV with the pink flamingo hanging off the spare tire."

My voice was calm but shuddered once when I felt the man shift slightly under my pressing hands.

"Got it."

Raven left the flashlight and ran in the dark with only a sliver of ambient light from above to guide her. A moment later, the Explorer's engine hummed to life and its xenon headlights pierced the night with utter brilliance. The tires slipped once, spitting loose gravel before gaining traction and driving off.

"Still glad we opted for the primitive site, Chance?" I said while rummaging around the first aid kit for medical tape.

"It's the best around. Secluded from the full-timers. Close enough for them to pucker up from all the commotion that's gone on in the last few minutes. These people, you know the type. They come looking fer adventure in these remote-type campgrounds, but one little bump in the night and they're folding up their chairs and heading into their camper behind closed doors for a game of Yahtzee or Trivial Pursuit."

"Yahtzee?" I said, finding a chuckle escaping. "You're probably right."

I held back my remarks on his minor profiling of the campers in the other sections of Rio Grande Village. Instead, I shifted the conversation to the man's backpack.

"Check out his bag. Felt heavier than I expected when I pulled it off."

Chance reached across the man's legs and hoisted the bag off the ground.

"Whoa. Ya ain't kiddin'. It's heavier than a bowling bag with a twelve-pounder cradled inside."

The man carried a canvas backpack. It had one main compartment enclosed with a cinch cord and covered by a leather flap that buckled to a clasp near the bottom of the bag. Chance set it on the ground, then reached his hand out to me.

"*Dame la linterna.*"

"What?" I said, giving him the stink eye.

"*La linterna.* The flashlight. *¡Ay, Dios!* Just when I thought ya were gettin' the hang of things."

I handed the light to him, catching a glimpse of his thick mustache curling upward at the corners of his mouth. Even in moments such as this, Chance had the uncanny ability to find a glimpse of blitheness which found a way to filter into everyone around him.

"Of course. La lanterno, or whatever it's called. Why shouldn't I have known that?"

The man stirred again, this time fluttering his eyes and mumbling words I could not understand.

"Hey. Buddy. Just relax. Help is on the way."

He continued to mumble, garbling what sounded like the same word or phrase over and over again.

"What's he sayin'?" Chance asked as he undid the strap on the backpack.

"Hand me my phone and I'll let Google Translate take over the linguistics. Oh. Wait. There's no service. OF ANY KIND out here."

"No, but his words sound familiar," Chance said matter of fact.

The bleeding from the man's chest soaked through the three gauze bandages.

"Shit," I said as I felt the warmth ooze into the pads of my fingers. "I need to change these already."

I found one fresh gauze pad in the first aid kit, but that was all.

It's not enough.

From that point, stopping the bleeding by any means necessary would be the difference between the life and death of this man.

"Hope you've had your shots."

I removed the towel from under his head and laid it across his chest. I was about to ask Chance if he had found anything worth mentioning in the bag when I heard him whisper something in Spanish to himself. As usual, I did not understand his words but the manner with which he muttered suggested that he had found something he did not expect.

"What is it?"

"I have no idea," Chance replied.

With one hand, he held the flashlight and aimed the beam onto a small, metallic-looking cube in his other hand. It was roughly the size of an extra-large Rubik's cube and did not appear to have an interface of any kind. The surface of each side was smooth and its filleted edges gave it a spacey, out-of-this-world look.

"What the hell is that?" I asked.

Chance turned it over and twisted it to get a look at each face of the object.

"Except fer some tiny inscription, the things as clean as a whistle."

"Inscriptions? What does it say?"

"Can't tell. Characters of some kind. A few numbers mixed in. Looks like chicken scratch."

A low moan rumbled like distant thunder in the man's throat. He tried to raise an arm, then let in flop back to the ground.

"He comin' around?" Chance asked.

"No. Drifting is all."

I looked up hoping to see headlights returning to our camp, but the night was dark and still and Raven was nowhere to be seen.

"*Bienvinedos*," Chance said, his voice carrying a tinge of frustration. "Looks like you got more than you bargained for, *amigo*."

I kept pressure on the towel and monitored his breathing while we waited for more help to arrive.

"Any ID in his bag?" I asked.

"Nope. Just this...thing is all."

I felt along his pants pockets, but they were empty. No wallet. No money. Nothing.

"It's so remote out here, there's no way he was traveling alone."

"That's what I'm thinkin', too."

Somewhere deep in the brush, a lone twig snapped. A well-timed coincidence, or was it that damn cow milling around again? I locked eyes with Chance.

"The border region down here is desolate, but don't let that fool ya. Ya know as well as I do that don't make a bit a difference. Hell, we could wade across to Mexico and back right now and no one would be the wiser."

"And if that thing he's carrying is important for some reason, I'd say that he may have someone on his tail. Don't think they'd have followed his trail directly, but..."

"Hey. Ju guys need some help over there?"

The new voice called out from across camp. Chance and I turned at the same time to see three figures walking toward us from the road that led to the main campground. Had Raven sent them? But where was she?

Another spoke as the threesome approached. It was a man's voice but his words, foreign, choppy, quick, and under his breath were not directed at us.

"Get ready," I whispered to Chance.

CHAPTER FIVE

The hairs on the back of my neck bristled like the hackles of a threatened Rhodesian Ridgeback. Chance placed the device back into the backpack and stood. Slow, concentrated breaths hissed from his nose. I could tell he sensed it too. Trouble had found its way into our camp.

"Everythin's under control, Park Rangers are on the way." Chance's voice boomed with authority, but the figures, all men now coming into focus, still advanced toward us. "Y'all mind yer step. It's pretty dark an' we've got our camp splayed out a bit."

None of them changed course or speed.

"¡Deténganse ahí, perros sarnosos!" Chance said, his tone direct, accusatory.

The Mexican man laughed.

"You should no say such things, my friend. It is no polite."

The whispering man spoke again, this time for all to hear.

"Gāndiào tāmen, ránhòu qǔ huí shèbèi." 干掉他们，然

后取回设备 ("Gahn dee-ow tah-men ran hoe chew hway shuh-bay").

I glanced down at the injured man. His skin looked clammy, like the surface of rotten Jello left out in the sun for too long. If help did not arrive soon, he would be a dead man. Looking up, I saw the men had fanned out and had slowed their pace. Their movements were cautious, deliberate. I continued to kneel next to the man while Chance engaged our uninvited guests.

"Don't get the lingo, but y'all er close enough. We've an injured man to see to. Please give us room."

"*Señor*, why waste time playing this game. The man is not your problem. He is ours."

The man's tone was calm. He spoke as if he were in control and knew there was nothing either Chance or I could do to stop what was about to happen.

"*Mira*, these men." He opened his arms, gesturing to the men standing next to him. "They are this man's... friends. But he has not been so friendly to them. Actually, he is a very dangerous man, so I think you should listen to me when I say..."

He paused when the whispering man grumbled another slew of foreign words from lips that wore an angry frown. It was clear to me that he grew impatient.

"Buddy, the best thing you can do for your friend is turn around and walk out of here," I said, watching each of them with a widening stare.

The whispering man turned his glare on me. My heart beat steady, but the ferocity of each pound echoed deeper inside of me. I exhaled and shook my head slightly. What had Chance said only a few days ago? "Come on, amigo. You need to get away. Find a calming place where we can slug a few beers and share a few laughs. No problems to deal with. No worries to get in the way." Glad that worked out for us.

"Enough!"

The whispering man was not so quiet anymore. He reached to his waist and pulled what looked like a Hawk-bill knife from his belt. The curved blade, its most distinctive feature, extended in front of him, appearing like a blackened hook emerging from the man's arm.

"No more games," the lead man said.

Chance looked at me, to which I simply raised my eyebrows, cocked my head to one side and smiled.

"Well, shit," I said. "I do like to play games."

The whispering man charged at me, slicing the knife through the air before him. I stood and took a defensive stance. My fists clenched. My knuckles cracked. A fire ignited along my spine.

He yelled his best battle cry as he closed to within three steps of me. That was a mistake on so many levels. Fighting, much like poker, is a skill where deception and intelligence are the most tactful of weapons to carry. Know your opponent. Play them, not the cards. The opposite side of the coin is to be careful not to give away your hand. Control your *tells*, especially when going all-in on a bluff. Every poker game has a donkey. He's the player that doesn't know when he's been beaten but acts like his hand is the most dominant. In the end, the cards speak for themselves. The whispering man, in layman's terms, was a definite jackass.

The second the whispering man yelled it cued my response, as this was his last move before making his initial strike at me. It also told Chance exactly when to act in my defense. With the simple press of a button, Chance clicked on the flashlight, shooting a brilliant LED beam into the whispering man's face. The bright white light wrecked the man's night vision, causing him to squint and flinch. Like the sun intervening on my behalf, the blinding surge jarred his momentum leaving him open to my swift counterattack.

He swung his blade, but I caught his forearm with my right hand and rammed my left palm into the point of his nose like a garbage truck flattening a VW Bug. The crunch and crack of violently displaced cartilage was music to my ears. On recoil, I felt the warm spray of fresh blood smear my skin. With a controlling grasp of his arm, I twisted it around, forcing it up and behind his back. At my command, and delicately placed pressure on his joints, he involuntarily bent at the waist. The Hawkbill blade dropped from his grasp onto the ground. He groaned as the muscles and tendons in his shoulder stretched beyond their limits.

The whispering man spoke but his foreign gibberish fell on deaf ears. Any Pitbull knows not to loosen its jaws until the fight becomes futile. Like a puppet under my total control, I turned him around to face the others.

"*Pinché cabrón*. You are a dead man," the lead man said through gritted teeth.

"Hey, Chance," I said with veiled sarcasm. "That, I understand."

"Me too," he replied, his voice lower, softer, more feral than I had ever heard before.

The lead man and his lone companion charged without warning. Their silent advance was direct, aggressive, and aimed at Chance. If they thought attacking the portly fellow at the campground was a good idea, they were in for a surprise. Even a mountain lion purrs from time to time.

The lead man appeared unarmed but the other produced a metal club no bigger than a billy stick. He swung it once, extending its telescopic end, furthering its steely reach.

"Chance!"

"I see," he said, eyes fixed on target and shifting his weight to the balls of his feet.

Tightening my grip on the whispering man, my muscles ached to let him go and jump in front of Chance. He squealed under the mounting pressure I placed on him, some purposeful, some as a result of my wanting to engage the others.

Chance outmanned both of his attackers by a few inches and at least fifty pounds, but his size and girth did not dissuade them. The lead man reached Chance first, winding up for a Superman punch as he leaped the final few feet that separated them. Chance raised his left arm and stepped into the man, deflecting the punching arm mid-air while grabbing the man's shirt with his right. He squeezed cloth and used their momentum to catapult the lead man into the path of the billy club man's swing. The two men tumbled over one another, the lead man catching the blunt steel shaft of the club across the neck. He grunted as they fell to the ground.

The billy club man yelled out words similar to phrases spoken by the whispering man, then said something in Spanish.

Who are they?

The men bounced back to their feet. Like pack hunting dogs, they maneuvered to place Chance between them. With hardened breaths, they snarled, waiting for just the right moment to strike.

Chance stood his ground, but I had seen enough. When the men charged, I pulled the whispering man's arm up and out, popping his shoulder out of its socket with one loud snap, then tossed him to the ground. He wriggled on the dead grass like a snake whose head had just been severed from its body. Lunging forward, I drove my full weight into the side of the man with the billy club, crashing to the ground on top of him. I landed two striking blows to his face, then grabbed the steel shaft of the club to keep its wild flailing from hitting me. I could hear Chance embattled with the lead man, and from the sounds of it, he had the upper hand.

That momentary pause was all that the man beneath me needed to sense my distractedness and catch me off guard with a solid knee to the groin. As dark as the night was, and as hard as the crisp sliver of moon worked to illuminate what it could, I saw bright lights appear before my eyes and felt a warm, building sensation roll in waves between my legs, coming to shore in the pit of my stomach.

Summoning all my remaining strength, I clung to the man, using my weight to bear down on him in a last-ditch defense. He wriggled side to side, each motion freeing him further, but my fists held firm to cloth and steel. Like a fish flopping on the sand, he worked his way out from beneath me. I could feel the pain in my midsection was dissipating, but the euphoric sensation of having squashed testicles remained like the lingering effects of inhaled helium. The gas made voices sound funny for a short time, but this was not funny at all.

The billy club man tried to get to his feet, but I rolled to one side, clipping his heels and twisting the steel rod in his hand. He stumbled once, then caught his footing in a dried patch of earth. Finding traction, he pulled himself from beneath me. The only thing keeping us together was my grasp of his weapon.

"You let go! I kill you!"

You son of a bitch.

A jolt of adrenaline surged through me, extinguishing the fuzzy feeling in my gut, but allowed the pain to remain as a reminder not to let my guard down again. I pulled on the billy club's extension, drawing the man closer to me while using his forceful attempts to shake me free as leverage to stand.

From my right, I heard Chance call out.

"You good?"

I squinted my eyes at the man who had threatened to kill me, said those exact words to my face, and felt a snarl curl out from my lips.

"Yeah, I'm good."

The roar of an engine and the bright beams of headlights appeared over the billy club man's shoulder. Raven! This had to end now before she pulled in.

I yanked as hard as I could, drawing the man close to me. With a heartfelt kick, I returned the favor he had so precisely laid on me. He grunted...loudly...but barely wavered.

The headlights engulfed us. They washed over the camp and swallowed every inch of dark that surrounded the ongoing battle between Chance, me, and the would-be killers who invaded our camp. I expected the Explorer to pull in and park, but I was oh so wrong. The engine revved. The headlights bobbled, then grew in brightness and precision as they barreled down on our position.

Behind me, I heard the whispering man's voice. He screamed more gibberish, causing the man I fought to disengage. He let go of the steel baton and ran out of the beams, disappearing into the night.

"Get back here!"

Chance yelled out as the Explorer skidded to a stop next to me. I turned to see the lead man helping the whispering man hobble away, his high-pitched groans of pain screeching into the night like the fading moan of a banshee.

Leaving the engine running, Raven hopped out of the Explorer.

"What the hell was all that?"

Ignoring her question, I answered with one of my own.

"Rangers on the way?"

"Yeah," she said.

Chance walked over to the man we had been caring for and protecting. Raven placed a hand on my face.

"You okay?"

"Yeah."

"Well, you look like shit."

I huffed once, then directed my attention to Chance when I heard him talking to himself.

"What is it?"

"The backpack is gone. The device, too."

He paused. In the beam from the headlights, I saw a look of defeat on his face.

"Something else?"

"Yeah."

On the far side of our camp, the road to the main campground filled with the hum and rattle of Ranger trucks coming to our aid. *Too little too late*, I thought. Raven and I walked over to Chance.

Looking down at the man we fought for, my heart sunk. The towel that had covered his chest had been cast aside. The chest-wide slice seeped, as did the fresh puncture around the steely blade of the hawkbill knife that had been plunged and left in him. His eyes, no longer fluttering or rolled back, stared lifelessly at the starry void overhead.

Damn!

CHAPTER SIX

Headlights from two National Park Service trucks and one spotlight mounted on the camp host's converted golf cart crisscrossed over the scene. Over our camp. Over the body. Raven sat with Miguel in our tent, with the flap pulled closed so he was unable to see what was going on. No language barrier could keep the gruesome image of a dead man with a knife in his chest from searing itself into memory. Miguel had already experienced too much trauma in his young life to have yet another nightmarish experience squat in his memory.

I stood in a huddle with Chance and the Rangers. It was obvious from the looks on their faces that they had never seen a dead body before. At least one that looked the way ours did. Accidents happen in the park, sometimes resulting in the death of a visitor. Heat stroke, exposure, dehydration, even sheer stupidity where someone goes too far to take a daring selfie and ends up falling off a cliff or getting too close to a wild animal. It happens. But this? A murder in the park? A crime such as this only happened one other time, and that was over twenty years ago. By the looks of our rangers, they might have graduated kindergarten by then, but that might be pushing it. Hell, none of them looked much older than Spencer, and he was just a sophomore in college.

"So, the victim," a younger and attractive-looking female Ranger asked.

She wore the standard issue National Parks Ranger uniform: gray shirt, National Parks badge over her left pocket, and green trousers. Atop her head was the iconic "flat hat," its stiff brim and high crown a staple among National Parks Rangers. A name tag over her right pocket read *Sonora Stone*.

"He wandered into your camp from..."

Ranger Stone paused and pulled a Maglite from her belt. Pointing it away from us, she pressed a button on its shaft. Light pierced the night, illuminating the tangled and ragged brush across the gravel loop road that bordered the campground. The beam penetrated through the bramble to the corn dog tips of tall cattails growing in the soggy mud near the banks of the Rio Grande.

"...there?"

"Yes, ma'am. That's exactly right," Chance said.

A second Ranger spoke up. His comments drawing our attention to him.

"Ain't no way a person could get through there. The mesquite alone would cut 'em ta shreds."

His mix of twang and proper English bugged me, but not as much as his insinuation that we were not being truthful. I glanced at his name tag. Brian Heckles. *Figures.* Holding back an insolent huff, I pursed my lips.

Ranger Stone spoke up before either Chance or I could reply with a tone suggesting that Ranger Heckles was not her favorite person, nor that what he said was of any help.

"Sheriff Gilbert—" she began, but Chance interrupted.

"Please. Call me Chance. Left the title back at the county line."

Guys like us are never off duty.

"Okay. Chance. Do you have any idea why the victim chose to come into your camp?"

"Lucky pick, I reckon. Or unlucky, dependin' on how ya look at it. Guess is he was lookin' fer help, saw our light, an' headed our way. He collapsed before we had a chance ta question him."

Ranger Stone turned to me.

"And your name is Callahan, right?"

"That's right. Cass Callahan."

"Anything to add."

Her line of questioning was so rudimentary it was almost laughable, but she was doing her job the best she could under the circumstances. I had to give her that.

"No. We had just enough time to send for help and administer first aid before the others entered the camp looking for him."

Ranger Hank Adams, the third Ranger, his voice more soft-spoken than his counterparts, said the one thing I had been wanting to say from the get-go.

"Shouldn't we go after the men who killed him?"

"Hank," Ranger Heckles said. "You gonna go after 'em yerself? In the dark? Hell, they're probably back in Mexico by now. No sense puttin' ourselves at risk."

I caught a glance from Ranger Heckles. His eyes looked overconfident, but behind the façade I saw a scared shit-less kid who did not know his ass from a hole in the ground. When our eyes met, his voice rose to a higher pitch.

"I ain't afraid er nuthin'. Just think we outta have, ya know, a plan?"

Oh, but you are, I thought. *Terrified.*

Ranger Stone eyed her motley crew.

"Hank, we're gonna need to call this in. Drive back to the Ranger station and get headquarters on the line. Tell 'em what's going on and get an ambulance out here to recover the body. Circle through the campground on the way. Maybe you'll see...something."

"Mind if I ride along?" Chance asked. "Don't want ta git in the way, but yer man could use a pair of eyes who knows what ta look fer."

Ranger Stone nodded her approval.

"Well, all right then." Chance turned to me. "Ya good ta handle anything else that pops up 'round here?"

"Yeah. I can—"

"We've got everything under control, gentlemen," Ranger Stone interrupted. "Mr. Callahan can assist securing the body until the ambulance arrives."

Chance smiled, knowing how I felt about being called Mr. Callahan. That was my father, and he had been dead for many years. I was Detective Callahan, or simply, Cass.

"Ranger Heckles, escort the camp hosts back to their campsite," she continued while motioning to the golfcart with two wide-eyed seniors who had seen more than they bargained for this evening. "Reassure them that everything is fine. That the campground is safe, and that..."

"Safe?" he interrupted, a snide chuckle reverberating through his voice.

I caught his gaze about the same time Ranger Stone did, but the authority in her stare outweighed mine by a mile.

"Okay. Okay," he said, raising his palms. "They're safe. We're safe. Everybody's safe."

I wouldn't go that far but get moving dip shit.

"Brian." Ranger Stone's voice hardened as she called him by name. "We are the wall between fear and the unknown. What you tell them, how you act, will set the tone for how they feel. You want to scare them? Next thing you know, the whole campground will catch wind of it and we'll have more questions thrown at us than we care to field, let alone answer."

The five of us stood together, though our huddle was sagging.

"Let's get moving," Ranger Stone said.

Chance patted me on the back, then followed Ranger Adams to his truck. Ranger Heckles sauntered through our camp en route to the curious camp hosts. I saw Raven poking her head out of the tent. Even in the dark, I could see the concern on her face. Maybe it was more of a feeling but it did not matter. I knew Raven. I knew the look.

"Do you have an extra sleeping bag that we could use to cover the body?" Ranger Stone's voice had softened now that it was just the two of us. "To be honest, I wasn't expecting this. We've had some pretty bad situations before, but I've never experienced a, uh..."

"Homicide?" I said.

It was the right word. *Murder. Killing.* Those painted a far more gruesome scene, but they would not be wrong. What else describes how this mystery man died? The wounds to his body tell one story, but the knife sticking out of his chest pretty much sums up the whole damn thing. He was murdered.

"That's not a word we hear around here. Ever," Ranger Stone said as we walked over to the body. "Unfortunately, there have been accidents, either due to bad luck or plain ignorance, but this is...forgettable."

It never would be, though. This would linger like the bad aftertaste of vomit following a hangover. The acidic burn. The convulsive thrusts. The pulsing thump of a heartbeat that migrates from chest to throat to head, and back again. Wave over wave, the shock runs its course until finally, muscles relax and regret begins to dissipate, but the memory never really goes away.

"This is where your training should kick in, Ranger Stone," I said.

"How long have you been in law enforcement?" she asked.

Her eyes found mine. Her gaze was innocent, warm. Not in a sensual way, but that of a child looking for something in a parent. Reassurance. Confidence. I held her gaze, feeling the weight of her unspoken plea.

"Feels like a lifetime."

"So, you've been in situations like this before?"

I knelt next to the body.

"More than I care to admit."

She knelt across from me. The beam from her Maglite flooded over the red stains on his clothing, over the cooling blood streaking across his bare skin. A reflection shimmered when light found the steel of the knife standing defiantly half-buried in the man's chest. It captured my attention but led me to a new discovery.

I reached across the body and grabbed the end of Ranger Stone's light, aiming it at the upper left quadrant of the man's torso. Though his chest and clothes were caked with drying sweat and blood, I saw an unnatural discoloration on his skin that disappeared beneath his shirt. I let go of the flashlight and used my hands to peel back the saturated cloth.

"Whoa." Ranger Stone's grip on the flashlight wavered.

"Steady," I said.

I pulled my cell phone from my pocket and took a picture of a very ornate, and very foreign-looking tattoo.

Hovering over a swatch of tightly wound bamboo

poles, each connected by strands of razor wire, was a red-inked bird. The bird's wings were spread wide, its feathers etched in delicate detail, giving the impression of a powerful yet graceful creature in flight. The crimson ink contrasted sharply against the cool greens and metallic grays of the bamboo and razor wire, making the bird stand out like a vivid flame against the darkness. Its sharp curved beak curled downward. Its fiery eyes gave a glassy, angry stare. Dangling beneath it, the bird's talons clutched the limp, scaly body of a dead serpent. At first glance, I might have mistaken it for a snake, but its head resembled that of a dragon. Hair protruded from its chin. Its nostrils were large and prominent. Short, pointy horns jutted out from the end of its snout. Its oversized eyes bulged from its head, and its tongue lolled lazily to the side of its mouth.

I found myself mesmerized by the intricacy of the tattoo.

"You ever see anything like that before?" Ranger Stone asked.

I did not answer right away. Instead, I took two more pictures, then stood up and slipped my cell phone into my pocket.

"I'll say this. I've seen plenty of tattoos over the years, but this ranks in the top ten on sheer artistry alone."

We both turned to footsteps approaching from camp. Ranger Stone aimed her light, flooding Raven's face, causing her to squint. She held a sleeping bag in her arms.

"Ma'am," Ranger Stone began.

I interrupted.

"This is my wife, Raven. Raven, this is Ranger Sonora Stone."

"Sonora. What a beautiful name," Raven said.

Only Raven could deflect the events of the evening

with a compliment, even when under the gun. But it worked. Ranger Stone lowered the flashlight.

"Mrs. Callahan."

"I overheard your need for a sleeping bag. I can only assume it's because, well, to...cover the man?"

I reached out and took it from her, then draped it over the body.

"Thanks, Rave. Miguel all right?"

"Yeah. I don't know how, but he's asleep." Raven looked at Ranger Stone, then back at me. "What do we do now?"

"We wait," Ranger Stone said. "Ambulance will be on the way, though it may take a while to get down here. I expect a few agents from the Department of the Interior, or possibly Homeland Security to show up. Until they arrive, we need to keep the scene secure."

Ranger Stone looked around, her gaze projecting into the darkness.

"You all opted for a remote site. Away from other campers?"

"We wanted a little more privacy and don't mind roughing it, every once in a while," Raven said.

"May be the thing that keeps sanity in the campground. At least until morning," Ranger Stone replied. "Mr. Call...um...Cass. I could use your help until the guys return."

I glanced at Raven. She shrugged her shoulders and smiled at me. Damn, that alone lifted my spirits. She had a way about her that continually reminded me how lucky I was that she picked me. Stuck with me. Tolerated me over all these years.

"I'll be in the tent with Miguel. Holler if you need anything," she said.

Raven turned and walked quietly back to camp. I

spoke to Ranger Stone as I watched the best thing in my life walk away.

"You drink coffee?"

"Not since this morning. Why?"

I turned to face her. The detective in me surfaced while the protector lingered just out of sight.

"It's going to be a long night."

CHAPTER SEVEN

anger Sonora Stone remained at our campsite throughout the night. We created a perimeter using crime scene tape I carried in the rear of the Explorer and watched over the body, waiting for Chance to return with the park rangers. Raven made coffee but left us to do our work. The coffee helped, but it was the underlying adrenaline that kept us both awake and on guard.

Chance and Ranger Adams were gone for hours. Ranger Stone's walkie chirped shortly after Ranger Heckles escorted the camp hosts back to their camper. He said he had found other things to do. Something about a contraband stash discovered by hikers who happened to be waiting for the camp hosts when they showed up at their site. Stone told him that it was not a priority and could most certainly wait until morning, but he played the "you're going out" and "I'm losing you" game. I could tell by the tone in Ranger Stone's voice that she was not pleased, but that she was not entirely surprised by the move. Trust is so important in our line of work. Without it, we lose our edge, and our operations risk falling apart.

Trust ensures that we can depend on each other in critical moments. Heckles going AWOL was fine by me.

The sliver of moon descended below the horizon. We kept our flashlights turned off to let our eyes adjust further to the deepening darkness. I could still see Ranger Stone, though the surroundings looked like the monochromatic settling of an old John Ford western. Guarding a dead body in the middle of nowhere, in the middle of the night, was not how I envisioned this jaunt into Big Bend going.

When the small talk between Ranger Stone and me died out, long moments of silence hung on the air between us. She was the most experienced of her crew, but even she was only a shade of green lighter than the patches on her uniform. What we were doing, guarding the body, was grunt work, but the weight of the whole scene resting on her shoulders was not one for which she was completely ready to handle alone. Her professionalism helped her manage her team, but once they were gone, her inexperience seeped in like slipping hands on a pull-up bar. I had to give her credit though. She hung in a long time. Longer than most in her shoes.

It was well past midnight when the first signs of help came our way. In the distance, I could hear a chorus of rumbling engines. As they drew nearer, the crackle of crushed stone popping under the weight of approaching tires accompanied the sound. A stream of headlights cut through the darkness casting long shadows behind the trees and path before them. Each vehicle operated under Code 2. No emergency strobes or sirens. As the motorcade approached, I saw that it was Chance and Ranger Adams leading a procession of official vehicles.

An ambulance, two US Park Ranger Law Enforcement SUVs, and two US Customs and Border Patrol trucks rolled along the gravel loop road behind the lead Ranger's vehicle. They pulled to a stop, surrounding the scene like a small band of Conestoga wagons and prairie schooners circling up for a night on the open range.

Chance was the first to hop out.

"Cass. How y'all holdin' up?"

"Fine, if you ask me. Ranger Stone has everything under control."

Chance smiled at Stone.

"It's been quiet since you left. And Cass has been a big help." She paused. I could see her leaning to look around Chance. "I see you've brought the cavalry."

Chance glanced over his shoulder.

"Yeah. Yer man, Adams, got on the horn once we arrived at the station. Had a clear signal clean through ta Lajitas. You know, those signal boosters are pretty handy. I may have ta look into that fer the county once we get back, Cass."

Car doors opened and closed behind us.

"Anyway. We got through to DOH as well as DPS. We got Border Patrol and National Park Law Enforcement here ta take over. DPS relayed our request for an ambulance. Everyone showed up about the same time."

"Any sign of our uninvited guests?" I asked.

"Nah. Not a one. They melted inta the woodwork like I'm sure they've done a hundred times before. It's bad luck, but what can ya do? Y'all find anything worth a plug nickel out here, or we just spinnin' our wheels in the dust?"

Before I had a chance to answer, two DOH officers walked over and asked for a briefing. I began but did not get two words in before being asked to step aside and let Ranger Stone take the lead. I stepped out of the way, the hairs on my neck bristling. Chance put a hand on my shoulder and led me away.

"They have no idea who we are, amigo. Don't let it git to ya."

I looked back, catching a quick glance from Ranger Stone while she gave her report.

"First opportunity you get to steal her away from here, take it, Chance," I said. "She's young. Doesn't have much behind her but school and a year or two with the parks, but I see something in her."

"That so?" Chance said.

"It's a feeling."

We watched Ranger Stone handle the DOH officers as best she could. Ranger Adams hung around like the unpopular kid at a middle school dance. None of the officials paid him any mind, but he remained attentive to Ranger Stone.

In what seemed like record time, DOH had released the body to the ambulance drivers. They were not your typical EMS workers but locally contracted ambulance attendants. If this was the best they could get, it would have to do though it made me wonder who would answer the call in the wake of a lifesaving emergency.

When the DOH officers concluded their initial investigation, they instructed the ambulance personnel to load the Chinese-looking mystery man, tattoo and all, into the ambulance and head out. I did not hear where they were taking him, but I figured a call to Dr. Frannie Lopez-Tasker, our friend and local medical examiner, would get us a seat at the table. If anyone could help us track down a body, it would be Frannie.

I hated to think that this would be another case wiped under the rug, but it was out of my control. This was not our jurisdiction. At best, in the eyes of DOH, we were victims of an unfortunate incident. The only thing left for us to do was try to understand what had happened: *a man emerged from the dark with injuries, most of which were caused by his attempt to run through the thick brush; however, his more serious injuries appeared to be the result of physical harm inflicted by another person or persons. The man passed out before we could question him. A mysterious device was found in his possession. Moments later, three more men approached the camp looking for the injured man and attempted to use force to take him. The injured man was fatally stabbed while unconscious during the fight to protect him. All three attackers escaped into the night, taking the mysterious device with them.*

Unanswerable questions were all that remained for us to ponder.

CHAPTER EIGHT

The rising sun painted the rugged terrain to the west and north of our campsite with warm pink and orange hues. The Rio Grande transformed into a shimmering flow of sparkling gold, an open treasure sought by more than the homeland with which its waters touched. Clear skies formed a massive blue dome overhead, encasing all the colors beneath it like a swirling marble as the last of the stars retreated behind the birth of a new day. There was no escaping the beauty, yet the blemish of death and unanswered questions from the past night's events remained a scar on the landscape.

It was early, but striking our campsite seemed like the only thing to do. Like it or not, our vacation was over. Rangers Stone and Adams, along with the DOH officials had rolled out just before dawn. Chance and I exchanged information with Ranger Stone and encouraged her to reach out should she ever need backup beyond the boundary of the park.

"I'll keep you in mind," she had said, and that was it.

The rumble of engines faded as the park entourage drove away leaving us behind at our campground crime scene as if nothing of any consequence had happened. A murder, one would think, might carry a little more weight around here. After taking our statements, removing the body, and determining the group responsible was most likely already back across the river and decidedly out of United States jurisdiction, they simply asked us to contact the authorities if something else were to arise. To me, it was a clean-up job where only the bare minimum was taken into consideration.

When the Explorer was packed and ready, I suggested that Raven and Miguel come with me on one last hike up the trail to the overlook.

"Come on, buddy," I said. "Want to see the Chihuahuan Desert one last time?"

I held my hand out to Miguel, but instead of taking mine, he grabbed Raven's.

"Keep trying," she mouthed.

Together, the three of us marched off leaving Chance behind when he passed on the offer to join us.

Miguel's eyes were puffy from lack of a good night's sleep, but he held Raven's hand as we walked along. He switched between kicking loose rocks and picking them up to study and would stop and listen to each sound as we made our way along the trail. It was early, and the desert was just waking. We heard the deep chirp of a bullfrog way off in the marshy waters between the trail and the Rio Grande and the fluttering wings of a pair of Marsh Wrens racing across the sky like bullets chasing a target. As we began the climb up the slope to the overlook, I looked back and pointed out the slow, graceful glide of a lone Blue Heron to Raven and Miguel. Such peaceful snippets in such a rugged country.

We followed the switchback trail to the top of a bluff that overlooked the campground to the west, Boquillos, Mexico and its field of solar panels to the east and provided an unobstructed view of the Rio Grande carving its way along the border as its waters headed south for the Gulf of Mexico. It was beautiful. I had hoped the hike would be that last delicious bite, the proverbial icing on the cake that sealed this trip with one lasting good memory. Raven and Miguel seemed content, but I found myself staring into Mexico, into the brightest rays of the morning sun, wondering where the men from last night were hiding out.

Questions erupted within me—were more lying in wait for the right moment to cross over undetected. Was our victim Chinese? Korean? He was definitely from Asia which begs the question: why was he *here*? What was the device he carried? And the mixed backgrounds of the men after him proved without a doubt that the Texas/Mexico border was now an international gateway inviting trouble from all over the world.

I shook my head and wiped the stubble on my chin.

"You okay, Cass?" Raven asked, placing a palm on my arm.

"Yeah."

It was all I could manage, though she knew better. Pulling my arm aside, she slipped into my chest and laid her head against me. Miguel looked up at us with his dark-brown eyes full of wonder. The blank look on his face was as innocent as the day he was born, then something happened. Still holding Raven's hand, he reached out, tugging hers with his, and pointed to Mexico.

"*Mama y Papa... ¿están allá?*"

I felt Raven press against me, then she slowly dropped to one knee and spoke to Miguel.

"*No lo sé, cariño. Pero si podemos encontrarlos, lo haremos.*"

She squeezed his hand and kissed him on the forehead.

"What'd he say?" I asked.

"He's missing his parents." Raven stood up and sighed. "I told him we would do everything we could to find them."

"But, Raven, you know that..."

"I know."

We stood in silence a moment longer, then quietly made our way down the switchback trail to the camp-ground. We found Chance leaning on the back of the Explorer fidgeting with his pocketknife. He flipped it into the air by the blade and caught the handle. Perfect every time. When he saw us, he straightened up and motioned to the car like a maître d' welcoming new guests to his fine establishment.

"How was yer walk? It's quite the sight, ain't it."

Raven mustered a smile when her eyes connected with his.

"It is."

Chance opened the rear door for her. She lifted Miguel into the back seat of the Explorer, then paused before hopping in herself.

"But I've seen enough on this trip to last me a while."

Chance shut the door, then turned his focus on me.

"You were hopin' ta see somethin' up there, weren't ya?"

I looked past him to the tangled mesquite and thorny brush for one final glance at the path our dead man had taken with hopes of escaping his pursuers.

"Hell, Chance. I don't know."

"Whelp, ya can't win 'em all. Ya may want to, but that ain't always how it works."

I nodded, then walked to the driver's side door. His voice stopped me before I could get in.

"Hey, Cass."

I looked at Chance across the black roof of the

Explorer. His face was a mix of stern authority and gentle understanding.

"I can see it in yer eyes, but hear me when I say, yer mission's over. This little trip was the first step ta put all that struggle of the past few months behind ya. Don't let what happened last night git in the way of that. Once we get back ta Brewster, we'll get back ta the way things were."

I nodded. Chance opened his door, got in, and closed it with a thud. I reached for the handle on my side and discovered my grip tightening to a point where my knuckles turned white and the skin of my palm screamed under the strain. I looked down at my hand and slowly released the pressure around my grip. From the back window, the soft form of a child's face found its way into my view. Miguel looked absently out the window. There was no wonder, no excitement for the return journey, but a distance in his stare that I wished I could understand. I suppose we were both struggling from recent events. Maybe, with patience and a little luck, we could find normal together.

I opened the door and pulled myself into the driver's seat. Chance wrapped his knuckles on the dashboard.

"Let's hit the road, *amigo*."

Crushed gravel popped beneath the tires. The hum of the engine was the one constant, as my mind raced with thoughts and memories and questions of which I just could not let go.

CHAPTER NINE

The hum of the tires rolling along Panther Junction Road and the subtle vibrations filling the cab of the Explorer acted like a soothing massage chair. Miguel fell asleep in his seat minutes after we hit the road. Raven propped her head on a pillow against the rear window. With eyes closed, her body gently lolled with the car as she, too, enjoyed a morning nap. Chance and I sat quietly in the front seats, each keeping to our own thoughts. The cockpit was quiet. With no cell reception, we had yet to regain contact with the outside world.

To the south, Emory Peak commanded attention as it jutted out of the Chisos Mountains, standing tallest among the peaks. A glance of it in my side mirror reminded me of a scene in *Close Encounters of the Third Kind* where Richard Dreyfuss becomes obsessed with recreating the likeness of what was really Devils Tower. It was the hypnotic call from the unknown that drew him in and caused him to make some life-altering and quite selfish decisions. As my eyes locked onto the reflection of Emory Peak in my side mirror, I could not help but feel as if it was speaking to me. *Warning me? What was it saying?* Its massive, rocky face seemed to follow us as we drove away from Big Bend National Park.

A road sign marking the change from Panther Junction Road to Texas Highway 118 must have also been an invisible barrier for any and all communication signals. As we converged onto the state road, the dome of silence was broken and the Explorer sprang to life with dings and whistles from our cell phones as text messages, missed calls, and voicemails chided us for being unreachable.

Raven, jolted by the sudden sounds, banged her head on the window. Miguel was startled awake but remained in a daze and was too confused to know what was happening. Chance reached for his phone while I pressed a button on the Explorer's dash screen to read out my missed texts.

"You have twelve messages," the Explorer's computer voice announced.

Chance huffed.

"Message one, from Levi Flint... '*Cass, call me. Wildfires in the Panhandle er causin' trouble for ranchers in the area. Wanna lend 'em a hand. Lemme know.*'"

"You hear about the fires?" I asked Chance.

He responded while reading over his messages.

"Ay-yuh. Thought they'd have a handle on it by now. Was just startin' up when we left a couple days ago. Looks like the wind played the devil's fiddle and caused some major problems. Fires burnin' over half a million acres so far." He pointed to his cell phone. "Bulletin went out yesterday with an update. Don't look like the fires er lettin' up."

"Message two, from Levi Flint... '*Cass, fires buildin'. Buddy of mine lost his house an' his livestock are in danger. I'm reachin' out. Seein' what we can do ta help.*'"

"Message three, from Levi Flint...'*Damn, Cass. Where the hell are you?*'"

Chance put his phone down and stared ahead.

"Ol' Flint's persistent, ain't he?"

"Understatement of the year, right there," I said.

"But he ain't wrong. What ya gonna do?"

I flipped my left blinker on as we approached the turn-off for RR170 and Terlingua.

"Something tells me Flint is already doing whatever needs bein' done."

Chance raised his cell again and continued scrolling through missed messages. I turned onto RR170, then pulled onto the shoulder and sifted through the remaining transcriptions of Flint's nine additional calls. As I was nearing the end, I heard Raven on the phone behind me. Turning around, I raised my eyebrows in question. She waved me off and continued listening. I could hear a deep voice coming over the line and knew right away it was Flint.

"Put it on speaker," I whispered.

Raven leaned forward, pulled the phone from her ear, and pressed the speaker icon. Flint's voice filled the cab.

"*...it's a goddamn shame. I told 'em the CR'd be happy ta watch over a few hundred head 'til the fires are contained and they git back on their feet.*"

"Sounds good to me," Raven answered.

"Flint. It's Cass."

"*Jesus, Cass. Glad ta hear yer still alive.*" Flint's sarcastic tone was tolerable. "*Git my messages?*"

"Yeah, Flint. All twelve of them."

"*Then y'all know what the Six M Ranch is dealin' with?*"

"Got the CliffsNotes version, but yeah?"

"What? Who the hell is Cliff?"

Raven smirked at me. I began to explain, but Flint cut me off.

"*I been tellin' them we got plenty of land to offer fer a time. That set right with you?*"

"Whatever you need to do, Flint."

"*Good 'cause the first load is pullin' in as we speak. Ms. Raven, you best git on back here. We got a shit ton ta do.*"

"We're on the way. Be there in about..."

Raven looked at me.

"An hour," I said, finishing Raven's sentence.

"Roger that," he said, then abruptly disconnected the call.

"This is turning out to be one hell of a mornin'," I said.

I pulled back onto RR170 and headed north. Passing through Lajitas, Chance gave a wave to a trooper he recognized as he sat in his cruiser at the entrance of the DPS highway patrol office. The trooper returned the gesture, then pulled out after we passed by and headed south.

The dips and peaks of RR170 and the curves that followed the snaking trail of the Rio Grande along the border meshed into one stomach churning blur as I sped toward the CR. Chance was busy on his phone. Raven slid to the middle seat and whispered soft Spanish words to Miguel, then translated them to English.

As we came to a rise in the highway, I recognized the stretch where our tire had blown out and we had met Chance before arriving at the CR for the first time. Chance noticed as well.

"Git ready to pull over."

"Pull over? Why?"

"Just received a message from Deputy Bostwick. There's been a break-in at Javie's Autoparts. Boss is waitin' fer me up ahead."

"I can—"

Chance interrupted.

"Git back ta the CR. Settle the family. See what Flint's got goin' on. I'll holler at ya if I need ya."

"You handling me, Chance?"

He turned to me. His mouth erupted its best Cheshire smile, teeth and all with mustache curling above his lips.

"I can, if that's what ya like?"

Waiting on the shoulder a hundred yards ahead with lights flashing was Deputy Bostwick's rig. I slowed upon approach, toggled on my hazards, and pulled over behind the county vehicle. Chance held out a hand, and we shook.

"Never off duty?"

"Never," Chance replied. "Good luck at home. I'll be in touch."

He looked over his shoulder and nodded to Raven, then hopped out of the Explorer and walked on stiff legs to the passenger door of Bostwick's patrol car and got in.

With a chirp of the siren and lights flashing, they pulled away. I followed behind, keeping pace with them until Raven leaned forward and read the speedometer.

"Uh, Cass? How about you bring it down to double digits?"

The turn off for the CR was approaching, so I let off the gas. Not because I was asked to, but because I might have sped right by otherwise. At least, that's what I told myself.

Gravel punched at the wheel wells once again, and dust rose in our wake. As we approached the CR, I slowed to a stop and looked ahead at a traffic jam of trucks and trailers lining the road in front of the ranch entrance.

"What the hell?" I said. "Looks like Flint invited all of North Texas to the ranch."

CHAPTER TEN

The CR had been in the Callahan family for over one hundred years. Now it was our turn to call it home. Leaving Houston last fall was a conscious decision to better our lives, though I could have done without the unexpected complications that literally crawled out of the ground to find us. Timing was everything. Through it all, Raven embraced ranch life, taking the reins and her responsibilities to levels I never expected. As I leaned back against the Explorer, the sight before me became more marvelous by the moment.

One by one, trucks pulling trailers full of cattle drove under the arch at the head of the ranch, entering the property in a swirl of dust and rumbling engines. As each rolled by, I could hear the deep lowing and shuffling of hooves in the trailers over the churn of each diesel-powered dually. I had seen cattle haulers on the interstate several times, but the memory that stuck with me was not the size of the rig, or the smell of its haul, but the look in the captive eyes of the cows within. Through the metal slats of the trailer, the bovine expression was hard to miss—forlorn, defeated, as if they knew the slaughterhouse was just an exit away. But I did not see that look today.

It was mid-morning and the CR was alive, bustling like the working days from generations past. I watched ranch hands hop out of a parade of pickups that followed the trailers. They huddled around Flint as he barked instructions. The message was clear. The language was raw. I did not hear everything he said, but the bunch went right to work. When they dispersed, a new chatter filled my ears. The hand's yips and hollers, body language, and chopped up, dialectical drawl created a cultural takeover of the CR in a matter of moments. Their communication alone would make an anthropologist pant.

Their work was fluid. Like red ants, they fanned out to the smaller trailers, unloading horses and gear, as the chorus of cows grew, hovering in the air like a herd milling about on the back of the morning breeze.

Standing next to Flint was Raven. Her eyes remained fixed, locked onto the controlled chaos that flooded the ranch. No sooner had I parked the Explorer had she jumped out with Miguel and ran into the house to change into her work clothes. Raven, the CR's newest ranch hand, was not about to miss out on this event. Where did my soft-spoken, schoolteacher-wife go? I dismissed the question with immediate haste. The answer did not matter. I loved who I saw. Flowing hair beneath her hat, a bright blue pearl-buttoned shirt with black, decorative swirls across each shoulder, jeans that hugged her hips, boots that knew a hard day's work, leather gloves covering her hands, and a gleam in her eyes that meant business. Her fingers twitched by her sides. I could tell she was itching to get involved. Her transformation on the ranch made her stronger, helped her regain her confidence, and was as sexy as hell.

"C'mon! Keep 'em movin'."

Flint's voice boomed across the staging area to the rails of the corral. A phatic communion surged from the men in response, then settled like a crashing wave against the shore. Flint looked over the sea of workers and caught my gaze. He lifted his chin, regarding me for a microsecond, then dipped his head close to Raven's ear. She nodded as he spoke. When Flint pulled back, she hightailed it to the barn and disappeared inside.

The front door to the house clanged, drawing my attention to the porch. Miguel walked with tentative steps to the edge of the porch and placed his hands on the railing. He watched the scene before him with innocent curiosity blended with the sleepy haze of having just woken up. I turned my back to the action and walked over to him.

"Hey, Miguel."

He turned his head and looked at me with dark-brown eyes that seemed filled with questions. I raised my hands in front of me and lowered my voice to levels I had not explored since Spencer was a child. Hard to believe my only son is a college man now.

"You see Raven?"

Miguel stared at me without answering. I lowered myself to one knee.

"Look, she's there," I said, pointing toward the barn as Raven emerged high in the saddle on the back of Robin, a mare she had become quite attached to following its delivery of a foal a few months back.

Miguel tilted his head, then turned and followed my finger.

"*Caballo*?"

His inflection matched his curiosity.

"That's right. Raven's on a horse. She's going to work for a while. Guess it's just the two of us until she gets back."

Miguel did not respond. Instead, he crossed his arms on the porch railing and rested his chin in the cradle of his knuckles.

I let out a puff of air, bulging my cheeks to ease the tension building in me. "*Patience*," Raven would say. "*It'll take some time.*"

I stood behind Miguel, giving him space to watch. Cowboys mounted horses, freshly saddled and ready for work. As the action migrated past the corral and into the pastures beyond, I stepped off the porch and turned to Miguel.

"Come," I said, waving him over. "Let's watch from over there."

I pointed to my eyes, then to the corral. Miguel lifted his head and turned around, scurrying back into the house without response.

"Well, damn," I said to myself.

I put my hands on my hips and looked out across the CR. A new swirl of dust lifted like a gentle dust devil as the herd of trucks and trailers, horses and riders cut a path through the pasture.

I followed Raven as she bounced along with the others while I stayed behind. It gave me a funny feeling to see her go. That was my job. I was the one who left her behind to wait while I went off to work. To war. This morning, our roles were reversed. I knew she would not be gone long, and that she was under the watchful eye of Flint even if she did not want it, but I immediately missed her and wondered what she would be facing. I worried, yet I was proud of the badass she had become. What a juxtaposition to be in, and what made it worse was that it was out of my control.

The front door slammed behind me, startling me out of my thoughts. Clomping boots under swift moving feet scuttled across the wooden planks as Miguel hopped off the porch and headed toward me. He was still dressed in pajamas but had pulled a pair of boots over his leggings. As the tiny bedhead cowboy neared, he spoke.

"*Quiero mirar.*"

He must have read the *I have got to learn more Spanish* expression on my face because he stopped, pointed toward the corral, and spoke again.

"L...l...look."

This was only the second time Miguel had offered any sort of unprovoked communication to me, and the kid was making an extra effort to speak so I, me, the adult, could understand him.

"Okay," I said, stepping aside. I motioned for him to walk by. "Lead the way."

I noticed the look on his face had replaced the blank stare from the porch with a sense of purpose. I instantly understood. Miguel was not caught up with the commotion of the workers and the excitement they brought to the ranch. He wanted to keep an eye on Raven, as if he would be the one to come to her rescue should she need it.

He walked past me, arms swinging by his side, boots printing tiny steps in the dirt, and headed on a direct path for the corral. In the weeks since his arrival, he spent nearly every waking moment by Raven's side. The corral was their place. It was where she introduced him to Luna, the CR's newest foal, and where he sat on the rails to watch her work with the young horse. It was where she talked to him, bonded with him, and sat quietly with him, earning his trust with small gestures and a kind voice.

He reached the rail and climbed to the top like a spider traversing its web. I followed behind and stood next to him once he reached his perch. The sun behind us cast long shadows of our bodies into the center of the corral, making us look like elongated aliens fresh off the ship. Miguel cupped his hands over his mouth and yelled.

"¡Vamos! Mami Raven. ¡Vamos!"

It was the first time I had heard a sense of excitement rally from within him. A feeling of surprise tickled my spine. He was cheering her on. But more so, had called her mommy. I watched as he lifted his hands and waved them over his head. The trail crew was too far away to take notice, but unless my eyes had deceived me, I saw the flash of a hand return his wave in the distance. Maybe it was Raven. Maybe it was a lucky coincidence or an inadvertent response by a cowboy signaling another. Either way, Miguel turned to me sporting the biggest smile I had yet to see him make. It shined across his face the way Chance's Cheshire grin lights up a room. I embraced the moment and placed a hand on his shoulder and smiled back. He did not flinch under my touch. Instead, he turned back around, and with my palm still resting in place, shouted again.

"¡Vamos! Mami Raven. ¡Vamos!"

This was a big moment. For both of us. It was the type of win where the celebration of victory went on and on, until at once, it halted. At least for me. The charging sound of a new vehicle driving onto the ranch pulled my attention away from Miguel.

Black smoke polluted the air as a massive truck surged over the cattle guards, roared past Flint's tiny house, and skidded to a stop in the center of the yard. Crunched gravel flew askew and dust surrounded the knobby tires.

The beast of a truck, complete with roof rack running lights, a blacked-out grill guard with the words KING RANCH welded into the design, and lifted chassis was owned by none other than Floyd Huckabee. His aggressive approach meant one thing, and one thing only. He was pissed about something and I was going to hear about it whether I liked it or not.

CHAPTER ELEVEN

Huckabee, southern neighbor to the CR and owner of the Flying H ranch, hopped out of his truck, disappearing behind its raised frame. The old bulldog was short and rounded in the middle and plagued with little man syndrome. If the Old West and Danny Devito could produce offspring, Floyd Huckabee would be the meanest runt of the litter.

I shook my head and pursed my lips, anticipating the rant I was about to hear. In a flash of brown, I saw him slap a hat atop his head, the brim of which bounced in view along the hood line of the truck. Rounding the front end and brushing his right arm against the iron grille guard, he walked toward me. His arms arched away from his body. The top two buttons of his long-sleeved shirt were snapped open revealing a swirl of brown and gray chest hair. His belly overlapped his waistline, covering the top portion of a large silver belt buckle. Aged skin, hardened from years of West Texas ranch life under a blistering sun, looked raw, as rugged as the Sierra del Carmen mountains across the Rio Grande. I have met with Floyd Huckabee many times and have known him to crack a smile a time or two. Genuine or not, his grin overshadows the gruffness of his face, but right now, he wore a snarled crook in his jaw. Huckabee mumbled to himself as he stormed over.

"You look like someone just spit in your beer, Floyd."

Huckabee huffed as he joined me and Miguel at the corral railing. He placed his right foot on the kickboard and tipped his hat back with an angry finger.

"Ya know..."

A surge of impatience inside of me knew right away that I was in for a long story.

"...I been livin' in these parts all my life. Near seventy goddamn years."

"Floyd," I interrupted, raising a thumb over my shoulder. "The kid?"

He lowered his voice, but his agitated tone remained.

"He talkin' American now?" Huckabee said, glancing at Miguel.

"Just try and keep it clean," I said.

Huckabee slid a finger into his mouth and swiped a wet sludge of expired tobacco from his gums onto the dirt near his feet. He spit the rest of the disgusting habit into the corral.

"Anyway, land out here gits harder ta come by. A few hundred acres here and there, maybe. But what good'll that do ya? Yer uncle Stewart'd agree with me." Huckabee turned and leaned his back against the fence. The wood slats groaned beneath the added weight. "Seems the only way to add meaningful acreage out here is ta profit from another's misfortune, or be the first in line with cash in hand when a neighbor dies."

Sinclair, I thought. *That's where this is going.*

"You planning to buy the Double SS? Hear it's coming up for auction soon. Only relatives the lawyers could find lived over in Boston. Apparently, they've been estranged for years."

Huckabee turned his head. His face soured as an ill-formed snarl returned. His eyes looked deep and hollow, like bottomless pits.

"That's that cotton-pickin' problem. The winning bid was *supposed* ta be revealed next week. Shady goddamn deal. Apparently, some highfalutin law firm from California undercut everyone. Horowitz, Lee, and Calderón. Those West Coast sons a bitches used some back channel ta git a lick on my property. An' fer what? What the hell are some flip-flopping tree huggers gonna do with ranch land here in West Texas? Build a shopping mall or some city crap like that? It's a crime if'n ya ask me." His eyebrows raised and he jabbed a finger on my shoulder. "Somethin' you an' the sheriff should look inta."

I chose to ignore his brazenness.

"Your property?"

"Hell yes! Ain't no one round here place a bid higher'n me."

"And you know this...how?"

Huckabee inhaled a deep breath, held it until I thought he would pop, then let it whistle out through the space between his front teeth.

"I know," he said, nostrils flaring.

I turned and looked at the activity filling the pastures. Brown specks of cattle began dotting the landscape between the trailers and the open expanse of the CR. Miguel was entranced, eyes fixed on the horizon. On Raven, wherever she was.

"Look, Floyd. I'm sure things like this happen all the time. It's a bad deal for you, but there's nothing I can do about it."

The veins in Huckabee's neck pulsed. His weathered hands clenched at his sides. Like a dog being let off its chain, he stormed back to his truck, grumbling the whole way. He thrust open the driver's door, hoisted himself inside, and fired up the engine. Black smoke polluted the fresh air. The diesel's rumble made Miguel jump, causing him to shoot me a concerned look. Before driving off, he leaned out the window and yelled.

"Yer a fool if this sets right with ya. Mark my words, you'll wish it were me over at the Double SS instead of Horowitz, Lee, and Calderón." He paused. His lips curled lower over his chin. "Or whoever they are workin' fer."

CHAPTER TWELVE

By mid-afternoon, the CR had taken in over three hundred bovine refugees rounded up from the Six M Ranch in Hemphill County and transported out of the dangerous path of rapidly spreading wildfires in the Texas Panhandle. I had stayed at the house with Miguel, watching through my Swarovski binoculars as the cowboy crew drew further away. The crystal-clear optics gave me a clean line of sight until the riders were too distant to distinguish apart. They also triggered a memory of the last time they were put to use—border crossing recon in Presidio preceding my undercover mission into Mexico when hunting El Despiadado. I fought to dismiss the resurfacing images. This was not the time for a flood of bullets, blood, and bad-assery to overtake my thoughts.

When the sun bent shadows to the east, I caught my first glimpse of the cowboy crew meandering back to the bull haulers. I watched them mill around the trucks and trailers until plumes of black exhaust signaled it was time to continue the parade back to headquarters.

Flint led the way. I expected to see Raven by his side,

but she was not there. Instead, a cowboy from the Six M rode next to him.

"Where you at, Little Bird," I whispered to myself.

I scanned the pack of workers, but she was nowhere near to be seen.

I focused on one rider after another, following the line of horses and trucks pulling empty trailers until I came to the back of the pack.

"There you are."

While most of the cowboys rode together in small groups, Raven and her companion rode apart. At first glance, nothing seemed out of sorts. Raven was the type of person that could talk to and get along with anyone, or at least tolerate another without revealing her true feelings. Had I not kept a fixed gaze on her, I would have missed the one telltale sign that she was not a happy rancher. Through the optics, I recognized the stone-cold glare on her face. The distance she kept from the other rider seemed deliberate, their estrangement palpable. She had been so excited to get to work today. What had changed?

I followed her through my glasses as she rode on and remembered something my uncle Stewart once told me when I visited the CR as a child. Riding drag on a trail drive was the worst assignment of all.

"Sure, it's an essential position, but not a desirable one," he had said. "If ya like ta eat dust, cause a fuss, and that's where the trail boss'll put ya."

Lowering the binoculars, I shook my head, wondering what the hell was going on with Raven.

I stepped into the house to check on Miguel. He was fast asleep on the couch with the TV remote clutched in his palm. *Go, Diego, Go!* played on the screen. I laughed to myself after recognizing the episode.

"Still saving the rainforests after all these years, huh, Diego?" I whispered.

Leaving Miguel where he slept, I crept back to the porch, then walked across the yard to the corral and waited.

Sweat trickled down my neck as the warmth from the afternoon broke the dam of tolerance around my body. It was not quite spring, but the sun blazed overhead. Each day was a mystery of its own when it came to West Texas weather. One minute, the clearest, bluest skies flood overhead like a Caribbean dream, and then the next, utter darkness and treachery form beneath the mightiest of thunderstorms. Temperatures have been known to fluctuate more than fifty degrees in a single afternoon, changing the landscape from summer to winter in a matter of just a few hours.

I caught Flint's attention when the cowboys reached the ranch. He rode over with the man from the Six M. They both dismounted their horses and looped the reins around the top corral fence beam.

"Flint," I said, extending my hand.

We shook and released.

"Cass, this here is John Morant. The Six M's been in his family near as long as the CR," he said, turning to the man standing next to him.

I offered my hand to him.

"Mr. Morant. Welcome."

John Morant was an elderly man. Beneath the brim of his hat, wrinkles outlined his leathery forehead. The look in his light blue eyes emitted a sense of warmth, but a glassy glaze of age and history coated the shine with a subtle fog. He grew a full, white mustache over a grin that looked as if he had a dozen yellow roses for teeth. My guess was that he was pushing seventy years old.

"Mr. Callahan," he said, taking my hand. His grip was like a vise and his knuckles were as bony as river rocks. He held on tight as he spoke. "Can't thank ya enough. It's hell on earth up in the Panhandle. From what I've heard this mornin', things are only gettin' worse."

I could feel the angst in his grasp as he shook my hand.

"I'm glad we can help, but thanks should go to Flint. He's the one who..."

Morant cut me off.

"Bet ya didn't know that me an' yer uncle Stewart go back a ways. Used ta sling beers behind the stands at the Tri-state rodeo up in Amarillo. We was kids at the time. No fear. No rules. Just lookin' fer a good time without findin' ourselves in the hot seat come mornin'. Those were the days, I tell ya."

When our hands parted, I felt the blood flow into my fingers, chasing away the pins and needles that had started to prick my entrapped palm.

"That so?"

We stood eye to eye regarding one another. More riders made their way onto the yard, clustering around the corral. I could hear chatter among the growing crowd, but my focus remained on John Morant.

"Ay-yuh. Was sorry ta hear of his passin'. Guess yer the new head honcho round here."

"Something like that," I said. "Just glad I have Flint to run things. My wife and I are lucky to have him."

I turned to Flint.

"Speaking of Ra..."

"Hold up there, Cass." He looked at a mass of cowboys assembling around the perimeter of the corral. "Somethin's about ta go down that you may want ta git in the middle of. Whatever happens, don't!"

I followed his gaze and saw the last of the trucks and trailers pull around the corral. In the swirl of their dust, Raven emerged, aiming her horse for the far side of the corral. The other rider followed behind her. As they reached the fencing, two cowboys hopped into the corral and pulled the gate open so they could enter. Raven reined her horse to one side while the other rider led her horse to the opposite rail.

"Flint, what the hell is going on?"

"Well, we're gonna have ourselves an ol' fashioned, West Texas barn burner."

Flint glanced at Morant.

"Yep. Got a couple bobcats that need ta get the scratch outta the way. No time ta settle differences on the range. Now that we're done, they kin git it outta their system."

I looked across the corral and saw Raven next to her horse. Her jaw was clenched tight. Her eyes held a look I had seen many times before...on the battlefield. Never from her.

I switched my gaze to the other rider who had entered the ring. From behind, all I could see was the braided end of a blonde ponytail dangling over a sweated shirt. When the rider turned around, a dusted female face glared at Raven. She removed her hat and tossed it to a cowboy nearby. A long, blue curl of hair fell over her face. She removed her leather work gloves and slipped them into her rear pocket, then tucked the strand of hair behind her ear.

I looked back to Raven. She had started to walk to the middle of the corral. With each step, she unbuttoned her cuffs and rolled up her sleeves.

"Flint?"

"I told ya, but it's best ta let this run its course." He leaned close to me and whispered. "Raven ain't told anyone her place here on the CR. It was her choice. Now, she's earnin' her place among seasoned cowboys. You git in the way of that, she'll never amount ta anythin' in their eyes. An' you'll look like a mother hen protecting its brood."

Morant placed a boot on the kickboard and folded his hands over the top beam of the corral fence. Flint leaned away and joined him. I stood with my arms dangling at my side. They felt heavy. I felt helpless. The only time I knew of Raven fighting was when she had been attacked, once in our home in Houston, and once here on the CR when La Sombra Negra tried to kill her. Both had been fights for her life. This was different. It looked to be a matter of anger, or pride.

CHAPTER THIRTEEN

Tension filled the corral like a sweltering August heat index as the two fighters approached each other. Sweat dribbled down Raven's cheeks. It ran down her neck. Except for the errant strand of hair tucked behind her ear, matted wisps of blue stuck to the other woman's forehead. Her face was flushed. It could have been sunburn, but her forceful chugs of breath between gritted teeth made me think otherwise. Cupping her hands around the top of her head and the bottom of her chin, she cracked her neck. The distinctive rat-a-tat-tat spoke to harsh life experience and brute preparation of which Raven should be sorely concerned. I sure the hell was.

Cowboys lined the fencing, ready and waiting for action. Flint pointed out a few from the Six M and a handful of neighboring North Texas ranches, naming who each was and told me a few ragged things about each man.

"And the girl?" I asked.

"Don't know 'er. Looks like Beauty and the Beast all rolled inta one, don't ya think?"

I rolled my eyes.

"Great observation, Flint. You gonna tell me what led to this?"

Flint answered as he looked ahead.

"Yep, but not right now. Don't matter what started it, just that it's gonna git finished right here."

The girls circled each other, silently staring down the other.

One cowboy whooped. Another shouted.

"Got yerself a wild one there, Blue Gil. Time ta break 'er in."

His words set off a raucous round of revelry around the corral. The enthusiasm for the ensuing brawl was akin to the crowd of Bartertown citizens perched around Thunderdome. *"Two men enter, one man leaves."* This was not a fight to the death, but it could get ugly.

I glanced over my shoulder hoping the noise did not wake Miguel. He did not need to see what was about to happen. I focused on the porch as long as I could stand it. Seconds thumped in my temples as the beat of my anxious heart kept the time. The front door did not open.

Turning around, I looked back into the corral. Into the ring. What I saw made my neck burn. Raven and Blue Gil stood poised and ready to fight—Fists clenched, eyes squinted, cheeks pulsing red, and nostrils flared.

Jesus, was Raven really doing this. And was I really going to let it happen? I knew the consequences of an intervention, but damn!

Like runners reacting to the sound of a starter's gun, the words "GIT IT ON" bellowed from the crowd, and the two girls charged.

Dust rose at their heels.

Blue Gil growled. Her voice rumbled low, gaining steam and volume as her war cry screeched above the rowdy crowd. As she closed on Raven, Blue Gil cocked her right fist and lunged ahead with a brutal swing.

I clenched my teeth together as I watched the punch fly at Raven's head.

At the last possible moment, Raven ducked left, then rammed her shoulder into Blue Gil's chest. A thunderous wail erupted from the fences when the girls collided.

That's it. Now...grab...sweep...stomp...

I found myself calling out moves in my head. Moves I would perform that would quickly cause my opponent to submit, or worse. If only Raven could hear me. She was not a fighter. A killer.

Raven swung, landing a left fist to the middle of Blue Gil's back. Unfazed by the blow, Blue Gil threw a sharp elbow into Raven's ribcage. The two girls parted, but only for a moment.

"That's not enough, bitch." Blue Gil said with a sneer.

"*Whoa's*" and "*oooh's*" rippled around the ring.

The lock of blue hair dangled in front of her face.

Raven did not waver. She slid her left foot back, bent her knees, and raised her fists in front of her. Her stance was impressive. Though she had never studied martial arts like Spencer and I had, it's not unusual for parents to become familiar with the most basic of lessons, even from the viewing section of the Taekwondo school lobby. Now she was beyond the safety glass, and instinct was her only ally.

With surprising quickness, Raven slid forward and jabbed her right fist into Blue Gil's mouth. Knuckles landed. Skin and teeth crackled. Blue Gil's head snapped back.

Don't stop. Keep the pressure on. Raven slid back to her ready position. *One punch is not enough.*

Swirls of dirt rose and settled around Raven's feet as she moved to her left. She flexed her fists. I could tell she wanted more, but I knew she did not know what to do next.

Blue Gil tilted her head, following Raven's movement, staring at her like a rattlesnake poised to strike. Slipping her tongue between parted lips, she licked a trickle of blood forming at the corner of her mouth. The taste— salty, warm, thick. I knew the feeling.

Shit.

Like a wild bronco, Blue Gil kicked Raven in the thigh, then charged with a flurry of punches to her bicep, stomach, and face. Raven's body rocked from the sudden attack. Blue Gil wound up for a mighty put-down. Raven twisted just in time for the punch to miss her face, but she did not dodge the powerful blow fully. The solid strike connected with her shoulder blade, sending Raven sprawling to the side. She lost her footing and fell to the ground.

Roll. Roll. Roll.

Raven did not roll. She did not have time. Blue Gill jumped on top of her, pinning her to the dirt beneath her weight. She punched Raven in the face. Blood sprayed from her nose.

"Still talking shit now?"

Raven wriggled beneath her.

God! I found myself leaning forward, toes curled in my shoes, hands pushing my body higher on the corral fence. I wanted to jump in. I wanted to pull Blue Gil off. I felt myself raising higher when a gripping palm wrapped around my forearm pulled me back.

"Not yet."

I whipped my head to the side, locking eyes with Flint.

"She's getting her ass handed to her."

Flint lowered his foot from the kickboard and faced me.

"What she's doin' is earnin' respect. Sure, it'll sting,

but take a look around. When this is all over, ain't a one of these hands that won't have her back tomorrow and every day after that."

Morant leaned back, eyes still on the ring, but added a final thought.

"It ain't explainable lest you walk it yerself, Callahan."

I shook my head. I knew that drill. I just never expected Raven to be on the violent end of acceptance.

"Fine," I said.

I turned back to the fight in time to see Blue Gil jab Raven in the ribs. My heart splintered.

"Come on," I yelled. "Dig, Raven. Dig."

I saw Blue Gil's mouth move but could not hear what she said. Raven's eyes bulged, then tightened as if she stared directly into the sun. Her cheeks puffed. A roar like no sound I had ever heard Raven make before blasted from deep within her. Tingles prickled my spine. A surge of excitement welled in me.

Using what energy she had left, Raven bucked and twisted. Blue Gil rode out the escape attempt but remained dominant. She leaned back for another power-filled punch, causing a small gap between her crotch and Raven's waist. Raven bucked again. She kicked out and up with both legs, landing the toe of her boot on the back of Blue Gil's head. The crowd crooned.

Another flailing jolt of her body gave Raven enough room to slink out from beneath Blue Gil. Like a scorpion, she scuttled away.

Blue Gil rose to her feet, shaking her head. Raven retreated to the corral fence. Her nose crinkled, and she gritted her teeth as she pulled herself up.

"Hell yeah!" one cowboy said, standing near her.

Hearing that phrase. That simple exaltation caused a rush of pride to wash over me.

Heads nodded and rugged encouragement sounded out from other hands near her.

I saw her knuckles tighten. I watched her suck painful breath after painful breath. Blue Gil stepped toward her. Stalked her. With a hair-raising yell, she charged.

Raven moved to meet her head-on. Blue Gil's arms swung wide. Raven stepped into her advance, kicked her right foot in front of her like a striker attempting a penalty kick, and landed a solid boot square between Blue Gil's legs. Lionell Messi would have celebrated.

A surge of air rushed out of Blue Gil. She doubled over, but Raven was not done. Just as the fight started, Raven rammed her shoulder into Blue Gil, knocking her over. As she tumbled backward, Blue Gil latched onto Raven's shirt, ripping cloth and popping buttons, and pulled her down on top of her.

The two fighters rolled over and over near the center of the corral. Dust clung to sweat, caking their skin and clothes with a layer of beige grime. Punches flew but the intensity of each blow lessened. Strained, exhausted grunts accompanied each burst.

Tangled in battle, the two women looked rough. Blood stained Raven's face, dribbling in dirty red rivulets from her nose. Across her lips. Into her mouth. Her right cheek looked on fire, puffing and bruised. Blue Gil's upper lip was swelling. The fiery look in her eye waned to a flicker. Instead, they looked spent, ready for an end.

The chatter and cheers around the rim of the raucous corral filled the CR. It echoed in my ears as I watched the two warriors, *my warrior*, take a stand against one another.

Movement out of the corner of my eye drew my attention to Flint as he climbed the fence and jumped into the corral. He strode with measured deliberation, calming the onlookers by his presence alone. Each step seemed to mute the surrounding chaos, drawing all eyes toward him as he moved toward the girls.

Stopping next to their continued entanglement, he spoke.

"Enough. That cuts it."

His voice boomed. I heard his words as clear as day, but the girls refused to heed his call.

"Goddamn it," he said, stepping forward. "I said enough!"

Reaching down, he grabbed Raven as she rolled on top of Blue Gil and tossed her to the side like he was slinging wood at the burn pile. He then reached down and pulled Blue Gil to her feet. She struggled once, but the strength of Flint's glare punched through her determination to continue.

I had to hand it to Raven; she was as wild as a tiger in a rage, brushing off her displacement by Flint and charging back in again.

"Rave!" I yelled.

Flint turned in time to point an iron finger at her, nearly poking her in the face.

"Cut this shit!" The look in Flint's eyes could tame a mountain lion just as easy as his firm jaw could gnash it apart. "It's done."

Raven stopped. Her breaths calmed, each huff's intensity diminishing as the adrenaline had done its job. Blue Gil brushed the loose dirt from her clothes.

I climbed the fence and hopped into the corral. Other cowboys did the same. Each of us walked over and surrounded the two fighters and Flint.

"Now," Flint said. "Don't matter what happened before. Only thing is where we go from here."

He turned to Blue Gil.

"Gilly, you've made your point."

He turned to Raven.

"And you. Damn, if you ain't one stubborn—"

"Son of a bitch?" Raven said, interrupting him.

A smile escaped Flint's lips.

"Something like that."

John Morant stepped forward and stood with Flint between the two. He looked at the crowd, connecting with each of them as he shared a glance.

"I can't say enough about ol' Levi Flint and the Callahan Ranch. We all know the trouble we're facing in the Panhandle, at our own steads, but it's people like this..." Morant laid a hand on Flint's shoulder. "...that reminds me that Texans and ranchin' are one big family. I've been friends with the Callahans for ages. Now that the elder's past on, it's time to foster a new relationship with the next generation."

He held a hand for me. We shook, but he did not let go.

"Cass Callahan, thank you for opening the CR to us in our time of need. Stewart would be mighty proud."

His eyes fell to Raven. Letting go of my hand, he stepped over to her.

"And you..." He paused to look back at his crowd of cowboys at Blue Gil. "Bein' a rancher, a cowboy, ain't easy."

Murmurs and head nods rippled through the crowd.

"It means long, tough hours. It's givin' all you got for a grander purpose. It's takin' what yer given and doin' more with it than ya thought ya ever could."

He turned and looked into Raven's settled eyes.

"And sometimes it means standin' up fer yerself when ya know you've done ever'thing ya know ta do, even if it ain't all right."

A rise in curiosity filtered among the crowd as Morant offered Raven his hand.

"Mrs. Callahan, I think ever'one'll agree with me when

I say you may not have been born ta be a rancher, but ain't no one gonna say ya ain't one right now."

Whoops and hollers rose from the crowd at the surprised revelation of Raven's true identity. Blue Gil shook her head. Morant let go of Raven's hand. Flint glanced at Raven, winked, and followed Morant to the corral gate.

As the crowd dispersed, I watched Blue Gil approach Raven and prepared to jump in the middle if tensions re-escalated. She stopped in front of her, massaging her swollen lips.

"Callahan? Mrs. CR, huh?"

"Yep."

"Didn't want anyone ta know? Maybe treat ya different?"

Raven nodded.

"I get it." Blue Gil offered her a hand. "Yer tougher 'n' shit."

Raven took her hand and shook.

"Call me Gilly."

"I'm Raven. Raven Callahan."

Gilly smiled.

"Goddamn right you are."

CHAPTER FOURTEEN

A pink glow hovered overhead like satin sheets draped among the clouds as the day slowed to a saunter. Most of our new North Texas friends had headed out, eager to get back to the Panhandle to lend a hand to the many other ranches in the literal line of fire. John Morant stayed behind with a group from the Six M.

"I want ya ta keep a few of my hands on as long as the herd is down here. Too much to ask fer y'all ta see to 'em on yer own."

Morant sipped coffee, black and steamy as requested, while he sat with Raven, Flint, and me.

"That's generous of you," I said, then looked to Flint.

Morant cupped his coffee in his hands and leaned forward in his chair.

"Generous? Yer makin' this sound like it's my show ta run. It's one thing ta offer up yer land. Hell, y'all did that without switch of the tail, but ta tend to them cattle on yer own? Wouldn't be right ta leave ya without some help."

"What'd ya have in mind?" Flint asked.

Morant relaxed back in his chair.

"Well, there's Jesse, Pedro, and Cody..." Morant paused, turning his attention to Raven. "...and Gilly."

We all turned to Raven. Clint Black's song *Good Run of Bad Luck* rose on the early evening breeze as the tune escaped the open windows of the Six M dually where the last of Morant's crew waited with cold beers in hand.

"You all are looking at me like it's my decision."

Raven reached for the cooler and pulled a fresh bottle of Corona from the ice-cold slosh therein. She twisted the cap, tossed it back into the cooler, and took a long swig. Beneath her eyes, red and purple puffy trails scorched each side of her nose. Her knuckles were scraped and raw. We all watched as she lowered the bottle and wiped her mouth with her sleeve.

"You *are* asking me," she said. It was Raven's turn to lean forward. "Let me answer with a question of my own. Mr. Morant, are these the best hands for the job?"

Morant smiled.

"Yes, ma'am. They are."

"Then that settles it. They can bunk in the spare house next to Flint. Should be enough room. And I think Gilly can handle herself among the boys? Or am I wrong."

"Not wrong at all, Mrs. Callahan. At the Six M, all my cowboys bunk together. Ain't no funny business goin' on after hours. Game of cards, maybe some drinkin' to wind down the day, but that's it. They know to toe the line and are aware of the consequences should they choose to cross it."

It was at that moment when I realized I was second fiddle to Raven on all things CR. She was the one that put in the range work. She was the one that proved her worth. She would be the one grinding away in the saddle every day. I chuckled to myself when the thought came full circle. I was fine with all of it.

A growing rumble caused us to turn away from one another and look to the road beyond the CR's fence line. Black smoke littered the air, soiling the glazing pink skyline. The noise grew until a line of massive diesel eighteen-wheelers barreled past the ranch. Solid black trailers in tow cut through the dust and exhaust, hauling who knows what.

"New neighbors?" Morant said.

"Looks like Huckabee was right," I said.

We settled back into our chairs. Flint cocked his head.

"Come again, Cass."

"According to Floyd, the Double SS was purchased in some shady, backroom deal by a law firm out of California. I hadn't heard a word about it until today. I knew the ranch had been cleared for sale, but that was about it."

"What's a law firm want with a ranch way the hell out here?" Flint asked.

"Your guess is as good as mine, Flint," I said. "Maybe I'll run by one of these days. See what's going on."

Flint gulped the final dregs of his beer, his eyes falling upon mine as he lowered the empty bottle.

"Lemme know when ya do. I'd like ta ride along."

I nodded at Flint. The ensuing silence brought a moment of curious confusion, cutting our fellowship time short. Raven stood.

"If you will excuse me, I'll grab the keys to the Six M house and let everyone get settled."

We all stood.

"That what we're calling it now?" I asked.

"You have another suggestion?"

"Nope. Sounds good, Rave."

"I'll head over with ya when yer ready," Morant said. "Won't surprise 'em that a few are stayin' here."

Raven disappeared into the house in search of the keys.

"My crew'll blend in. They're a good bunch. A little rowdy at times as you are well aware, but they'll sure as fight for the CR as they would the Six M. Your scrappy wife saw ta that already."

Raven returned with jingling keys in hand.

"Ready, Mr. Morant?"

"Lead the way Mrs. Callahan."

Flint and I stayed behind as Raven stepped off the porch and headed over to the Six M crew with John Morant.

"Cass," Flint said. "I gotta tell ya, Raven impressed the shit outta me today. If you'da told me when ya first arrived that she was gonna be one of my ranch hands, I mighta laughed you back ta Houston. But, damn! Look at her now."

"Yeah."

It was all I said, all I could say at that moment. My attention was fixed on watching her approach the Six M bunch. Gilly was the first to see them walk over. She raised a beer, signaling for the guys to take notice. Chatter rose from the group like it did when they first arrived and got to work. It was welcoming, rugged; A lassoing of Texas lingo that said, "Yer one of us now." The dialectical drawl and cowboy speak was foreign to my ears, but it connected with Flint. He grunted, shifting his weight from one foot to the other. A quick glance at his face showed me his cards, if only for a moment, but I caught something I had not seen in him before. One distinctive emotion. Pride. I memorized the look and filed it away with the other minute details about Flint I kept secured in my head, then returned my gaze to Raven and Morant.

Morant lifted both hands to quell the rowdy bunch. When he spoke, all heads turned to him. Duty and respect fell in line as each cowboy listened to what he had to say. I watched as Gilly stepped over to stand next to Raven.

"Any reason to think we'll have another situation in the corral?" I said to Flint.

"Most likely, no. But these guys are born tough. Sometimes fightin' is what they need ta let off some steam. But that ain't why ya asked. What ya really want ta know is if Gilly an' Raven'll go another round. Don't take a genius ta know what yer thinkin', Cass."

I looked at Flint. He smiled like we were old buddies and he was yanking my chain. Flint and I had our problems in the past. Like Raven and Gilly, we duked it out and the two of us are now in a good place. Trust born through fire is as strong a bond as one can make with another. Time will only tell if Raven and Gilly will walk the same road.

CHAPTER FIFTEEN

TWO WEEKS LATER

I am so tired of the chase. Of the blood. Of the killing. Illegal activity along the Texas border had spiked, and although the terrain north and south of Brewster was rugged and barren, we were not immune to this surge. Incidents were becoming a daily occurrence, pushing the Border Patrol, Texas DPS, and the Brewster County Sheriff's Office to their limits. The federal government had mobilized some National Guard units, but this proved insufficient. In an attempt to address these shortcomings, Governor Abbott mobilized his own National and State Guard, financing their efforts with state funds to address growing international hotspots along the Texas border. Even with this initiative, desolate South Brewster County received only limited assistance. Our resources were stretched thin, taking a toll not only on law enforcement but on the community as well.

Every day for the last two weeks, the sheriff's office had responded to reports of illegal transients on private ranchland, burglary of local businesses, automotive theft, and in one case, murder. Such crimes were not surprising in cities with international crossings, but for small-town Brewster, the increased criminal activity had citizens on edge. The absence of a strong border policy provided an open invitation for the world's worst to exploit its vulnerabilities, pushing those most committed to entering the country illegally away from populated areas to what some referred to as a borderless region. The increased volatility had us all working overtime.

Further complicating matters, the Brewster County Sheriff's Office had been involved in the arrest and detention of individuals from a wide array of countries, underscoring the diverse and international nature of the issues we faced. The days of intercepting the traditional Mexican migrant were a thing of the past.

"This shit is getting outta hand."

The gruff voice of Detective Ray Porter, my former partner and ex-Army lieutenant, rattled the speakerphone of the Explorer.

"You wouldn't believe what we've had to deal with here in Houston."

Once "No Filter Ray" got going, it was hard to get a word in edgewise.

"It's not like the old days when wetbacks made a run for it. Bust a cattle rig hauling beaners or a camper crammed like a clown car headed for who knows where. No. Now we've got fuckers from all over trying to sneak in and through Houston, for Christ's sake! North Africa, Syria, fucking Iran..."

I turned the speaker volume to level one and let Ray's rant blend with the hum of the Explorer's tires as I drove down RR170. I was coming off another long day with the sheriff's office and was ready to throw out the blood-spattered jeans I was wearing. When things went to hell, I usually found myself with Chance at the center of it all. Today was no different.

Needing to decompress, I had called Ray to check up on him and see how his injuries were healing. My friend, the old battle axe, had been shot during our black ops hunt of the Camargo cartel and El Despiadado. Call it luck, fate, or that he was just too damn stubborn to die in Mexico, Ray suffered our escape flight back to the States and pulled through. Hearing his voice was both therapeutic and annoying, but I loved the guy.

A brief pause on the line made me think he had dumped his load and was waiting for my reply. *Wrong.* I raised the speaker volume in time to hear the beginnings of round two.

"A hodge podge of Eggplants and Slant Eyes were busted at the port just last week. Cass? Ya hear me?"

"I'm with you."

"It's like I said, this shit is getting outta hand. I can only imagine what you're having to deal with. Thought the whole reason you moved out west was to get away from this crap."

I paused, reflecting on his last words—*get away from this crap.* He was not wrong. The trajectory of my life, of my intentions, had taken a serious turn since we arrived at the CR. Focus on Raven. Focus on family. Move on from law enforcement.

How's that workin' out for you, Cass? I thought.

It has had its rewards, but as of late I have found myself sinking further and further into the sludge Raven and I had attempted to leave behind in Houston.

"Cass?"

"You're right. It's been a cluster fuck from the beginning. Especially these last two weeks. Even tried to disappear into Big Bend but couldn't escape the monotony."

The ping of a call waiting invaded the line.

"Big Bend? Haven't told me about that yet."

The line pinged again. I huffed and read the caller ID.

"Gonna have to wait, Ray. Gotta take a call."

"Roger that."

I clicked the *accept* button on the dashboard controls and connected with the incoming call.

"What can I do for you, Special Agent Sharp?"

"It's Special Agent in Charge now, Callahan."

"No shit? What happened to Zuñiga?"

"Washington snagged him up. Bunch of bureaucratic rearranging going on."

"Lemme guess. You're happy to take the post but pissed that you didn't get the call up to the big leagues as well. Why be a bench player on varsity when you can be the star on JV?"

"Nobody wants to be that guy, and yeah. Pissed, but I can deal."

"No choice but to."

"There's always a choice, Callahan. You know that."

All too well as of late, I thought.

"Yeah. So, you didn't call to sing your own praises. What's on your mind?"

"Heard you had a run in a week or so back down in the park. Seems like there isn't a place in the world where trouble can't find you."

"How'd you hear about that?"

"Special Agent *in Charge*, Callahan. I have become all-seeing."

Great. Just what I need. When I first met then Agent Dylan Sharp, he was an infectious thorn in my backside. To say I did not like the guy was an understatement. Loathing comes to mind, at least until recently. He elevated from definitive asshole to tolerable prick when he saved my life and Ray's life on our mission to Camargo. I should also acknowledge that he flew me back into

Mexico under the radar once I located El Despiadado, so I could give him a special, heartfelt sendoff. *BOOM*. A normal person might think that friendships are formed by such things, but Agent Sharp, now *Special Agent in Charge* Dylan Sharp soaked in too much of the glorified Kool-aide after our mission and did an immediate about-face. The guy's social skills were a mess. Maybe he was bullied as a kid. Maybe he was the last one picked at dodgeball. Maybe his prom date ended up dancing the night away with another guy. Whatever his baggage was, he let a growing hero complex overshadow all things, and I mean *ALL* things, causing the chaffing between us to return red, hot, and irritating as ever. I will always owe him my life, and he knew that.

"Sharp, I don't have the time or the patience right now to..."

"But you will want to hear this. When I saw your name flash by in a joint terrorism task force brief, I too a closer look."

Terrorism?

"Seems like your run-in with the Chinese douchebag and his multinational friends struck a chord somewhere up the chain."

"You're not making any sense, Sharp."

"I'm just saying that you might have been at ground zero for something pretty damn big."

The road ahead dipped low, then climbed again like the Rattler at Fiesta Texas before it was renovated. As the road peaked, I had an open view of RR170, the surrounding rugged terrain, and a car stopped on the shoulder about a half of a mile ahead.

"Maybe you'd like to come up to El Paso and sit in on a few meetings? Say the word and I'll have an official badge waiting for you at the security desk. Agent Cass Callahan. Has a nice ring to it, don't you think?"

Now a quarter of a mile away, I saw steam rising into the air. Two figures paced back and forth at the front of the car. They both looked small in stature. I pegged them as teenagers in need of help.

"Not interested," I said, my eyes locked on the stranded vehicle and its passengers.

"Cass. Come on. This is a big chance for you."

"It's not, really. More like a big pain in the ass." I activated my hazard lights and pulled onto the shoulder. Loose gravel and broken bits of asphalt crackled under the weight of the tires. "Look, the information is interesting, but it's not something I want to get involved with."

"Could be a..."

"Look, Sharp. Hard pass. Thanks anyway."

I could hear the hiss of frustration over the line as Sharp breathed into his phone.

"You'll change your mind," he said, then ended the call.

"Not a chance," I said aloud, as I slowed the Explorer to a stop behind the disabled vehicle.

I looked ahead and saw two black-haired, frightened-faced figures peer around either side of their car, then glance back at each other. Intuition kicked in taking, and labeling, mental snapshots of everything I saw. Blue Ford Escort. Mid to late 1990s model. Two middle-aged persons. One male. One female. Black hair. Both stood roughly five foot four to five foot six. Slight figures under loosely fit clothing. If I had to guess, they were both Chinese.

I opened the door and stepped out. The air was a mix of warm and cool, fluctuating with the breeze as sun and the wind danced delicately over the dips and peaks of RR170. Hiding caution behind a friendly smile, I waved my hand and walked over to greet them.

"This is a lonely stretch of road. Do you need a hand?"

Neither answered. The man stood near the front left side of the steaming car. As I approached, the woman joined the man, taking a subservient position behind him. High cheek bones on the woman gave her a demure appearance. She bowed her head, staring at the ground.

The man squinted his eyes as he watched me approach. His look seemed both cautious and afraid. I stopped at the rear of the Ford. Paint peeled in faded strips from the bumper and the roof of the old car. Rusty screws held a dusty Texas license plate in place. Something felt...off, like I was not supposed to be here.

"You all okay?"

I saw the man slowly move his right hand across his waist and reach for something in his pocket.

Alarms went off in my head. Angling my body to use the rear of the car as protection, I lowered my stance and put one palm out in front of me. My other hand reached for my gun.

"Keep your hands where I can see them," I said, my detective's voice sounding off with professional determination.

CHAPTER SIXTEEN

"No! No! *Diànhuà*...I...no..."
Broken, frightened English gushed from the man. I kept my eyes locked on him as he waved his hands in a flurry of pleading gestures. He stepped forward one step then stopped, leaned to one side, and looked past me. The woman moved in sync with his every step as if she were latched onto him but never raised her head. As if watching a car pass in slow motion, the man twisted his head around to look over his shoulder in the opposite direction. I followed his gaze. RR170 was empty as far as the eye could see. When he turned back to face me, he slowly dropped his left hand to his side and raised his right hand to his ear. Resting his right thumb on his earlobe and curving his pinky around in front of his mouth, he froze like a street mime working for tips.

"Phone?" I said aloud, my inflection offering understanding and curiosity. I placed my hand near my ear to mimic his action.

The man's cheeks relaxed. His eyelids fell into their natural resting place. He shook his head.

"F...f...ohh...ne."

I lowered my hand and straightened my stance. Stepping into full view of him, he looked me over, his eyes stopping and fixating on my legs. I looked down at my jeans.

The blood, I thought.

Spatterings of red stained my jeans from an incident I had been involved in earlier today.

"Okay. Okay," I said. "Is your phone in your pocket?"

I patted my left front pocket, then pointed at him.

He reached for his pocket with tentative fingers, patted his leg twice, and nodded. By the man's actions, I could tell he understood.

"S...ank yu...f...f...ohn...ne..."

I watched as he slipped his fingers into his pants and pulled out an iPhone. A brand-new-looking iPhone. He swiped his finger across the screen, then tapped something into the device. A moment later, he held it over his head, and Siri spoke to me.

"The car is broken."

When she finished, he lowered the phone and tapped again. Curiosity piquing, I waited for his next message.

"Thank you. We do not need your help. Thank you."

Siri's voice, as condescending sounding as ever, repeated the announcement twice before the man lowered the phone.

I looked at the car, then walked closer.

"You sure about that? There's nothing for miles around."

One glance at his phone verified what I had been thinking—the newest, most expensive phone on the market. Interesting how he could afford such an expensive device and yet he drove a Ford POS. And their clothing? Plain and well worn. It did not add up to me.

The man shrugged his shoulders. With raised eyebrows, he shook his head.

"No."

I thought I might try Google Translate to communicate with him, but I was not certain which language to use in reply. He looked Chinese to me, but could very well be from Taiwan, or Mongolia for all I knew. Even if my profile was spot on, the number of multiple dialects within the Chinese language itself would make it difficult at best for me to effectively communicate. I settled for English.

"Let me call you a tow truck."

The man's face showed an absence of understanding while retaining a calm, indifferent demeanor.

I raised one finger, then pulled out my phone. Four generations older than his, but still got the job done. I swiped through my contacts until I found the number for Hector Chavez, a local wrecker driver. The man's eyes followed my every move. I lifted the phone to my ear and gave him a courteous smile.

The line buzzed three times before a quick talking, high-pitched woman answered my call.

"Hector's tow. What you need?"

"Is this Marcella?"

"Yeah."

"Hey Marcella. It's Cass Callahan. Can you get Hector out to south RR170..." I paused and looked along the road for a mile marker. "...just past marker seventy-eight? Got a couple stranded with an old Ford Escort. Looks like a bad radiator."

"Okay. Okay." Her voice sped over the line. *"Gimme a minute."*

I heard the thud of her laying the phone on a desk or counter, followed by static from a CB radio. Short, muffled bursts of Spanish rolled off her tongue. She was persistent, repeating the same words until Hector responded. After a back-and-forth that sounded like a frenetic Spanish-dubbed conversation between Charlie Brown and his teacher, Marcella spoke to me.

"*Okay, Cass. Hector will be there in twenty.*"

"Thank you, Marcella."

"*Jus' make sure they can pay.*"

The line went dead before I had time to reply. I slipped the phone into my back pocket and leaned against their car. The steam from under the hood slowed, which only meant the engine was cooling. If they tried to drive it anywhere, it would overheat in a matter of seconds. Their only way out was with Hector.

"I've got someone coming to help you."

The man wrinkled his face and tilted his head, then said words I did not understand to the women still shadowing him. The woman nodded with quick, tiny bursts. The man tapped his finger on his phone again, then held it out for me to take.

"You want me to...?" I said, standing up straight.

I started to reach for his phone when a loud engine roared over the rise south of us. It caused both of us to turn and have a look. A lone truck barreled down RR170 like the driver was racing for the checkered flag at Daytona.

If that's you already, Hector, slow it down. But how could he have responded so quickly?

On cue, the driver pulled onto the shoulder but did not slow down. Wrecker drivers, at least back home in Houston, are better referred to as reckless drivers in pursuit of their next haul. It always amazed me that they were not the cause of more accidents, especially during rush hour. For wrecker drivers, speeding through congestion on the Sam Houston Tollway was like playing Frogger, with them as the frantic croaker trying to reach the lily pad.

I stepped away from the disabled Ford and onto the

road. I wanted a clear view of the driver and for whoever it was to see me. Only one of us won that round. The sinking, late afternoon sun blazed with intensity, creating a glare that shimmered across the front window, blocking my view of the driver's face. While I was curious who was driving, one thing I knew for sure: it was not Hector.

This...thing...was decked out with thousands of dollars of aftermarket upgrades—knobby, off-road tires, lift kit raising the chassis at least eight inches, rock sliders, custom chrome grille, custom light bars fixed to the roof and grille guard, snorkel kit, a vented hood, and a matte black paint job. The make and model of the truck was almost unrecognizable. It was like Alex Murphy after he became *Robocop*.

I glanced back at the man to see his wife's eyes peering over his shoulder. Enlarged, fixed on the truck, like she had seen something she should not have seen or done something she should have done. The woman was afraid. The look on the man's face was less obvious, but I could not help but feel that he, too, was uncomfortable with whoever was coming.

At the last possible moment, the driver slammed on the brakes. Tires screeched out in pain as RR170 claimed a layer of its skin. The rumbling engine could have very well been a guard dog prowling for trespassers. A glint of shine reflected from something inside the cab just before the door swung open.

CHAPTER SEVENTEEN

My spidey senses tingled. My fingers twitched. The air seemed to grow hot and stale like the inside of a parked car baked by hours of direct sunlight. I watched as a mammoth of a man stepped out of the driver's side, easily reaching the ground without needing to slide out of the raised cab. The truck rocked, relieved from carrying the added weight. Leaving the door open, he stepped away from the truck and placed his hands on his hips.

He stood at least six foot six, maybe more. His barreled chest and bouldered midsection looked solid. He wore pointed-toe black boots, a belt buckle over jeans that looked like a manhole cover, and a button-down, long sleeve Wrangler shirt. His sleeves were rolled up above the elbow and three buttons on the front of the shirt were unbuttoned. Oddly enough, as working a man as he portrayed, his clothing looked new. He held his jaw firm, which bunched his cheeks under eyes of which I could not see. Black aviator glasses covered any sign of relief or contempt he may have been feeling. My gut told me it was the latter. His speed. His body language. Hell, just his massive presence aroused suspicion. But the most important detail of all was this...I did not know and have never seen the man before.

"Mr. Kang. Mrs. Ping. Why don't y'all get in the truck."

His deep voice rumbled like his truck's engine.

"I'll get ya back home."

He raised one hand, then waved them over with his fingers.

The man, Kang, hesitated. The woman, Ping, nudged him in the back causing Kang to bark at her in sharp foreign bursts.

"None of that," the man bellowed. "Come get in the truck."

I stepped forward.

"Howdy, friend."

I knew the man had seen me, and it was clear that he had ignored my standing across from Kang and Ping. Now that I had addressed him, he turned to look at me.

"Tow trucks on the way. Shouldn't be long." The man let out an exasperated stream of breath. The air whistled through his teeth. Stepping closer, I continued to engage with him. "You from around these parts?"

"You ask a lot of questions...friend. If you don't mind, we'll just be on our way."

He looked back at Kang and Ping, who were both now staring at me. They wore a sheen of fear like a loose scarf threatening to slip from each of their necks. Or was it a noose?

I had no legal leg to stand on, no real way to keep the man from taking the two. If they got into the truck voluntarily, they would have to deal with whatever problems they faced with him on their own. The car was my only card, but it might as well have been a seven of clubs. Worthless, but worth a bluff.

"You know, I hear the county impounds deserted cars.

They should stick around at least so they can tell the tow truck where to take it."

The man removed his glasses. His eyes threw daggers at me, but with one slip of the tongue, he changed his tune.

"You know, you're right." He paused long enough to contort his grimace into a forced smile. "Listen, friend. These two are needed back at the ranch." He shifted his gaze to Kang and Ping. "I've told you before that you don't have to worry about going out for supplies. I'll have everything you need shipped in."

The man shifted back to me again.

"These two, Kang and Ping, are cooks out at my ranch."

I shook my head as if I gave two shits but played along as I searched for more information.

"Bet they're good, too. I've always loved an authentic Chinese meal. Peking Duck, Kung Pao Chicken, they all taste so good. It should almost be illegal."

I stared at the man, my eyes saying what my lips did not. He replaced his glasses and stepped over to me. His shadow dragged out behind him. Sunlight reflected in bright starbursts from his sunglasses as he stared down, and I do mean down, at me. I was tall, but this man made me look like the last one picked at dodgeball. If Andre the Giant had a little brother, he could have been him.

"Something you'd like to say, friend?"

His nostrils flared.

"What ranch did you say you were from? I can't say that we've met before."

"You're right," he said. "We haven't. And, I didn't say. If you must know, I'm running the Three Bar."

"That so? Never heard of it," I said.

"Just acquired it last month."

"Well, then we're practically neighbors."

The man chuckled, standing firm and tall, like a rock waiting to roll.

"*Zǒu ba!*"

A new, sharp voice called out from the truck. A quick shift of my attention caught Ping flinch. Kang's lips were pursed. It looked as if he were holding his breath. I glanced at the truck, then back to the giant in front of me.

"Got someone else in the truck?"

The man cocked his head and clenched his jaw.

"Mister..."

So much for friend.

"...you ask a lot of questions. One might consider that a problem. Do we have a problem?"

I looked at the man square in the face, my glare carving through his dark glasses.

"Sir, I only stopped to help these two. Just being neighborly. If you see it differently, maybe there is a problem."

"I don't see it that way, especially with a gun bulging on your hip. It's the way of the west out here, I guess. Maybe you thought you were helping. Maybe I got here just in time. Either way, it doesn't matter. I'm going to take my cooks and be on our way. You'd do well not to get in the way of that...friend."

Friend again? What an ass.

The man turned and marched to the truck.

"Kang. Ping. Load up," he said, giving them a firm wave.

They followed, but Ping gave me one final look. It made my skin crawl. What I saw in her eyes looked like a final, pleading stare of someone who was drowning but just beyond the reach of my outstretched hand.

The man opened the rear door of the truck. I watched

as they climbed in, all the while thinking I should flash my badge and keep them here. If I called for assistance, Deputy Boss or Leo could back me up until we had some real answers as to who these people were. As it stood, no laws had been broken. My plan may buy some time but could also stir up a harassment suit which was not something the county had time to deal with at the moment.

The man slammed the door behind them. Slammed, as if put out by their predicament. Before he got back in, I yelled out to him.

"And the car?"

He stepped onto the rock slider and looked at me over the top of the driver's door.

"Keep it."

The truck lurched under the man's weight and size, the shocks seeming to groan as the mountain saddled up. He closed the door, shifted into drive, and revved the engine. It growled like a caged wolf, then darted ahead, fishtailing around as the tires screeched across the loose blacktop shoulder.

As the truck sped off, I saw the image of a different man's face looking in the passenger-side mirror. Dark hair, dark eyes, Asian facial features. Tingling sensations pricked my neck when I saw him.

Had I seen this man before?

I burned what information I could about him to memory as his image raced away. With a roar of the engine, the truck disappeared over the south rise on RR170.

I turned back to the Explorer, pulling my phone out of my pocket as I walked along. Chance may have more information about the Bar S and maybe the giant man as well. He never offered his name, but a guy like him would be easy to recognize. The line rang three times before voicemail intercepted the call.

"Hey, Chance. Sending a car to impound. Need to run plates and dig up any background info we can find about the owners. I'll call it in. Keeping you in the loop. Call me back."

As I finished my message and ended the call, the chug of an older truck sounded out in the distance. I looked north toward Brewster and saw a clanky, old model Chevy clomping its way toward me. Yellow flashers beamed out over the cab as its popping muffler announced its arrival. It was Hector.

I stepped into view and gave a wave. Hector pulled up next to me, the truck idling with knocks and bangs. He leaned over and rolled the passenger-side window down.

"Hey, *ese*."

"Hector," I said, leaning my arms on the window frame.

He looked past me.

"Real piece of shit there. This ain't yer car, *Ese*. Where's the driver."

"Long story. Haul it back to the impound yard, will ya? You can settle up with the officer on duty. County will cover this one."

"As long as I get paid."

I stepped away and slapped the side of the truck.

"Thanks, Hector."

He pulled forward and set to work securing the vehicle.

I got into the Explorer and sat in quiet, replaying every instance of what had just happened. I had little to go on, but that's how casework starts, putting the little pieces together to form the bigger ones. Soon, patterns of information begin to take shape. That was my hope, and the car may be the key. Abandoning it was the man's biggest mistake. Come morning, I would dive into the vehicle history and records. From that, I felt confident I would find something, anything that might warrant a formal visit with our new neighbors. If not, maybe it was time I drove out with Flint and gave them a proper West Texas welcome.

CHAPTER EIGHTEEN

Twilight on the CR has always been tranquil, a melting pot where day and night come together as if bound by a curse where one could see but not fully touch the other. The swirls of color painted across the sky splash onto the distant mountainous faces where shadow and light explode in gloaming luminescence. Light of day, dark of night, like star-crossed lovers, one runs after the other. The cooling air and gentle flow of the breeze's soothing grace cause ripples of goose bumps to form on bare skin. It's time best spent with arms wrapped around Raven and eyes cast on the open range. Dusk's calming effect was unique to West Texas, evidence again why the land within the CR was also called the Gateway to Paradise. The array tonight went on without me.

Rumpled vibrations surged through the Explorer as I drove under the archway and over the cattle guards at the entrance to the ranch. My mind weighed heavy with thoughts from today—the late morning foot chase and arrest of two illegals caught stealing Twinkies and Yoo-hoo from the Sinclair gas station. Who the hell steals

Twinkies and Yoo-hoo? *Hungry, desperate folks do.* Breaking up the bloodied, tangled mess of undersized men with oversized egos at *Tio Andres*. The bar fight sent one man straight to county lockup, while the other first took a detour to Brewster Regional for stitches to the back of his head. Both men will pay the price for their idiocy. As for me, I dove into the splash zone to break it up. Good deeds never go unpunished? No shit. In doing so, my new blue jeans became the canvas for blood spatter and dripping sweat, but the job got done. And to frost the icing on the damn cake, my hope for a quiet drive home followed by a rest-filled evening got railroaded. Coming across the couple on the side of the road started out as no big deal, but now I am faced with a large, and seemingly unpleas- ant, problem. Who the hell did they drive away with, and who was the passenger in the truck?

I pulled past Flint's tiny house and the Six M barracks as they have come to call it, rolling to a stop just past Jesse's truck. Jesse acted as foreman for the Six M crew and was a hell of a nice guy. He was as tough and as knowledgeable as a well-worn saddle, and Texan all the way. His ranching experience was natural. Pedro and Cody leaned on the tailgate, chewing, jawing, and spitting. I rolled down the passenger-side window.

"Hey fellas."

"Mr. Callahan," they both answered in tandem.

"What's the word?"

The men glanced at each other, then at back me, eyes squinting, faces curious.

"What's up? Any issues with the land or the herd?"

Pedro spit, then spoke.

"Been out saddle draggin' 'long the fence maze since sunup. Them devil lines are more riddled than a parched creek bed in July."

It was my turn to look stupefied.

A smirk cracked along Cody's lips.

"Pedro ain't the most eloquent of us," Cody said, smiling at his friend. "He's sayin' we've some fence work ahead of us if'n we aim ta keep the cattle from wanderin' off property."

Cody walked over and leaned against the Explorer as we talked through the window.

"We're headin' inta Brewster for a couple beers. Ride along if ya like."

A day like today merits a few beers at least, I thought.

"Maybe," I said nodding. "Gotta check in with the boss."

Cody's smirk returned.

"I get you. Leavin' in ten er so," he said, backing away from the window.

I pulled up to the house and went inside. Miguel sat on the couch, Optimus Prime in one hand, a G.I. Joe action figure in the other. Raven had found a chest of Spencer's childhood toys. To Miguel, it was heaven in a box. He clashed his hands together, the two heroes engaged in a fight to save the world.

"Aren't they the good guys?" I asked.

Miguel paused long enough to thrust Optimus Prime toward me.

"More than meets the eye!"

The image of the large man in the pickup burst into my head as I watched the fight resume. Miguel's eyes followed each action, his lips curling and vibrating as he made battle noises.

That's it!

I moved into the kitchen and pulled out my cell phone. Sitting down, I swiped through pictures until I found what I was looking for. Flipping back and forth between two images of the dead Chinese man from Big Bend, I shook my head, replaying the sequence of events from that evening—the cow, the man stumbling into camp, the three men approaching, their demands, the pop of the first man's arm as we fought, the bright lights, the sight of the knife buried deep into the injured man's chest, the chatter. I closed my eyes and focused on every detail I could remember.

"Their voices," I said to myself. "Foreign words. Spanish. Chinese? The whispering man."

My bulged eyes open, and I slapped the kitchen tabletop with both palms.

"Son of a bitch!"

"That good of a day, huh, Cass?"

I twisted around to see Raven standing behind me.

I stood up and wrapped my arms around her. Without letting go, I leaned back to look in her eyes.

"No, it sucked. But you're not going to believe this."

"Your *son of a bitch* epiphany?"

I let go of her and reached for my phone.

"I saw one of the guys from the camp out."

Raven walked around to the refrigerator, pulled out a jug of Borden's chocolate milk, and poured two glasses.

"From Big Bend?"

"Yeah. Rave. I think I saw the killer today. It just hit me."

"How can you be sure?"

I glanced at the picture of the dead man one more time, then slipped the phone into my front pocket.

"That's just it."

Raven stepped forward, handing me one of the glasses of milk.

"I caught a glimpse of a guy today."

Miguel ran into the kitchen, stopping in front of Raven. He squeezed the G.I. Joe under his arm pit to free up a hand for the other glass of milk.

"Go on," Raven said, nudging him back toward the living room. "Back to saving the world, little man."

Miguel walked carefully out of the kitchen, sipping his milk along the way.

Raven turned her attention back to me.

"A glimpse of a guy? What were you doing?"

"I had stopped to help some people whose car had broken down just north of here. Asian, probably Chinese, couple. Didn't speak English. Long story short, a truck arrived shortly after I did, and they rode off with the driver who claimed to be from the Bar S ranch and they were his cooks. Huge SOB. Real ass, too. Ray would've hated him."

"And you let them go with him?"

"What was I supposed to do? Arrest him for being an asshole? I had no probable cause. The woman looked frightened, but they went with him voluntarily. Anyway, as they drove away, I saw a new set of eyes glaring at me in the passenger-side mirror. Distinctive. Memorable. I just couldn't put my finger on it until now."

"And you're sure it was the same guy?"

The growl of a diesel engine roared to life in the yard.

"Pretty damn sure. But I'll confirm that hunch when Flint and I pay the Bar S a visit tomorrow."

"Don't you need a warrant or something? You already said you didn't have cause."

"You're right. But there's no law against being neighborly."

A horn blared twice above the thrum of the diesel rumbling outside. Raven looked over her shoulder.

"Going somewhere?" I asked.

Raven looked back at me and smiled.

"It's Miller time."

CHAPTER NINETEEN

Darkness fell over the CR like a bowl of black bean soup spilling across the kitchen linoleum. Cirrostratus clouds spread over the ranch, blocking the moon and stars, snuffing out their usual ethereal glow. Lights on the barn and the porch bulbs of Flint's house and the Six M barracks fought against the blackness. Their attempts to overpower the impenetrable shadows proved futile, their luster fading into liminal space.

Alone, after putting Miguel to bed, I stood on the front porch and gazed into the heart of the CR. Black-and-white images spun in my head, flickering like the film strip of an eight-millimeter movie. I could hear the clicks and hum of the projector motor. Its warm, burning smell filled my nose. The fabricated Proustian memory transported me to the back of seventh-grade science class when all I wanted were answers without having to sift through the mounds of meaningless information our teacher drilled into us. Right now, I felt the same. All I wanted was answers, but I had none. Was it what I felt on the inside, what I saw, or rather, did not see in the distance that consumed me? Darkness. Uncertainty. Nothing.

I closed my eyes, searching for focus, for something that might cast a hint of light on the turmoil that swirled in my head. Moments bled into seconds, then into minutes of pulse-pounding quiet. It was The Nothing, like that of a childhood story, that shrouded my thoughts.

"Ya stand like 'at much longer, may roost a kettle of turkey buzzards for the night is through."

I opened my eyes and saw Flint ambling through the shadows toward the house.

"What ya call it? Watch yer six?" he said, walking onto the porch. The wooden planks creaked under the clanking of his boots.

"That's right. With the crew heading to town, I figured I had the ranch to myself."

I offered Flint a hand to shake.

"Nah. They need a chance ta blow off some steam. Cuss me out without my hearin'. Plus, I'm gettin' too old for that shit. I'd rather pop a top and kick back where I ain't gonna be bothered."

"I hear ya. Have a seat and I'll grab us a couple."

Opening the front door, I could hear the soft sounds of deep slumber snort out of Miguel's room. Reverting to ninja parenting skills I had no reason to summon until recently, I slipped into the kitchen, retrieved two Coronas from the fridge, and was back outside again without disturbing him. I handed one to Flint and took a seat across from him.

He lifted his bottle in gratitude, then took a long draw, followed by a wet-sounding belch.

"You hear anything about our new neighbors?" I asked.

Flint shook his head.

"Not a word. Figured we'd cross paths by now."

"And the others?"

"Same." Flint polished off his Corona in two thirst-quenching slugs. "And that ain't the strangest part. I ain't seen stock of any kind grazing the land, 'cept ours of course."

The beer was cold and felt good going down as I drank to match Flint's pace.

"Ya'd think that if a man was a rancher, he'd buy land and use it fer what it was intended. All I've seen is empty range as far as the eye can see. Couple new buildings on the horizon, but not one head of cattle. Not one horse, neither. Hell, I ain't seen a thing."

I leaned forward, placed my empty bottle on the wood slats at my feet. Resting my elbows on my knees, I looked Flint square in the eyes.

"I've been pulled so many different directions lately, but I think it's far past time we head over and meet the neighbors. Welcome them to the neighborhood."

"Meet the neighbors?" Flint's inflection mocked, his voice dripping in suburban sarcasm. He huffed, twisting the empty Corona bottle between his fingers. "Bullshit. You wanna know just like I wanna know what the hell is goin' on over there. Can't be nuthin'."

"Nothing wrong with a little West Texas recon."

I saw a glint in Flint's eye, and a thought occurred to me. Call it a hold-my-beer kind of moment. I relaxed back into my chair and smiled.

"You're thinking what I'm thinking."

Flint gave a subtle nod.

"Why wait?" I asked.

The ensuing silence between us spoke volumes. I twisted my head and looked over my shoulder, squinting my eyes as if I could see into the dark that blanketed the CR. Beyond the corral and the fences and deep into the night was the Bar S, formerly the Double SS. I played out viable scenarios in my mind until finally I settled on what I considered to be a plan with acceptable risk.

I turned back around and crossed my legs at the ankles.

So, I thought. *Ride out to the burn pile near the north fence line and cross onto Bar S land. From there, head northeast until we see something or come up empty. It is so damn dark we will be in and out before anyone knows we were there.*

I reached into my pocket for my phone and noted the time.

9:17

I stood up and slid my phone back into my front pocket.

"Soon as the crew gets back from town, we'll head out."

Flint nodded, and the silence returned. I had no idea what I expected to find, but the itch in my gut urged me to proceed. The idea might not be the best, and the legalities we faced if we got caught could fracture an already strained, yet practically nonexistent, relationship between the Bar S and the CR. But hell, I wanted to have a look around. And it would be just me and Flint. What could go wrong?

CHAPTER TWENTY

It was just past midnight when Raven and her rowdy crew of Six M wranglers arrived back at the ranch. Slamming truck doors, laughter, and gritty chatter replaced the rugged thrum of the diesel engine that had growled to a stop in the center of the yard. I stepped to the window and looked outside. Like cattle huddled in the grove during a storm, the drunken bunch seemed to cling to each other near the lowered tailgate of the Ford F-250 dually.

I saw Raven standing next to Gilly. She had one arm around her shoulder and waved the other in the air. I watched the girls sway back and forth and heard their voices howl an off-key rendition of Steve Goodman and John Prine's *You Never Even Called Me by My Name*. Raven was a fun drunk. She could hold her liquor with the best of them but suffered just like the rest of us come morning. With only a few hours to recover before hitting the saddle, I surmised Raven would remember this night for a long time.

I walked to the kitchen, filled a glass full of water, and took it to the bedroom, placing it on the nightstand next to her side of the bed. I set a bottle of Advil next to the glass and returned to the front of the house. Good deed done, but I had to go.

As I opened the door, the huddle had already begun to disperse. Gilly and the Six M crew ambled to their barracks while Raven made her way toward the house. When she saw me step off the porch, her eyes lit up, and a smile stretched like the wide-open prairie across her face.

"Better turn back around there, cowboy," she said, pointing a swirling finger at me. "This party ain't quite over."

Damn, she looked beautiful—ruffled hair, boots and tight jeans, top button of her shirt popped open, and that carnal look in her eyes. My heart thumped as rising urges fought against the responsibilities I faced.

When we came together, she wrapped her arms around me and dove in for a passionate, beer-flavored kiss. The soft press of her lips, the tickle of her tongue against mine, the feel of her body grinding closer and closer, it all felt so good. So natural. Her fingers trailed down my back, then moved along my waistline. I felt the tug of her hands at my belt and the nip of her teeth on my bottom lip.

Son of a bitch, I thought.

I must be the dumbest man on the planet, destined to unmitigated self-shaming and regret, but I had somewhere else I needed to be. Turning away from what was assuredly going to be one wild rodeo of a bedroom romp, I cupped her hands in mine and slowly pulled away.

"What is it?"

Raven looked at me, her lust-filled gaze teetering. Moments ticked by as I forced myself to say the words.

"I can't. Not right now, anyway."

Voices in my head screamed like a stadium of disbelieving football fans, watching in horror as a player ran in the wrong direction.

"Why? What are..."

Raven stepped back. Pulling her hands away from mine, she looked me over. As her head lifted and our eyes met again, I saw her desire had been replaced with disappointment.

"Why are you dressed like that? All blacked out."

Tactical pants, skintight dri-fit shirt, field boots, utility belt—I was dressed for invisibility under cover of night.

Truth, Cass. It's always been truth between you.

"Heading out on a hunt with Flint."

Half-truth? Dumber still, Cass!

"At this time of night?"

Raven's voice pitched higher as she crossed her arms and shifted her weight to her hips. I knew she was not buying what I was selling, but she was also still well within alcohol's fuzzy boundaries. Not balls to the wall drunk, but past a point where logic and reasoning were still on siesta.

"You'd rather go on a stupid hunt than go inside with me?"

"That's not it at all, Raven. Why don't you go inside. Get some rest. I'll be home soon, and then..."

Raven pursed her lips and rolled her eyes. I reached out to her, feeling the frustrations of my poor choices being rattled by a foolishly missed opportunity to be with my wife. Was that not the whole reason for moving to the CR? To be with her? Focus on her?

"Maybe I can..."

"Nope," she said, cutting me off and waving a hand between us. "Too late."

She started to step around me.

"Rave?"

"You go have your fun with Flint."

Her boots clomped across the porch. Hinges creaked as the wood-framed door opened, then clanged shut behind her.

Damn.

Having made my bed, there was nothing left to do but proceed with my mission. I headed for the stables, feeling the weight of each step like an invisible tail dragging in the dirt behind me. As I entered the barn, the musty smell and dank air inside filled my nose. It tingled my senses and triggered memories from childhood summers spent on the CR with my uncle Stewart. I'll never forget discovering a rattlesnake in the barn, falling from the saddle near the grove, or shooting my first gun when I was eight years old. Each of these experiences acted as a catalyst for my love of adventure, my embrace of risk, and my pursuit of their inevitable rewards. It was why I trained for competitive fighting in Taekwondo as a teenager, reaching the pinnacle of success as the 1997 AAU National sparring champion. The urge continued to fuel my being which led me to join the military, and ultimately become a detective following my honorable discharge from the Army.

I lingered in the shadows of the barn and let those thoughts ruminate until a rustling at the far end of the building caught my attention. I flipped on a wall switch that activated a string of lights leading to the stables and saw Flint walking my way.

He was dressed in jeans, a dark print Wrangler shirt, boots, and a black felt hat. He wore a weathered leather holster on his hip that cradled his Colt 1911, a relic in its own right and gift from my late uncle.

"Ya ready?"

"Yeah. You too, I see."

I motioned to his sidearm. Flint's jaw shifted under grinding teeth.

"You learn anything about West Texas yet, Cass?"

I nodded.

"More than I'd like to admit. This'll be quick. In and out. Observe what we can from a distance. Run of the mill sneak and peek, that's all."

"Run of the mill, huh?" Flint cocked his head, then spit a stream of black tobacco juice into a patch of dry hay near a fifty-gallon rusted-metal trash bin. "You go on thinkin' that."

"Something bothering you, Flint?"

"You know about them climbers over in Nepal? The ones that pay out the ass to try an' reach the top of Mt. Everest? I'd bet a six-pack of Modelo Especial that they had the same thought on their mind. "Run of the mill," just as long as they follow their guide. That was their first mistake. Underestimatin' what they was about ta do. Just because ya think ya know what lies ahead, don't make it so, 'specially way out here."

"I hear you, Flint. Expect the unexpected." We started walking toward the stalls. "Watch each other's six, and we'll be back in time for me to buy you that six-pack."

When the horses were ready, we saddled up and headed out. Our pace was slow. Quiet. Overcast skies formed a dome of darkness over the CR. A thin film of cool brushed my face as a distant scent of rain filled my nose. Lightning scratched the horizon with jagged flashes of brilliant electricity, its thunderous groan muted by land's wide expanse and time and the invisible border that seemed to encapsulate the CR and all of its surroundings.

As we descended into the darkness, the pad of hooves and the thump of my heart kept time like the click of a metronome set to guide a musician through their piece. I had heard a similar tune before, but instead of hooves, it was the rumblings of tank treads, and the pounding in my chest was not the beats of my heart, but the punch and recoil of gunfire.

UNDER THE SHROUD OF NIGHT, *Dragon Company, bolstered by a platoon of M1 Abrams tanks from the 3rd Infantry Division, readied for a critical operation on the fringes of Baghdad. Under a new moon, night covered us like spilled oil across the desert sand. A foreign sky pulsed in various degrees of brightness overhead but was not strong enough to illuminate our position below/ Conditions were ideal for an ambush. My joints tensed with anticipation of facing the Iraqi armored units.*

I drove an armored M1151 Humvee for Lieutenant Tucker, my operation's commander, as we accompanied the tanks into battle. Sitting behind me was Specialist Daniker and Sergeant Murphy. Murphy sat in an elevated turret, manning the Humvee's M2 .50 caliber machine gun. An abnormal quiet filled the cab. Murphy kept his bad-tasting jokes to himself. Lieutenant Tucker stared out the front window. The dim, green glow of night vision paved the way as I followed the convoy to our attack position. Even behind the wheel of the Humvee, I could feel the powerful vibration of the tank's engines and the rumble of metal and rubber tracks as they rolled ahead, demolishing anything in their path. It gave me both a sense of power and one of nervous reservation.

As we positioned our platoon along the anticipated route of an Iraqi armored column, Lieutenant Tucker confirmed final positions over the radio. His voice was hushed, calm, firm. Radio discipline ensued once positions were taken.

Time seemed to slow to a stop, at least in my head, as we waited for the Iraqi forces to arrive. Questions loomed, uncertainties festered, but the image of Raven, my beautiful young wife, acted as a saving counterweight to the mounting pressures I faced.

As the Iraqi column approached, marked by the distant rumble of engines and the faint silhouette of tanks against the desert night sky, we held fire until they entered the kill zone. On Lieutenant Tucker's command, the night erupted. Our lead M1 Abrams tank, Thunder 1, fired the first shot, striking the lead Iraqi tank and setting it ablaze. What followed can only be described as night turning to day, with fire and explosions and terror the fuel that lit the way.

The ambush was swift and devastating. With tactical precision, our platoon fired at the Iraqi convoy. Thunder 4 targeted the rear guards, disabling the transports and trapping the column. My ears rang even through my protective head-gear. My body trembled with the aftershocks of each blast, the fuzzy spasms of adrenaline and warfare rippled over the entirety of my skin. The overwhelming firepower of the Abrams tanks was decisive. The rapid, heavy thuds of the Humvee's .50 cal firing as Murphy took aim at the enemy made this fight, this attack, more personal, as if I were pulling the trigger myself. Confusion reigned among the Iraqi forces as they scrambled under the relentless assault.

There was no escape for our enemy. As the Iraqi tanks burned, their ammunition cooked off in spectacular explosions. The Third Infantry Division pressed the attack, ensuring no vehicle was left operational. The air was thick with the acrid smell of scorched metal and burning fuel, a stark contrast to the quiet of the desert night before the engagement.

Like a dragon, our tanks breathed fire and boomed thunderous roars. Yet, when the ambush was over, silence returned as if we soared through the air on outstretched wings. I saw the twisting flames burning amid the destruction. Plumes of black smoke covered the stars above with a hot, thick layer of blackness. The few Iraqi survivors retreated on foot into the night, leaving their dead behind.

With the mission accomplished and the Iraqi armored column effectively neutralized, Lieutenant Tucker ordered the *retreat. I eased back in my seat and raised my hand before my eyes. My fingers shook. I tried to make a fist, but the muscles in my hand were unresponsive.*

"It'll pass," Specialist Daniker said. "Always does."

I nodded, but kept my eyes locked on my hand and wondered if what he said was true.

We were an overwhelming force. With rumbles and metallic grinds of tank treads over packed earth, Dragon Company withdrew leaving behind chaos and destruction as a clear message to any Iraqi reinforcements.

The ambush had significantly degraded the enemy capabilities near Baghdad, buying time and strategic advantage for coalition forces. It had also carved scars deep within me. A hidden place where nightmares and visions lurked, waiting for an opportunity to surface once again.

CHAPTER TWENTY-ONE

Trespassers. That's what we were. Not neighbors, or fellow ranchers, but trespassers. Flint used pliers on his Leatherman and snipped the barbed wire fencing marking the property line near the burn pile. Once the sharp strands were pulled aside, we proceeded onto Bar S land, walking our horses northeast. Our route zigzagged from the CR, but Flint knew the land well enough to lead us in the right direction through the dark.

My only experience with Bar S land was when it was owned by Roy Sinclair and called the Double SS, and even then, my time on the property was limited. Old Sinclair made it obvious from our first meeting that I was not welcome in the territory, nor did he have any interest in giving me a chance to prove my worth. First impressions tell a lot about a person, I of all people know that. As it turned out, a murder investigation I was involved with led me to head up a raid of the Double SS to arrest Roy Sinclair. All clues pointed directly at him. Truth be told, there was no love lost when the final warrants were obtained and carried out. As I was about to place old Roy

Sinclair in custody, Joe Sinclair, his cocky grandson, showed up looking for a fight. He tried to deflect blame, he stumbled over his words and all but confessed to being the real murderer.

Poor Joe. He did not have much of a role model in Roy Sinclair. My guess was he was trying to prove himself a tough guy but went about it all the wrong way. He was an inexperienced kid who fell in with the wrong people from the wrong side of the border, which gave him quite an unpleasant disposition. He had shot and killed a small band of Mules that carried product for him from the Camargo cartel. What he did not know was one of the men was an Undercover FBI operative carrying materials sensitive to the cartel. To Joe, he was just another expendable Mexican. Most criminals, Joe included, think they have an airtight plan to avoid the law, but I have yet to meet one whose plan actually worked.

When the truth was revealed, Roy Sinclair lost control and attacked his grandson. The scuffle ended with a gunshot that tore through Roy and hit Sheriff Gilbert in the shoulder. Joe ran for his truck while Chance and Roy lay in a tangled heap of blood. He sped away cross-country, barreling through fences and onto the CR, racing toward the border. His off-road escape attempt was short-lived when he tried, and failed, to complete a *Dukes of Hazzard*-style river jump into Mexico. His truck caught some air but landed precariously upside down in the Rio Grande. I dove in and had to work fast to pull Joe from the cab before he drowned. But that was the job—confront the bad guy, chase the bad guy, save the bad guy if necessary, and arrest the hell out of him.

Now, I broke the law with Flint as we continued our trespassing path deeper onto Bar S land. Our objective was to get a look at their headquarters using night vision optics and see what, if anything seemed out of place, but my curiosity pulled me to investigate the new buildings Flint had seen first.

"These buildings you mentioned. How far would you say they were from here?"

I spoke in a low tone, my voice registering just above a whisper. I could hear Flint inhale before speaking.

"Prob'ly 'bout two, maybe three sections away from where we are now."

Sections?

"Humor me, Flint. How far is a section?"

Flint chuckled. The leather in his saddle stretched as he shifted positions before answering.

"Damn. The green ain't washed off ya yet. A section is a square chunk of land. Six hundred and forty acres. One mile all 'round each edge."

I shook my head.

"Then just say it's two to three miles. How is that so different."

"It's different cause that's how any rancher in these parts would say it. Best git used to the lingo. Maybe there's an app ya can download on yer phone that'll help ya out with 'at."

I paused, allowing Flint his bit of fun, before speaking again.

"Let's check those buildings out first," I said.

"This is yer party."

Flint reined his horse left and led the way. The high-altitude clouds that cloaked the land in blackness began to show wear, as if large moths had chewed holes in their textured coverings. Looking up, I could see patches of stars peeking through, their ambient light cascading through the openings in the clouds. As we walked on, the distant wail of coyotes caused our horse's ears to prick up, but a calming 'shush' from Flint settled them both. They knew his voice and trusted his signals.

When the yips and yowls subsided, quiet returned like water filling a hole in the sand at the beach. Silent, rapid, unyielding. It was then, a thought struck me.

"Earlier, you said you hadn't seen any new cattle or horses on the property, right?"

"A-yuh. Not a one."

Instinctively, I looked around.

"Too dark ta see hardly anythin'. When ya gonna bust out them fancy goggles. Maybe that'll let ya see what yer lookin' fer."

I pulled back on the reins bringing my horse to a stop and reached for a pouch on my utility belt. With a quick rip of Velcro, I retrieved a PVS-14 Night Vision monocular I had squirreled away for special occasions and looked through its lens. Twisting in the saddle from left to right, I scanned the land in all directions.

"Nothing."

I lowered the device.

"Mind if I give'r a go?"

I handed the monocular to Flint and he placed it in front of his right eye.

"Woo-ee. Ain't that somethin'. Night vision. Who the hell came up with that idea?"

As he raised it again, I heard a faint rumble, like the hum and grind of a small motor. Sound travels across the open range, so it could have been quite a ways away. Still, I recognized the sound.

"Here," I whispered, holding out my hand.

Flint returned the monocular to me. I looked through the lens, adjusting the focus and settings as I scanned the black terrain.

"You hear that?" I asked.

Flint responded, but I missed his reply. At that moment, I saw movement through the monocular. A subtle, green glow that looked like a ball or orb moving along the ground came into focus.

"There," I said, my voice carrying on louder than I would have liked.

The distant sound and the blip in my night vision optics meshed and instantly I knew what I had seen.

"ATV. Like ours, probably."

"Can't see. How far ya reckon?"

I lowered the monocular and looked at Flint. My horse stomped its front foot.

"Half a section. Maybe more."

Flint huffed.

"Don't sound quite right when ya say it, but nice try. I git the jist."

The holes in the clouds continued to pull apart. The lightning in the distance was but a flicker as the weather conditions took a turn for the better.

"Let's follow. See where its headed. I'm curious to know why its running black," I said.

Flint's horse bobbed its head, its ears pricked and shifty.

"Whoa there, girl." Flint's voice was deep, soothing. He leaned forward and rubbed its neck. "We're headin' out."

The crack of a single gunshot and a sudden flood of light rang in my ears and blinded my sight. The horses jumped, startled at the unexpected sound. With reins in hand, we whirled around to face the brightness. I raised my hand to my face, shadowing my eyes from the intense light.

"Keep your hands where we can see 'em. Move again, and we won't miss a second time."

CHAPTER TWENTY-TWO

A feel of electrified adrenaline surged throughout my body, yet with no release, it caused a fiery heat to radiate from my gut to the nape of my neck. Blinding light shone in our faces. We held our position and waited. My eyes squinted against the harsh glare.

"You fellas lost?"

That voice. I know that voice.

"¿Habla inglés?" it said from behind the shadow of surprise and drawn guns.

"We speak English," I said. "How about lowering the light a bit?"

The beams held firm.

"How about you answer my question. A man's likely to find trouble for himself out here if he isn't careful, so let me ask it again. Are you fellas *lost*?"

Before I had a chance to reply, Flint spoke up.

"Damn, mister. Ain't nobody lost. I been seein' ta this land since before that prickle in yer pants knew what the fuck it was good fer."

Low toned laughter bellowed behind the lights. Next

came the sharp click and swift glide of a fresh round being chambered.

"You have a foul mouth, friend."

"If ya have a problem with my mouth, how 'bout steppin' out an' facin' me like a man?"

Hooves clomped on dry earth. Moving into view, the form of a horse and the massive size of its rider blocked the beams directed at us, creating a starburst radiance around the approaching figures of man and beast.

"Friend, I don't think you understand the trouble you're in. Trespassing is a serious crime around here. For all I know, you could be running drugs, or illegals, or looking to steal from me and my people."

"Yer *people*?" Flint said. "You part of some commune. Second coming of Davd Koresh er somethin'?"

Flint was almost as bad as Ray, both sharing a talent for pouring kerosine on an already blazing fire.

The man pulled back sharply on the reins, halting his horse just inches from Flint's, nearly causing the animals to collide. As the sky cleared overhead and the blinding beams were diverted from view, a faint glow enveloped us, allowing my eyes to adapt to the dim light.

The tension between us was tangible. As my eyes adjusted, I could both see and feel it growing. In an instant, I recognized the man's face—it was the second encounter we'd had in just one day.

"Hold on a minute," I said, attempting to defuse the situation. "I can understand your cause for alarm. It's late, and from your perspective, we look pretty damn shady, but I assure you, we are not a threat."

The man kept his eyes locked on Flint.

"I'm Cass Callahan, owner and operator of the CR. Our ranches border one another." I pointed in the direction of the property line. "We've had some trouble with coyotes recently. Figured a night hunt might scare 'em off. The ones we don't kill anyway. Probably should've given y'all a heads-up, but our relationship with the previous owner was pretty fluid. He grazed cattle on our land, we hunted on his. Didn't cross my mind that our being over here might cause a fuss."

We were still under the gun, but as silence lingered, I felt a slight ease escape the mounting pressure.

"That so?" the man said, looking at me. His eyes, merely slits on his face, opened wider. He recognized me as well. I was sure of it. "Times are changing around here, Mr. Callahan. You'd do good to remember that. What may have been in the past won't work for us going forward. We catch you trespassing again, I won't hesitate to shoot first and ask questions later."

"Look," I said. "We've gotten off on the wrong foot. Why don't we..."

The man reined his horse to one side, clearing the way for the blinding beams to stab at us once again.

"I'll say this once," he said, his voice as gruff as it was when he ordered the two Chinese cooks into his truck. "Take your horses and get off our land."

I was never comfortable turning my back on a man with a gun, but we were left with no choice.

"Come on, Flint. Hunt's over."

I reined my horse around, but Flint did not follow. Instead, he guided his horse closer to the man, riding right up alongside him.

"I know you," he said. "I know all about men like you. Ain't a fella around here that wouldn't disagree with me when I say this ain't yer world. Ya ain't gonna last. Mark my words. Yer gonna find a reason ta move on."

"Blind threats won't do you any good, friend."

"That ain't a threat, mister. It's a fact."

Having had his say, Flint reined his horse around and rode over to me. We moved away at a slow, cautious pace.

The beams behind us cast long shadows across the ground, then without warning, turned off. Darkness fell. Silence followed. The tension remained. I peered into the distance, straining to see and hoping to catch the hum of the mysterious ATV. It was long gone.

Minutes passed. Thoughts raced in my head. *How did they know exactly where to find us? And at this time of night?* I did not get a look at who was holding the lights or the guns. Just the man. The same damn man from earlier today. Both meetings left me empty-handed and full of questions.

My body rocked along in the saddle to the steady rhythm of my horse's gait. I closed my eyes and saw puzzle pieces scattered across a blank floor in my mind, but there was no image to follow. No clue that confirmed my uneasy feelings. My intuition had always been reliable, but to a judge, or to Chance would mean absolutely dick.

Opening my eyes I saw clear skies before me. Stars blazed overhead. The ridgeline along the cliffs across the Rio Grande glowed as the moon climbed into the early morning sky. My thoughts drifted again. An echo from somewhere deep inside me grew louder. "Oh, mister moon, moon, bright and shiny moon, won't ya please shine down on me." Was it a song or jingle? A lullaby Raven used to sing to Spencer. Why on earth was that surfacing now? What was the rest? Add that to list of *things* I could not quite put my finger on. Over and over, the lyrics played like the scratchy tune on a broken record. I shook my head attempting to clear my mind, but scrambled as it already was, all that resulted was a throbbing ache from my temples.

Maybe I was overreacting. Maybe there was nothing going on other than my amped up psyche looking for the next disaster. The past few weeks, months even, have been a roller coaster ride from hell. The rise and pitfalls of emotional turmoil had been enough to send any normal person on a terminal spiral, but not me. Not Cass Callahan. I could handle anything. I just could not figure this out.

"Cass."

I heard my name but did not react to its calling.

"Cass?"

Louder still. I felt a tingling sensation on my tongue, as if I had dipped the tip into a Molcajete filled with habanero salsa. A thought was materializing. If I could just hold on to the feel, the thought, experience might lead me to a realization.

"Hey, Hoss. Ya plan on rejoinin' the living?"

And just like that, I lost it all. Flint's voice was loud and direct. He slapped a palm on my shoulder. The jolt sent tremors throughout my body. Creators cringe at interruptions, often never being able to reassemble the same thought or verse or lines that were imagined when in such a deep, imaginative state of mind. Being ripped out of the moment is their worst nightmare. My worst nightmare.

I glared at him.

"Damn, Cass. You been out of it the whole way back."

Back?

I looked around. The burn pile was to my right. On the other side, fence posts stood at attention, growing smaller and becoming blurred in the distance as their long line guarded the CR. Coils of detached barbed wire lay on the ground between two posts waiting for repair. Waiting for us to close the door on our failed trespassing escapade.

"You wanna hop down an' give me a hand, or ya just gonna sit there an' watch?"

I took a long, slow breath, then twisted my body and

eased one leg over the saddle. My feet felt heavy once on the ground. I faced Flint without speaking.

"Can't say I've ever seen ya act like this, Cass. Ya need a drink or a long ass sleep if ya ask me. Prob'bly both."

The rugged aftermath of demolished thought remained in my head, but the dust was beginning to settle.

"Maybe you're right," I said.

Flint tipped his head back, looking at me out of the bottom of his eyes. Curiosity, concern, doubt—a true mix of thought swirled in his gaze, but he kept what he was thinking to himself. With eyes locked on mine, he pulled his Leatherman from his belt.

"Come on. Grab that end of wire and let's get to work. Can't leave this mess behind."

CHAPTER TWENTY-THREE

My bare feet hung off one end of the couch while my head lay on a decorative pillow at the other. A colorful Afghan that had seen more years on the ranch than I ever had draped across my midsection. The whir of the ceiling fan overhead created a soft breeze that cooled my toes as they poked out from under the small, hand-knit throw. The old house creaked as if looking for that perfect restful spot in which to sleep but had no luck finding it. The kitchen wall clock *tick, tick, ticked* causing my mind to subconsciously keep the time.

I drifted in and out but never truly slept. Each time I closed my eyes, I saw the man from the Bar S. His eyes were dark like oily pits. He squinted while nodding his head like he had figured me out, like he knew something I did not. A brilliant flash followed, and a full moon took his place. Beams of white light streamed down over the rangeland, illuminating tufts of sage and patches of cactus. Spindly branches from mesquite trees formed long shadowy fingers that reached out as if looking to latch onto something in the distance. The strange childlike tune began to echo as if played through a distant tunnel, and then darkness swooped in and swallowed it all.

The abruptness jolted my eyes open. When the blur of restlessness subsided, I watched the ceiling fan blades swirl above me until my lids grew heavy. Closing my eyes, the cycle would start all over again.

I grew too tired to care about any meaning hidden in the fog of my hypnagogic state. I would have plenty of time to tackle that, as the sequential images and earworm tune had burned into memory.

When the black sheen of night began to meld into a harsh purple, I sat up, gave up, and decided to face the day.

I stood, letting the Afghan slip off me onto the couch cushions, and walked on bare feet into the kitchen. The linoleum was cool to the touch. I filled the coffee pot with water and set it to brew while I took a seat at the table and waited, twisting my empty coffee cup.

"You just got Litt up."

I twisted the cup again watching the words on its ceramic face scroll past.

"Louis Litt," I said, lifting it in front of me. "You were such an ass, but good when it counted."

Raven and I had binged the TV show *Suits* on Netflix over spring break the last year she taught elementary school. The show is about an office of high-powered attorneys who take on the most crucial cases, ultimately winning and taking home the prize. Louis Litt was the quirky, often inconsiderate, and sometimes inappropriate attorney who struggled to step out of the shadow of the lead characters, Harvey Specter and Mike Ross. Despite his flaws, Louis was a talented lawyer, and I felt sorry for the guy. I loved his slogan, which is how I came to have the coffee cup. Raven thought it jokingly fit my personality and suggested I use the phrase whenever I arrested someone.

"Cuff'em," She would say. "Then step back, point a finger at the perp and tell'em 'You just got Litt up.'"

Time seemed simple back then. Before the troubles. Before the move. Before the murders. Before...

"You stay up all night?"

Raven stepped into the kitchen dressed and ready for a day on the range.

"Not by choice. Lots on my mind."

A sizzling stream of scalding water began to fill the coffee pot. A heavy, aromatic smell of fresh ground roast filtered around the kitchen. I started to get up, but Raven raised a hand, motioning me to stay put.

"I got it."

She grabbed a cup from the cupboard, removed the fresh pot from the coffee maker, and sat across from me at the table. Her hair was pulled back behind her ears. Her eyes showed dark circles beneath them, a consequence of her late night with the Six M crew, but I did not hear one complaint.

"Look," I said as she filled my cup. "Last night. I...well, something is going on and I am having trouble figuring out exactly what it is."

She filled her own cup, then set the pot between us and took a careful sip from the brim. I watched as she placed her coffee on the table. She reached across and opened her palm, inviting my hand to hers.

"You have been under a lot recently. More than usual, if you ask me. And all of it since we came out west. Maybe you need to tell Chance that you need time off. Step away. Like when we first arrived. You were gung-ho about the ranch back then, before everything, you know...hit the fan."

I rested my palm on hers. The warmth of her skin on

mine, the feel of her fingers' gentle caress, it was medicinal. But, she had it wrong. Deep down, I knew what she meant. What I heard her say was, *"you're acting mental, it's time you fix yourself."*

"I'm fine, Raven. I just need to...the new neighbors. Something is going on at the Double SS. It's now the Bar S, but you know that. I'm sure you've noticed, too. Where are the cattle? Where are the horses? Why buy a ranch if you're not going to use the land? And don't you think it's strange that a law firm was the one to buy it? And the man who runs it...he's a real prick. I told you what happened on the road yesterday. And last night..."

I stopped short of finishing my statement and took a quick drink of my coffee, burning the roof of my mouth. Hot, black brew sloshed from the cup when I set it down on the table. Streams of coffee stained the exterior of the cup, drawing lines between the etched words: You|Just|Got. The second row of words were cut in two, dismissed as unimportant.

"Fill in the blank," a snarky, mental image of Louis Litt told me, his eyes full of disgust, his teeth protruding. "Then go cry to your mommy."

Raven reached behind her for the paper towels and tossed one to me. Her face twisted with curiosity.

"Last night? You said you were going hunting. Right?"

I wiped the table, then folded the spent paper towel and placed it under my cup.

"Yeah, well Flint and I share a dislike for what we think is going on at the Bar S, so we decided to check it out."

Raven shook her head in disapproval.

"That'd been a dumb move. What if you had found something? Then what? It's not like you had permission to be on their property. What if you had gotten caught."

Raven paused. The look on her face changed from disapproval to realization. "Wait."

I had years of training, both in the military and through my years of law enforcement that taught me to control my facial expressions, hide my tells that might reveal the truth or lack thereof. Right now, none of that mattered. Raven saw right through me.

"You did get caught."

I pursed my lips, feeling the throb of scorched, tender skin within my mouth.

"Yeah, we did. But even that was weird. How the hell did they know we were there? And in the middle of the night? It was like they were waiting for us."

Raven blew on her coffee, then took a longer sip. The blue digital numbers on the microwave seemed to pulse over her shoulder in the dim light of the kitchen.

5:16

Shades of day tickled the blinds at the kitchen window forming jail bar shadows on the floor.

I was trapped. Trapped by Raven. By the Bar S man. By actionable negativity of which I can never ignore. Maybe she was right. Maybe I did need to step away from everything. I could take Spencer on a fishing trip in Galveston, or rock climbing in the Hill Country. I pulled my hand from hers and pressed my palms together, rubbing them as if I were cold.

Raven stood up and walked around the table to me. Using her thumb and pointer finger, she gently pinched my chin and rotated my head to look at her. My cowgirl wife, tough as a bucking bronc, and more beautiful than a patch of bluebonnets in springtime, leaned over and kissed my forehead.

"If I know anyone who can fix whatever is going on up there..." she said, tapping my head, "it's you. You simply have to remember why we are here and for what purpose."

Looking at her eyes, deep and inviting, a lump formed in my throat. The last time that happened was when I learned my father had died. Why the hell was it happening now?

"You may think we only came out here for me," she continued. "But you needed this place just as much as me. Don't forget that Cass."

She leaned further and wrapped her arms around me. The strength of her grasp and her unyielding love for me caused my muscles to melt beneath her. I pressed my cheek to her chest. The thump of her heart reverberated across my face, throughout my body, into my soul.

"I'm gonna reach out to Charlotte Huckabee later today. I heard she hasn't been back to work at Dairy Queen since..." She paused.

Since Spencer went missing and the whole town faced the killer, EL Despiadado?

"Anyway. I'll see if she can come by and watch Miguel for a bit. She's a good girl and more than capable of caring for our little guy. Maybe even make it a daily thing if she is able."

She squeezed me again, then let go. The coolness of the air-conditioned kitchen replaced her warmth like completing the viral ice bucket challenge.

"I'll see you tonight, Cass. Take the day. Try and get some rest, okay?"

She blew me a kiss as she walked out of the kitchen. I heard the front door open, then swing closed, and the clomp of her boots across the front porch. Raven had found her place out here. I had, too, or so I thought.

I looked at my coffee-stained mug. Was it half full or half empty?

"Such is the life of Cass Callahan right now, eh Louis?"

He did not answer. No longer steaming, I finished my cup, cleared the table, and went out to the porch to sit.

The CR was a living, moving thing. Ranch hand chatter, horse and riders appearing from the stables, the orange glow of Flint's morning cigarette flashing next to his house, and the crack of dawn turning away the night, it all looked right. It felt right, like Craig Johnson's thirty seconds of Zen posts on Facebook. Moments have meaning, regardless of their length.

I stayed seated, feet propped on one another and watched my riders, my Raven grow smaller as they headed out for a day of work. I watched the sun rise. Its large, orange face overtook the horizon beyond the entrance of the ranch, then reached across the Gateway to Paradise to paint the faces of the rocky Mexican cliffs overlooking the Rio Grande. Through the cascades of orange and yellow, a single shadow flustered about as a barn owl raced against the light to find its darkened cavity within the rafters of the barn.

Warmth from the young day brushed my face. I closed my eyes and imagined my cheek pressed against Raven once again. She was the only person in the entire world who could handle me, whether I liked it or not. I opened my eyes, shook my head agreeing with myself that if today was to be different than yesterday, I would have to make it so.

Do what she said for once, Cass. Take the day. You can't afford to make any more mistakes.

CHAPTER TWENTY-FOUR

Alone in my office, I sat at the helm of my uncle's desk, tracing the dark walnut grain patterns with my finger. The large desktop was empty except for a copy of Louis L'Amour's *Hondo*, a favorite of my uncle Stewart's that I had not the heart to get rid of once we moved onto the CR. Its paperback body showed age through the wrinkles and creases on the cover and spine, like my uncle in his later years, no doubt. The pages had turned brown over time, but the words within its bindings had not changed one bit. I picked it up, feeling the weight in my hands. Scents of old vanilla and musty sawdust mixed with a hint of tobacco wafted from the literary carcass to my nose bringing with them an antiquated blend of real life and imagination. I could hear Uncle Stewart reading to himself, whispering the words so that each syllable, each description filled not only his mind, but the room around him. I had sat outside his door on more than one occasion and listened. I was too self-conscious to enter, fearing interruption, yet too interested not to stick around and hear how the chapter ended. It was not until later in life that I learned he had read aloud not just for his own enjoyment, but so that I could hear every word. Sneaky old bastard.

I smiled and set the book down on the desktop. Shifting positions in the oversized leather wingback chair, my feet nudged the chrome cast reinforced aluminum tactical case I stored in the kneehole beneath the desk. I felt the cool of its exterior against my toes which triggered a mental rundown of its contents. I knew what lay locked away inside and hoped I would never have to put them back in service.

A creak in the hall just outside the door caught my attention. I looked up as a small face peered in just below the strike plate. Tiny fingers held the door frame for balance.

"What'cha doin' out there, Miguel?"

Sliding further into view, Miguel's head appeared like a gopher poking its head out of its burrow.

"Wanna come in?"

Miguel did not move. I smiled, huffed, then asked again.

"¿Ven aquí?"

Without hesitation, Miguel scurried into the room, zoomed around the desk, and climbed into my lap. It seems I had made progress in areas other than speaking simple Spanish.

He looked at me, then around the room. With eyes filled with wonder and specks of crust pasted to his lashes, his gaze landed on my uncle's book. He looked at me again.

"Go on," I said. "Take a look."

After a moment of contemplation, Miguel smiled, then pointed at the book.

"You want to hear the story?"

I reached across the desk and retrieved the book. As I leaned back into the chair, Miguel nestled in, digging the back of his head into my chest. With knees bent, his legs dangled over my thigh.

"Comfy?"

"*Lee el cuento*," his tiny, accented voice whispered.

My curious look and lack of reply was enough for both of us to know that while my grasp of Spanish as growing, I had a long way to go.

Speaking slowly, and with determination, Miguel tried again.

"Stooo-rie. Ree-ad."

Flashes of Spencer crawling into my lap when he was a child and asking for a story graced my thoughts.

"You bet."

I opened the book to chapter one.

"*He rolled the cigarette in his lips, liking the taste of the tobacco, squinting his eyes against the sun glare. His buckskin shirt, seasoned by sun, rain, and sweat, smelled stale and old.*"

In the corner of the room, or maybe in a deep pocket of my mind, I saw Uncle Stewart, and he was smiling.

CHAPTER TWENTY-FIVE

By mid-morning, reinforcements arrived. I was rinsing syrupy plates from an Eggo Waffle and Little Smokies sausage breakfast Miguel and I had enjoyed following our morning read of Louis L'Amour and heard a knock at the front door. I wiped my hands on a dish towel, and walked through the house to see who was there. I opened the door to find Charlotte Huckabee standing on our porch. She had a backpack slung over one shoulder and wore a smile as inviting and warm as a summer's breeze.

"Mornin' Mr. Callahan."

"Good morning, Charlotte," I said, tilting my head as I recalled Raven's mention of reaching out to her. "You here to hang with the little man?"

"That's right. Raven, Mrs. Callahan, sent me a text this morning. She said you could use some backup. She said if things worked out that maybe we could make this more permanent."

"Sure, come on in. Miguel is playing in the back room. Follow the sounds of superheroes saving the world."

Charlotte smiled again, then walked past me into the

battle zone of childhood imagination. I started to close the door when my cell phone rang. I stepped onto the porch, pulled it from my pocket, and glanced at the caller ID before answering: *South Brewster County Sheriff's Office.*

I pressed the green accept icon and answered the call.

"This is Callahan."

"Good morning, Cass. It's Beverly Poole over at impound. We have that Ford Escort that Hector towed in yesterday. He said you'd be looking for the works."

"Yeah," I said. "That's correct. Thanks for calling. You beat me to the punch, Bev. Pull what you can from the VIN—registration, bank liens, flags on the vehicle, accident history, previous owners. Have one of the guys go out and search the car for anything that we can use as identifiers. Receipts, notes, insurance card. I need a clean sweep of the vehicle. Under the seats, glove box, trunk, the works."

"You got it, Cass."

"Thanks, Bev. I'll swing by this afternoon."

"Roger that." There was a pause on the line. *"Mind my asking why all the fuss over an abandoned car?"*

"Following a hunch, that's all."

"Good enough for me. I'll see what I can dig up."

I pressed the red end icon, and Beverly from impound was gone. And none too soon as a new call buzzed my phone. This time it was Chance.

"Hey, Chance."

"Buenos dios, amigo. How are things at the hacienda this morning?"

"Fine Chance, but that really why you called?"

"No, not so much, Cass. I got a call from California this mornin'."

Son of a bitch!

"You don't say. Who do you know out there?"

I could hear breathing over the line before Chance

replied. The kind of subtle huffs that suggest there is more to come and that I may not like what I heard.

"*It's not who I know, Cass. It's who knows you. Or about you at least. The call was from a law firm. Horowitz, Lee, and Calderón. Seems like there was a little trouble over on the Bar S last night. You wouldn't know anything about that, would you?*"

Shit!

"*Nevermind. Don't answer that over the phone. Just hear me when I say that yer new neighbors have some powerful connections. They threatened a TRO, Cass, an' I ain't got room to put your sorry ass up with me.*"

"What did you say?"

"*I told them that a restraining order was not necessary and that I would handle it on my end. Slap you with a fine, that kind of thing.*"

"A fine?"

"*Yeah. They agreed, so the next round of margaritas is on you, amigo. But...*" Chance's voice became serious. "*Ya do anything to get under their skin again, the consequences may be out of my control.*"

"How could I do anything to get under their skin?"

"*I know you well, mi amigo. Come in and let's have a powwow. Fill me in, cause I know there's more ta the story.*"

The line went dead before I could reply.

"So, there is more to you than meets the eye after all, Mr. Bar S man," I said to myself.

Innocent screams of joy burst out the front door as Miguel ran at top speed over the porch and into the yard with Charlotte following close behind. Her arms were outstretched above her head and her fingers were curled like claws. Man, that little guy could move, and in boots, no less. He scampered to the rails of the corral, and in three quick motions, was up and over before Charlotte had the chance to stop him. She leaned over, placing her hands on her knees, her chest rising and falling from lack of breath. She caught my glance and stood up straight and gave me a cheerful wave. That told me everything I needed to know. Miguel was having the time of his life, and Charlotte was here for the long haul.

I made an about-face and headed into the house to change clothes. Raven had asked me to take some time for myself. Chance had asked me to come in for a chat.

Guess we'll see where the day leads.

CHAPTER TWENTY-SIX

Brewster, Texas, the county seat for South Brewster County, was caught in a downward spiral of failing economics and growing crime. It was evident everywhere. Dilapidated buildings, growing homeless population—no doubt a result of the surge of illegals crossing the Texas/Mexico border in droves—businesses that had flourished were now faltering, even the church had seen a decline in attendance. Gang life had no significant impact on the population, but I saw signs of its growth every time I drove to work. A new, colorful tag on an abandoned building, growing groups of thuglike characters hanging around the bars or gas stations. When they were not at the bars, they would line the streets like they were waiting for a Fourth of July parade. It reminded me of things I had seen driving down Westheimer or Richmond Avenue inside the beltway when on duty in Houston. The town was going to shit, and there was very little I could do to stop it. Brewster was just another victim of the current administration's lack of concern for the little guy. The big guy had everything he needed. Why should he care about some tiny town way out west?

I pulled into the parking lot at the jail, found my spot, and cut the engine. The sheriff's office was still sharing space with the county jail until construction of a new South Brewster County Sheriff's Office was completed. Its destruction at the hands of the late killer Carlos Ruiz-Mata, El Despiadado, had been devastating, but each day brought progress to erase the physical reminders of that fateful day. If only it were that easy to rebuild the images burned into my memory. The video playback of our deputies being murdered, the burning rubble and smoking piles of cinderblocks and office supplies and lost friends—it had all been too much, too heavy. Reconstruction might mend the building's facade, but mending my mind was a different battle, one that required more than concrete and fresh paint.

I stepped out of the Explorer and walked to the front door, pausing once to look back at my car when I realized I had forgotten to swing by impound to see what information Beverly had ready for me.

After I talked with Chance, I thought.

Turning back around, I walked to the front door and scanned my ID badge on a card reader posted at the entrance to the jail. A loud, awkward *buzz* sounded, and the door clicked open.

The gray atmosphere inside the building was enough to dampen anyone's spirits. Being jailed was not a walk in the park. The mix of cinderblock and thick steel bars, sliding doors and reinforced glass windows was not what one might call a fertile working environment, but it would have to do for now.

I nodded at the accusatory yet despondent eyes behind the receiving window and walked around to the first security checkpoint. A guard with whom I had become familiar manned the metal detector along with a young lady who looked like today might be her first day on the job.

"How's it going, Jimmy?"

Jim Knotts. Just a kid by the looks of him, was a transplant from East Texas, like me. He spoke with a thick, back woods accent.

"Mornin' Investigator Callahan."

"How many times do I have to tell you, Jimmy. Call me Cass."

"Yessir, Investigator Callahan. I'll remember that next time."

I tossed my keys into a basket that looked like it had been stolen from the local Dairy Queen, then removed my gun from my SOB holster.

"Still can't get used to this," I said, placing the gun into a small lock box that the guards would secure until I left the building.

"It's procedure," the young lady guard replied.

She avoided eye contact with me while she stowed my side arm.

"He knows that, Sofia," Jimmy said, his East Texas drawl emphasizing and contorting her name into Suh-feeya.

"That's okay, Jimmy. She's just doing her job. First days can be a little tense...for everyone."

Sofia finally looked at me instead of past me. Her deep brown eyes and smooth almond skin did not fit the bland jailer's uniform. She was naturally beautiful. I smiled, trying to lighten the moment, but even then, she was sharp as stone.

"You can retrieve your weapon from the armory staff once you are on your way out."

She handed me a ticket like I was checking a coat at a party and pointed to a sign with an arrow indicating the way to the secure exit.

"Thank you, Sofia," I said.

"It's Guard Bishop, sir. Have a nice day."

I glanced at Jimmy. He pursed his lips but did not say a word. A light atop the security scanner turned green as I stepped through.

"Dodged a bullet there, huh," I whispered to Jimmy as he handed me back my keys. "Watch your back, my friend."

"Yessir. You have a good day Investi..."

I stopped him with a flick of my pointer finger.

"It's Cass, Jimmy. All my friends call me Cass. You should, too."

My voice echoed throughout the hall as I walked away, not waiting around to be called Investigator Callahan again. I never liked the title, special investigator, but it fit the job I agreed to do.

I navigated the maze of hallways until I came to the wing repurposed as the temporary Brewster County Sheriff's Office. I stepped through the door and was greeted by Deputy Marie Bostwick.

"Hey, Cass. You been called to the Principal's office? Again?"

"Something like that, Boss."

"Wouldn't expect anything less."

Deputy Bostwick, or Boss as everybody calls her, and I had walked through fire together these past few months. We had become friends beyond the badge, so her ribbing at my expense was not unexpected. In fact, our entire team of deputies were close knit. It was an oddity by some standards, but it worked for us out here. Back on the force in Houston? Not a chance in hell. Chance had a unique grasp over all of us. If asked what *it* was that kept everything running smooth, especially during a crisis and the rebuild of our presence in Brewster County, I would say that unless you live it, *it* was hard to understand. Chance's *it* worked.

"You heading out?" I asked her.

"Yep. Back to the blacktop and lonely stretches of highway. Gotta protect the house. You know."

"I do. Be safe out there, okay?"

"Always."

I saw Chance standing in the doorway to his office. He motioned me over, then disappeared inside, leaving the door open. I gave Boss a nod and left her to her duties. Telephones rang, keyboards clicked, the air conditioning hummed overhead, but it was the returning earworm that invaded my ears again.

Mister freaking moon...if I could only remember the rest, maybe I could make sense of it.

I poked my head through the doorway and saw Chance waiting for me behind his desk. This office was a mere afterthought compared to his previous space. It was plain, undecorated, institutional. But it was how Chance wanted it.

"This is only temporary," he had said. "We'll be outta here in a jiffy, even if I have ta move mountains myself."

"*Que paso*, Chance?"

"Shut the door, Cass."

I sensed an immediate tone of how this meeting might go. Deciding not to question his mood, I closed the door and took a seat across from him.

"Everything all right, Chance?"

"Not hardly. Yer buddies, Horowitz, Lee, and Calderón. They're up my ass again. Guess they assumed you'd get the good ol' boy treatment. S'pose they were right on that front."

"Kinda hard up about a simple misdemeanor, don't you think?"

"Was thinkin' that, but they're within their right to

complain if they want. You an' Flint shouldn't have been over there in the first place."

"Chance, there's some weird shit going on over there. I can feel it."

"But ya can't prove it."

"You know me, Chance. I'm not wrong about this."

"Yeah. I know ya. I know yer passionate about gettin' the bad guy. You've gone above an' beyond an' even more ta prove it..." He paused to fold his hands where I could see them. "...and at a cost greater to yerself than ta any other on the planet. I see it. Raven sees it. The only one who don't see it is sittin' right there across from me."

"You've been talking with Raven?"

"Ain't what ya think. Ain't goin' behind yr back er nothin' like that. Look, Cass. We're friends, no doubt about it. She's simply worried about you, that's all. Fact is, I am too. I could ignore this. Joke it off and let you be, but you are more than deserving of a break, *mi amigo*. I know I pulled you out of yer original plan when ya first came out here. Situations kinda helped that along, too. But the world is as even keel as it's gonna be right now. You gotta find a way to find that balance yerself. The good, the bad. Each has its place. You just got things all jumbled up which makes the negative shine and the positive go dark."

I sat and looked at my friend, my boss, my sheriff, and allowed his words to sink in. If he had simply asked me to take a leave of absence to get my act together, I might have told him where to stick that suggestion. The fact that he had the wherewithal to see my life, my work through the eyes of a human being, not only as an employer, is why he is so widely respected by all, and loved by his closest friends.

"Maybe you and Raven have a point."

Chance nodded, then relaxed into his chair. He leaned back and let a long breath settle his hidden nerves.

"Go see Spencer. Take a guy trip."

I eased back as well. My body overtaking my mind as it began to accept what was being asked of me.

"You know, I had that very thought this morning."

"Ya see. All you have ta do is let go, even if fer just a moment, Cass. Go be that dad, that friend, an' when you come back refreshed, an' if it's what ya want, work beside me once again."

His words rang in my ears. They meant something. When Chance speaks, his words always do. I began to answer when my cell phone buzzed the lining of my pocket. I looked down and decided to let voicemail answer the call.

"Chance, why don't I…"

My cell phone buzzed again. If I were truly going to let go, I would have to start now. I reached down, felt for the buttons through my pants, and clicked the call away.

"You were about ta say?"

Chance raised an eyebrow. His genuine, trademark smile began to form across his previously stern face.

"Yeah, I think I'll…"

Chance's desk phone buzzed to life. Its antiquated ring pierced the air between us, the ferocity in its tone crippling our coming together of the minds.

"The universe does not want to let you go, I think," Chance said, smiling. "Hold that thought."

Chance picked up the receiver and held it to his ear.

"Sheriff Gilbert speaking."

I could not hear the voice on the other end of the call, but I did not have to. Chance's smile disappeared in an instant. His eyes became focused. The call was brief, but the message must have been heavy.

"Got it. Don't do anything 'til we get there."

Chance shifted his gaze to me, then hung up the phone.

"Guess ya should've answered yer phone."

The nerve endings on the back of my neck prickled. A cool wash of adrenaline flooded my arms and legs. My fingertips began to tingle.

"Tell me."

"Seems Raven and her crew found somethin'."

"What did they find, Chance?"

He took a deep breath.

"We got a dead body out on the CR, Cass."

CHAPTER TWENTY-SEVEN

"Just when I thought I was out, they pull me back in."
Michael Corleone, *The Godfather Part III*.

Such was my life.

The whir of the siren and chirp of the horn were the only sounds I heard as we sped through town. With Chance behind the wheel, I looked out the window and watched the world swirl into a blur of color and light and watchful, curious eyes. He had insisted on driving us to the CR, citing that the 4x4 capabilities of his new Ford Interceptor Bronco would carry us all the way to the river with ease.

"Yer car is pretty an' all, but the Bronc has it where it counts."

There was no sense or time for argument, so I hopped in and away we went.

When we passed the city limits on the south side of town, I saw flashing lights fall in line behind us. I reached for the CB and spoke into the mic.

"That you behind us, Boss?"

"10-4. Callahan? You riding shotgun?"

"Roger that."

The echo of sirens carried through the speakers.

"Brave man."

Chance gave me the side-eye.

"Tell 'er to pipe down or I'll issue her a billy club an' have 'er walkin' the streets for a month."

"You do that, and she'd have this place cleaned up in a week."

Chance nodded

"Prob'ly so."

I changed my voice to mimic Chance's unique drawl, and activated the mic.

"Boss, Chance says he's *'glad yer taggin' along.'*"

"*Ay, cabrón*," Chance muttered. "Tell 'er we're droppin' to Code 2. Siren's givin' me a headache."

"Run Code 2. Rendezvous at the CR. DB on property."

"Ten-four."

I started to replace the mic when Boss spoke up again.

"Is the family safe, Cass? Raven, and..."

"Everyone is fine. Raven called it in. We'll know more upon arrival. Looks like the crew she's working with discovered a floater stuck in the reeds along the banks of the river near the grove."

"Isn't that where you found the last ones?"

"Yeah. Same vicinity, anyway."

"That ain't right, Cass. Bodies popping up all over the CR."

"I'm a crackpot magnet. What can I tell you? Out."

I slid the mic into its cradle and sat back in my seat. My nerves were calm, but my anxiety was building. Boss's comment about bodies piling up created a mental image within me of mounds of corpses stacked higher and higher, growing until the tops disappeared from view. I lost the time as I sunk deeper into the wakeful nightmare. I saw myself walking around the stacks, counting the dead, reaching numbers even I could not believe. Was I responsible for them all? I stepped closer. I looked closer. Their faces, gray and empty, skin swollen on some, tight and leathery on others. The piles swayed as I circled each decaying mass. Like pillars lining a great hall, they towered around me. Walking between them, I saw the shadow of a man come into view. Stepping closer, the man's face remained hidden in darkness, but his bare hands and bare feet stuck out of his clothing. He looked like a pauper asking for handouts. His shirt and pants matched, their plain tan fabric stained with sweat at the armpits and around his waist. His fingers were caked with dirt. His feet showed fresh scrapes. Blood trickled between his toes.

"Where am I?"

I whispered as I approached but I might as well have screamed out. My voice rose, echoing in the dark, swirling around the stacks of the dead, then soaring past my own ears as if caught by a boomerang that was meant to never fall from flight.

The figure before me raised his arms, then twisted around so that his torso appeared to rotate a full one hundred and eighty degrees. I heard popping sounds which reminded me of snapping twigs. When I realized it was the sounds of bones cracking, my lunch found its way into my throat before settling back into my stomach. I could taste the acid in my mouth. It burned into my nose. I stopped within arm's reach of the shadowy figure and watched him twist back around to face me.

"Who are you?" I asked.

The man lifted his hands to show that he was holding something now. At first, I thought it could have been a baby animal in his palms. He cupped his hands, concealing whatever he had, then peeling back one finger at a time, I began to see what it was.

I glanced to the man's face, realizing that with each

pull of a finger, a silvery light began to shine where his teeth should have been. I looked back at his hands. Reflective waves of brilliant light pulsed from his palms.

"What the hell?"

An insidious rumble of distinct laughter rose from inside of the shadowed man. His mouth, stretched wide, gaping open, revealing metallic silver shards where his teeth should have been. They chattered up and down as the laughter strengthened.

I forced myself to look away but could feel...*FEEL* myself being pulled back to bear witness to the terrible sight. The pressure around me was real. Pulling, pulling, pulling. My eyes bobbled back and forth from the man's face to his hands. Teeth to mysterious light. Shadowed figure to stacks and stacks of swaying dead. Back and forth. It was like watching a tennis match in hell. I glanced at his hands. Pulsing. Pounding. Waves of growing brilliance. Back and forth. Then to his face. His mouth. His gnashing mouth.

And the laughter, once low and guttural had reached pitches so high it could have been mistaken for screeching tires, or the squeal of a pig amid slaughter.

"Stop! Stop! Who are you? What are you?"

In a moment incalculable to measure, darkness and silence fell around me. The mounds of dead were gone. The man was gone. All the light and laughter and horror had vanished. I looked down and could see my own hands. They trembled as I lifted them before my eyes. As I lowered them again, I saw something on the ground where the man had been. I stepped forward, giving it a long, hard look. I saw a small box. A simple, plain, unmarked, metallic box.

Reach out. Go on. Pick it up.

I knelt and stretched both hands out to grasp the box. It was right there. So close. If I could only hold it and see what it was, how it felt, maybe I could make sense of this. All this. My fingertips brushed its edge.

"Cass...*CASS*. Com'on *amigo*. Snap out of it."

I jolted in my seat. Had I been asleep? Dreaming? In some sort of trance or mind-altering state. *What is going on with me?*

I looked out the front window to see we were pulling under the archway at the entrance to the CR. My eyes itched. My stomach felt queasy.

"Hey. You all right? Want me ta stop at the house b'fore we head out on the property?"

I turned my head slowly to look at Chance.

"No. No. Let's keep going. I...I..."

"You looked like a zombie. *Pareces un muerto viviente*, Cass. I let you be, figurin' you'd come around, but damn *amigo*. You were somewhere else. Sure yer okay?"

Chance's face showed real concern.

"I leaned my head against the headrest, stretched my eyes open wide enough to feel the skin on my forehead and cheeks pull. I shook my head, clearing away what cobwebs were left dangling in the dark empty space between my ears, and pointed out the front window.

"Drive."

CHAPTER TWENTY-EIGHT

The crystalline sky overhead, it's wide expanse reaching the ends of the earth in all directions, made for a perfect afternoon had we not been enroute to identify and recover a dead body. The terrain was rough and the seemingly lawless location had a history of its own, but, damn, share the wealth. Too much life had been lost on the outskirts of the CR over the past few months.

Images of the Six M crew huddled around their horses came into focus as we pulled around the grove. I saw Raven standing among them. She must have seen us, too. I watched her step away from the group and raise a hand to wave us over.

Chance slowed the Bronco to a crawl as we rolled onto the hardened path that led to the river. Surfacing along the river's edge, this stretch of packed earth resembled rocky fingers stretching from the cliffs across the Rio Grande, clinging to the dirt as if being pulled into the murky waters.

With the green grove of shade trees only yards from its tips, the rocky joints could not quite reach the safety of the oasis canopy. As if angered by its lack of reach, its fingers clawed at the dirt, creating fissures in the ground —fissures that sometimes held more than rattlesnakes and scorpions. I knew that all too well. Looking out the window, I watched as we rolled past the darkened crevasses, each seeming to grin at me, each a harbinger of mystery and time lost in the rugged West Texas terrain.

Chance parked the Bronco on a stiff patch of ground twenty yards from the river's edge. Deputy Bostwick pulled alongside us. Raven was already walking over to us as we got out.

"Hey," she said, her face wearing a mixture of relief and concern. "Sorry to pull you out of...whatever you were doing."

"Don't worry about that," I said, giving her a welcomed hug. "Sorry you found what you found."

"Hey, Chance."

Raven spoke over my shoulder before letting go. My fingers lingered at her waist, clutching at her like the cliffs did the earth.

"You okay, Cass?"

Her voice softened, her inflections notable.

"Yeah. Yeah. Just happy to see you."

Chance stepped around the front of the Bronco.

"Hello, Raven."

Raven pulled away from me and gave Chance a sidearm hug.

"The guys over there," she said pointing to a lumpy saddle blanket draped across the ground near the water. "The guys pulled him out. He probably would have floated on by, but he got tangled in the reeds near shore."

"Let's go have a look," Chance said.

Raven greeted Boss, and we all walked toward the body. The Six M crew stayed in their huddle, acknowledging us with head nods as we passed. I returned the silent sentiment, then turned to Boss.

"Go talk with the guys. Take their statements."

"On it," Boss said.

As we neared the body, the ground turned soft again. My shoes sunk into the moist ground.

We stopped and looked down at the rumpled covering. Of all its years doing its job on the back of a horse, I bet this blanket never figured to be draped across the body of a dead man.

Where were my thoughts going?

Chance knelt and pulled back the edge that covered the corpse's face.

"Whelp. Ya don't see that ever' day out here." He paused and looked up at me. "'Cept, we have. Similar anyhow."

On cue, I both recognized the man lying on the ground and understood what Chance had said.

"Holy..."

I knelt next to Chance.

"Looks like the guy from Big Bend," Raven said.

I looked over my shoulder.

"Didn't think to mention that over the phone?"

Her gaze sharpened.

"You didn't *answer* my call, Cass."

"Whoa, now. Let's not lose our heads, folks. Let's check his pockets. Maybe he has an ID."

I stood up.

"Don't need to," I said.

Chance looked up at me.

"How ya figure?"

"I know this man. He's the one from the broken-down car yesterday. The Chinese man with his wife. The ones I let go with the man from the Bar S."

Chance stood.

"You sure about this, Cass?"

"Positive."

Chance put his hands on his hips, twisted his body to look north, in the direction of the Bar S, then spat over his shoulder into the river.

"Well, if that saddle don't fit the rider, we'll be neck deep in cow pies, *mi amigo*."

"Oh, it fits, all right."

Chance stepped back, then whistled at Boss. She acknowledged, finished writing something on a pad of paper, nodded again at the Six M bunch, and walked over to us.

"Sheriff?"

"Need ya ta get Dr. Frannie on the horn. You'll need ta drive back to the house ta get a good signal. Tell'er what we got out here and that I need a full report. Need ta determine a cause of death."

"Drowned, if you ask me," Raven said.

Chance, Boss, and I all looked at her at the same time.

"Just my two cents," she said, her face looking sheepish.

Chance smiled, breaking the awkwardness of the moment.

"Yer prob'ly right, Raven. Just need an official statement."

She glanced at me, her eyes filled with accusations. I should have been the one to speak up.

"Look, we've got to get back to work. If you need to talk to any more of my guys, we'll meet you back at the house tonight."

With that, she walked away. No, "goodbye." Nothing. I turned to go after her.

"Raven."

She kept walking.

"Rave?"

I reached out and tugged her arm. She whirled around, cheeks huffing as if ready for a fight.

"What?" she said, her voice carrying weight.

"Hey, I just..."

"Go on, Cass. Go solve the murder, or whatever it is you all are calling it. It's what you want. More mystery. More danger. More trouble. God damn, Cass! You can't seem to live without it."

"Hold on just a minute." I could feel the heat rise in my temples. My chest became solid with irritation, accusation, frustration...contempt. "I was all set to walk away from this. From Chance. From the life I have lived and devoted myself to. I was in the chair when you called. Don't make this sound like I was looking for this. It found me."

Raven's face melted. Her eyes fluttered, then filled with tears that just would not fall.

"That's my point. You can't escape it, Cass. That's what frightens me so."

The crackle of rocks and dirt beneath Deputy Bostwick's cruiser filled the air between us as she drove back to the house to relay Chance's instruction to the medical examiner. My mouth sagged open, but no words cleared my lips. Raven closed her eyes, breaking the dam that held her tears. As she opened them again, wet streaks carved through the thin layer of dust that covered her working cowgirl cheeks.

"I gotta go."

I stood and watched her return to her crew. Gilly reached out a hand to her, which Raven ignored. She mounted her horse and reined it away. The others followed, but not before I caught a fierce glare from Gilly. A blue lock of hair dangled in front of her.

I broke off from her, turning to see Chance kneeling over the body once more.

Two dead Chinese in less than a month? And where was this man's wife? Was she in danger, too?

I walked up to Chance.

"They aren't gonna like it, but it's time we make an official visit next door."

"Bar S?"

"Yep."

Chance stood up.

"Maybe you ought ta sit this one out."

I looked down at the body, at the man I had tried to help only yesterday. I closed my eyes and saw the look of fright and uncertainty on his wife's face before they got into the Bar S truck. Before he ended up dead.

CHAPTER TWENTY-NINE

If luck had been on our side at all, it showed up in the form of Dr. Frannie Lopez-Tasker, Medical Examiner. North and South Brewster counties collectively made up the largest county in Texas, covering over six thousand square miles yet with the population being as sparse as it was, there was only one ME to service the entire area. As it was, Frannie had been down in Terlingua when she got the call from Deputy Bostwick and was able to drop what she was doing to make the short drive north to the ranch. She arrived within the hour, and with two members of her team to boot. Boss met Dr. Frannie's ME van at the ranch and escorted them across the property.

"Kinda ironic, don't you think?" Frannie said, stepping out of the passenger side of the van.

"Come again?" I said.

"Don't play dumb, Cass. You growing deadheads out here or what?"

Frannie was no stranger to the CR. She had played a vital role in my investigation following the discovery of the first bodies we had found on the property by partially identifying our main victim before he was collected in a startling coverup by the FBI. Her digging triggered a flag that the FBI wanted to keep under wraps. That was key, the truth becoming obvious once revealed. She and Raven hit it off like sisters, and she's been a friend to us ever since.

To Chance, on the other hand. He was sweet on her like sipping lemonade in the summertime. When he saw her, his mouth curved wide with the glee of a ten-year-old boy seeing his first crush walk down the hallway at school. His face lit up when he spoke to her.

"Dr. Tasker, thank you for being so...expedient in your coming."

"That's what she said," Frannie replied without missing a beat.

I shared a glance with Chance as Frannie walked over to us. Boss followed, doing her best to hide her laughter.

Frannie smiled with a radiance only a woman who knows she was attracting attention could make. And she liked it, too. Although she was at least fifteen years his younger, it was clear Frannie had expectations of her own when it came to the sheriff.

As usual, Frannie looked stunning, choosing comfort and style over what she dubbed 'boring business attire.' Her snakeskin boots, tucked into navy-colored slacks by Theory, complemented a red silk camisole and a fitted blazer matched to her pants. Her black hair flowed behind her, save for a single strand draped across one cheek. Dark eyes, perched above a smile worth its weight in gold, fixed on us—it was a look that belonged on a runway, not approaching a potential crime scene. Chance had every reason to be smitten. I was a happily married man, and a friend of Frannie's, but there was no denying she was sexy as hell.

"What do you have for me this time, fellas?"

"Single victim. No signs of visible trauma," Chance began. "Let me show you."

He stepped to the side and waved an arm to lead her away. Boss continued to crack up under the collar. My mood swayed, too, but not so far as to get rid of the acidic tasting backwash left in my mouth following Raven's departure. I know she would have liked to see Frannie, but that would have to come much later.

Chance uncovered the body, and Frannie, designer clothes and all, donned a pair of latex gloves and set to work right there on the banks of the Rio Grande. She talked to herself as she examined the body.

"Nail beds and palmar surfaces unremarkable, cervical swelling present without overt external signs of strangulation."

Gently manipulating the victims eyelids, she continued.

"Ocular findings include bilateral petechiae, commonly associated with asphyxial deaths, yet no periorbital ecchymosis noted."

Maneuvering her hands over the surface of the corpse, she examined his skin, most notably his midsection as it had swollen like a pufferfish in distress. "Postmortem submersion effects evident with marked generalized edema, particularly notable in the abdominal region, consistent with aquatic bloating."

Frannie pinched the outside of her right glove near the wrist, careful not to touch her skin, and peeled it off, turning it inside out as she pulled. She removed a small plastic bag and a cell phone from her blazer's interior pocket. She placed the glove in the bag, then held it out for Chance to take.

Still speaking to herself, she retraced her thoughts as she took video of each affected area of the body, thoroughly documenting any abnormalities present. Her voice sounded clear, professional, like what a documentary on The Learning Channel might produce. She moved from one side to the other, finishing her initial assessment and saving the video. Blowing the lock of dangling hair from her face, she stood, transitioning to taking photographs of the river in the direction the body was discovered.

"Can you estimate a time of death?" I asked.

Turning, with eyebrows raised and mouth curved and smiling like a sly fox, Frannie replied. "Of course. That's why I get paid the big bucks."

She peeled her left glove off, ensuring the contaminated exterior was contained within itself, then held it out so Chance could add it to the plastic bag.

Such a lapdog, I thought to myself.

"Preliminary analysis, factoring in ambient water temperature and observed postmortem changes, suggests time of death within the last twelve hours."

"Well," Chance said. "That gives us something."

Frannie smirked, suggesting that there was more beneath the surface.

"You might need to dig deeper on this one, Chance. On the surface, it looks like a drowning. At least that's what we were made to think. I'd bet an eggroll at the local buffet that this guy was murdered, then dumped into the river."

Chance shook his head. "That leaves us with a suspect pool of anyone on either side of the border, not to mention those that have other *business* in these parts."

"True." Frannie walked around behind us like we were the focal point of an interrogation. "But here's the thing. While there are signs of drowning, look at his neck," she said, pointing after circling back and kneeling beside the body. "I'll need to confirm with tests and an X-ray, but this isn't a typical neck break from strangulation."

Franne looked up at us.

"Please, continue," Chance said.

"Typically, and you boys probably already know this, but when a strangulation occurs the victim will have markings around the circumference of the neck, specifically where the attacker's fingers and hands squeezed. This doesn't show any signs of that. See?"

She waved a finger back and forth like Vanna White. Can I buy a vowel, Pat?

"No, this break is precise. Violent." Frannie stood up and walked behind Chance. "Let me put it this way."

With a flash of speed and agility, Frannie wrapped her arms around Chance's neck and squeezed. It was a gentle example but caught both of us off guard. Chance instinctively raised his arms and grabbed Frannie's hands.

"Whoa there, tiger." She loosened her grip but allowed her hands to rest on Chance's shoulders. Her fingers caressed Chance's tense muscles, sliding back and forth, brushing the skin of his neck. "You see? If he had been strangled, there would have been signs of a struggle. Skin under the victim's fingernails, specific bruising to his hands, fingers, and neck. Our guy has none of that."

"Which means?" Chance said, relaxing in the arms of our medical goddess.

I chimed in before Frannie could answer.

"It means whoever killed him was highly skilled. Military training, martial arts, possibly both."

"Bingo," Frannie said, sliding her arms from Chance. "I'll get the body back to the lab and run some more tests."

"Thanks, Frannie. I'll tell Raven you stopped by."

Frannie gave me a friendly smile, then turned to Chance.

"I'll call you later, Sheriff, if I find anything further worth mentioning...maybe even if I don't."

She winked at him, then turned and strutted back to

her guys waiting at the ME van. Her presence, while professional, was always a sight to behold. She could command a rhumba of rattlesnakes with the flick of a finger, a finger in which Chance was tightly wrapped.

"Partner, there's a surefooted boot right there begging to be worn," I said, nudging Chance in the ribs.

"¡Para, para!" Chance shifted his gaze to the running waters of the Rio Grande. The reeds cradling the body swayed under the river's current. "Looks like yer gonna git that visit to the Bar S after all."

CHAPTER THIRTY

Our three-car cortege passed the grove and crossed the barren stretches of rugged terrain between the river and the ranch house. There was nary a well-wisher or mourner to pay their respects to the dead, save for a line of vultures that swooped overhead like slimy ambulance chasers looking for an easy buck.

I hung my arm out the window. The warm afternoon air brushed over my hand and into the silent cab of the Bronco, ruffling my shirt in the breeze. I glanced in the side mirror and saw Dr. Frannie's ME van following three car lengths behind. Deputy Bostick brought up the rear. Shifting my gaze to the horizon, I noticed movement in the distance. Through the wavy distortion of heat rising from the ground, pinpricks of color ambled around specs of brown. The mass moved like a slow blob crossing the range. I surmised it was Raven and her crew. Who else could it be? It seemed fair to say that her life on the CR had taken a drastic turn for the better, while mine had spiraled downward as I fought to keep everything in my world from burning down.

When the barn and house came into view, Chance reached for the radio. Pulling the mic from its cradle, he clicked the transmission button and spoke.

"Hey, Boss. You go an' folla Dr. Lopez-Tasker inta town, then get back out on patrol. Ya can file a report of the cowboy's statements at the end of yer shift."

He clicked off. His wrist hung in the air with mic in hand as he waited for her reply.

"Ten-four, Sheriff."

Chance returned the mic to its cradle, then spoke to me as we approached the corral.

"You and me are gonna head over ta the Bar S. Call it a wellness check. See who and what we kin see. Tell 'em who we found."

"That's all?"

"Ain't jumpin' the gun on this one a'tall. They already have the backing of some West Coast law office who, by the way..." Chance shot me a glare. "...don't like you too much."

"Give me some time. I'll give them a reason to really hate me."

"Cass."

"You think I give a shit about their feelings? I saw our corpse yesterday. Alive. On edge. His wife looking at me like she was guilty of something and had just gotten caught. My gut is telling me there's something seriously wrong going on."

"I ain't challenging that. Not one bit. What I am sayin' is we need ta make sure that when we do find somethin', we haven't shot ourselves in the foot. One misstep and I guarantee their law dogs'll find a way ta keep 'em clean, even if they're as dirty as a three a.m. sheet in a Tijuana whorehouse."

I let the stench of that thought sink in. Chance was right. But so was I. I turned my attention out the window again in time to see Charlotte and Miguel standing on the front porch. Charlotte gave a wave. Miguel stood at attention, surprising me with a tiny salute as we approached.

"Son of a gun," I said.

"That boy thinks yer a hero, Cass."

"How you figure?"

"I've seen him play with those soldier toys of his. Even at his age, he's picked up on one thing plenty of adults haven't."

"And what's that?"

"Respect, *mi amigo*. Respect. Why does he salute you? Because that's what soldier's do. In his eyes, you're a soldier. You're a hero. Prob'ly his hero. You and Raven, anyway."

As we drove past, I sat up straight in my seat, raised a flattened hand to my forehead, and returned the salute. Chance chirped the siren and flashed the Bronco's light bar. The noise startled Charlotte, but Miguel's face beamed with elation. I followed his image in the side mirror when he fell out of direct view. He stood and watched each of us pass by. He waved at Frannie in the ME van. Boss flashed her cruiser lights as well, causing Miguel to erupt in a volley of hops and waves. It seemed our cortege found one onlooker who took the time to pay respect and enjoy themselves at the expense of an unfortunate incident.

We left the ranch and broke off from the group, en route to the Bar S. With a hefty job before us, the image of Miguel remained in the forefront of my thoughts. I could not help but smile, which made me wonder, was his attention, his show of respect, a silver lining? Or was it the calm before the storm.

CHAPTER THIRTY-ONE

"What the hell?"

Looking ahead, the Bar S had kept most of its predecessor's regional West Texas flair, but behind that façade, a distinct change rushed into view.

"Is that a guard shack?" I said, leaning forward in my seat.

The metallic drumming of a cattle guard bending under our weight vibrated through the Bronco as we pulled onto the property. The crackle and pop of stones shooting from beneath the Bronco's tires along the gravel road entrance seemed loud enough to announce our arrival. We rolled up and stopped in front of a lowered security gate, its newness shining as if just pulled from the packaging.

"No southern hospitality here, I reckon," Chance said.

Through the driver-side window, I saw a man open the door of the guard shack and size us up as if we had just run over a family pet. Chance lowered his window.

"Howdy."

The man, clad in jeans and Western-striped Wrangler

button-down, plain black boots, and a new Stetson, glanced from the door of the Bronco, then back at us.

"Have an appointment?"

I know what I would have said, but Chance took a more tactful approach. "No, sir. Would like ta speak with someone in charge, though."

"About?"

The man wrinkled his nose, digging for more information."

"Well," Chance started, hesitating.

Come on Chance. Don't let this mall cop get in our way!

"I could share it with you, but let's not wrestle around the pigsty on this, *amigo*."

"Yeah. I'm gonna need more than a..."

The buzz of a telephone rang out from the guard shack. The man turned around, stepped inside, and answered the call. I looked out the front window and saw a small security camera focused on us.

"Don't look now, we're on Candid Camera," I said.

On cue, the gate lifted. The guard leaned out the door and signaled us to pull ahead. He scowled and took two steps toward the Bronco when I fingered a wave at him, but Chance drove off, leaving the guard to eat our dust.

"I feel like we're in one of those 1980s crime dramas where the bad guys always seem to be watching and waiting with an unlimited supply of bullets jammed into a single submachine gun magazine."

"Don't the good guys usually win?"

"Yeah, but one of them typically eats a bullet."

"Not again, *amigo*. I've had my turn here already."

No kidding he had. Chance was the recipient of a two birds, one stone bullet, taking the shot to the shoulder during our raid of the Double S.

We drove into the yard and parked on what appeared to be a fresh layer of decomposed granite. Golden flecks of color sparkled within a field of tan and gray stone that stretched from the corral to the main house, then trailing off and becoming lighter, blending in with the old gravel beneath.

As we stepped out of the Bronco, an eerie hush hovered over the ranch.

"This is weird," I said. "Did we drive into the *Twilight Zone*?"

"You spooked by change, Cass?"

"No. I'm spooked by what I can't understand. Where are all the workers? The livestock? Even the horses that were used to track Flint and me last night?"

"Stables, most likely."

"Okay, I'll buy that, but..." I glanced down at the ground, at the fresh layer of earthy stone. "Where's the horse crap? Stains? Anything that might give a clue that this is actually a working ranch?"

With perfect timing, a door on the main house and a swinging door on the barn opened wide. The large Bar S man I had previous run-ins with stepped out of the house, followed by four other men, all wearing similar western-style clothing, all of which looked straight off the Boot Barn rack. They all walked toward us with a determined gait.

"Keep yer cool, *amigo*. That's an order," Chance whispered.

To keep from balling my hands into fists, I flexed and curled my toes inside my shoes. It was not nearly as relieving as having a hardened fist at the ready.

Chatter from the barn drew all of our attention. The Bar S man stopped, pointed out the door to his men, and whistled loud enough that its report could have echoed to Mexico. A man in the barn popped his head out the door in time to see two of the Bar S men double-timing it toward the opening. I caught a glimpse of his face, which was all I needed to know without any misgivings at all, that he was not from around here.

"See that?" I said.

"A-yuh. Looks like there's at least one other 'round here like the guy Frannie's about to dissect."

"Correct me if I'm wrong, but have you ever seen so many..."

"What can I do for you fellas this afternoon," the Bar S man said, stomping forward. "We are kinda busy around here. Lots of daylight left."

"It's, 'We're burnin' daylight, friend,'" I said. "John Wayne? Ever heard of him?"

So much for keeping cool.

The man brushed off my comment and spoke directly to Chance.

"Mind telling me why you're here? And with this..." He paused, then forcefully added, "Gentleman?"

"I am Sheriff Chance Gilbert. This is Cass Callahan, my top special investigator."

"Special Investigator?" He turned to the two men who remained with him. "You see anything *special* about him?"

When he faced us again, our eyes locked. I could feel the crunch of bone at the behest of my fist on his nose, but I held back. Professionalism was not lost on me, but my emotions had me by the balls.

Ignoring the Bar S man's insult, Chance continued.

"May I have yer name. Always like ta know who I'm speakin' with. An' feel free ta call me Chance. Most do 'round these parts."

I knew what Chance was trying to do, but I also knew that these were not the type of men to fall into a casual coaxing and exchange of information.

"If it so pleases the sheriff." The Bar S man spoke with a crassness that bordered on flippant. "You're speaking to William S. Tankerton, Operator and lead manager of the

Bar S ranch. Call me Mr. Tankerton. *Everyone* around *here* does."

Chance continued as if nothing Big Bill said bothered him.

Sure as hell bothered me.

"Mr. Tankerton. I wonder if you are aware of anyone missing from the ranch? An employee, perhaps?"

Big Bill—fuck him, that is what I will call him—Big Bill squinted causing crow's feet to scatter from the corners of his eyes. He raised his hands to his hips and let out a slow, controlled, breath.

"Come to think of it Sheriff Chance Gilbert, I am down a man."

"Mind tellin' me when ya first noticed he was missin'?"

The two men behind Big Bill crossed their arms, though their tough guy look had no sway over me. Their attempts to buff up were futile when standing behind their gargantuan leader. That, and I knew I would have them both on the ground in three moves tops.

Big Bill stroked his chin.

"Hmmm. Guess it was first thing this morning. Unusual for him not to be around, seeing as how he's one of our cooks."

He lowered his hand, sliding both into his front pockets.

"I'll say this, and your man there," he said nodding to me. "He knows this too. Our cook went AWOL just yesterday. In fact, I found him and his lovely wife broken down on the side of the road, stuck in an uncomfortable situation with none other than...*him*. It's a good thing I rolled up when I did. Who knows what Mr. Special Investigator might have coerced them to do. Man like him sees someone different, he may want to start asking questions he doesn't have any business asking."

"You mean why they both looked scared shitless when you told them to get into your truck?" I said, my fingers twitching by my side.

Big Bill took a step at me. I began my forward march but felt the pressure of Chance's commanding palm on my chest.

"I ain't gonna have none of that. Not today. Far as I'm concerned, don't matter why they left or where they were goin'. If they got into your truck on their own, that's on them. What ain't on them is this..."

Chance lowered his palm. I stepped back to stand even with the sheriff. My temples pulsed. This was the moment of truth—the moment I would read Big Bill's face, find his tell, uncover his lies, and see his guilt.

"We pulled who we think is your man outta the river just a few hours ago."

Big Bill did not move a muscle. If he were seated at the world series of poker, Daniel Negreanu and Phil Hellmuth would be left scratching their heads, wondering what move he would make next. Big Bill was solid as stone. However, his henchmen-in-waiting uncrossed their arms, their movements a synchronized display of unease. Tweedledee and Tweedledum-ass just said without words what Big Bill did not. They already *knew*. My problem, and it was a big one, was now I had to prove it.

CHAPTER THIRTY-TWO

"Pulled him from the river? DOA? That it?" Big Bill was irate. "You come out here with heavy news like that, and with a possible suspect for Christ's sake?"

Suspect?

"Mr. Tankerton," Chance said with patient professionalism. "The man we pulled from the Rio Grande just south of your property was positively identified by Special Agent Callahan. He had expired some time earlier. We are waiting for a report from the county medical examiner. Should have that before the end of the day. Lettin' procedure roll out b'fore we make any assumptions."

"You didn't answer my question, Sheriff. This man..." Big Bill pointed a firm finger at my face. "Not only did I find him harassing my people. We caught him and another man trespassing last night." He turned his attention to me. "Seems to me that my attorneys have more to look into, Sheriff, which is what *you* should be doing. This is your county after all. Consider all possibilities? The mere fact that Mr. Special Investigator, who by the way, never once identified himself as such, was snooping around last night, the same night you say we lost our man, and you don't have him under suspicion? Horse shit work if you ask me."

"He's not asking, Bill," I interjected, having heard all I could tolerate of his ridiculous accusations. "What he is saying is..."

"Callahan." Chance's voice overtook mine. "Head on back to the Bronco. I'll finish up here."

His words were simple yet searing, a command not a request.

"Chance."

He turned to me and leaned close to my ear, whispering.

"Check yourself, Cass. Get in the damn car."

Emotion is like alcohol. In moderation, it is enjoyable, but too much all at once and everything goes off-kilter. I felt like I had just run the gauntlet of spinning chair shots and keg stands at a frat party. Unease filled my stomach. Billowing anger swirled in my chest. The tumultuous gravity of Chance's simple directive was as hard as stone, and I was the glass house.

"This is bullshit," I said.

I glared at Big Bill. His face swelled with victory, radiating imperiousness. I looked at the men behind him. My rage cringed at their impudent smiles. One man mouthed something I interpreted as "See you soon," which nearly catapulted me into full-on attack mode. Heat pulsed from my ears. I dug my fingernails into my palms, forcing myself to hold back.

As I turned for the Bronco, I caught a glimpse of movement in a window on the side of the house. I dismissed the image and stormed back to the Bronco. Before getting in, I was drawn back to the window when I saw the curtains pulled to one side and a face linger in view.

Son of a...

The woman. The wife! Even from the distance, I could see the same worry on her face that she showed yesterday, except now, her complexion looked splotchy. Had she been crying? I opened my mouth as if to speak, but in that instant, she violently disappeared from the window as if having been yanked away.

"Hey," I yelled.

There was no more holding back. Call it probable cause or exigent circumstances, I was going in after her. I raced ahead, closing the gap between me and the house, with Chance, Big Bill and company the only obstacle in my path.

"10-33."

My voice sounded sharp, direct.

Big Bill's men stepped into my path, slowing my rush on the house. I could hear Chance shouting in the background, but the rising growl in my head took over. Tweedledee put his hand out like a 1900s traffic cop. His mouth moved, but I paid no attention to his words. I surged past him with ease, brushing off his failed attempt to grab me. More shouts filled the yard. I rushed past Tweedledee but was hit from the side by Tweedeldum-ass. He tackled me to the ground like a linebacker. His frame and build were smaller than mine, but an assault on the knees will topple most anyone. Hitting the dirt, I rolled right and kicked out, escaping his hold of me. Scrambling to my feet, I dodged a second attack by Tweedledee. With fist flying, I took one punch to the gut, but blocked and held onto a soft left hook aimed at my face. With one fluid movement, I grabbed his hand, rotated my stance into his body, drove an elbow into Tweedledee's ribs, then flipped him over my shoulder and onto his back in a power-driving jolt, knocking the wind out of him.

Tweedledum-ass had regained his footing and charged again, but the chirp of emergency sirens and commanding yells from voices of which I was unfamiliar stopped his assault. This gave me the crucial chance to advance toward the house, driven by a deepening worry for what might be happening inside. I continued on when the words hit me.

"Stop where you are and get on the ground!"

What? No! You don't know what I saw!

"Now!"

"Cass!"

Just a few more steps and I would reach the porch. Closer. Feet pounding the ground. Heart pounding my chest. Then, lightning struck, and the world flashed white before my eyes. My body froze like a Myotonic goat fainting midstride. I fell to the ground, twitching. My muscles contracted. My teeth clashed shut, biting my tongue. Metallic tasting warmth filled my mouth. Convulsions swept over my body as wave after wave of electrical currents shot into me. In a flurry of spasms and trailing voices, I heard Chance's above all else like an echo in a distant cavern.

"Stand down! Stand down!"

CHAPTER THIRTY-THREE

When I moved, I discovered two things—a searing pain radiating from the small of my back the likes of which felt like a thousand wasp stings, and that I was face down on the ground with my hands cuffed behind my back. Blackness turned to shades of gray, then bright white as I tried to roll over and sit up. My eyes fluttered open as my consciousness fell into a hangover from hell. The world spun around me, shifting in and out of focus. A frothy, film clung to the roof of my mouth. I had the urge to heave but swallowed my stomach's attempts to punish me. My muscles ached. All of them. My ears rang like church bells on Sunday morning.

"Stay still, Cass."

Chance's voice both comforted and angered me, but I did not have the strength to speak my mind.

"What...did you just...*TASE* me?"

Chance's shadow blocked the sunlight from my eyes as he knelt next to me.

"Nope. State Police."

"Staties? Here? Why?"

"A-yuh. They rolled up just as ya ran fer the house. Acted before I could intercede. One of them took ya down.

"This all smells like..."

"Hang onta that thought, pard. I'm still figurin' things out. Sit tight an' I'll get ya outta here soon enough."

Sunlight bit my face as Chance stood and walked away. I swirled my tongue, feeling the raw, tender chunk of missing flesh against the inner lining of my cheek, and spat out a mass of saliva and blood. Looking up, I saw Chance speaking with the two state policemen and Big Bill. Though I could not hear what was being said, Big Bill's body language, complete with flailing, pointing fingers, told the story.

I took a deep breath, flexed my stomach muscles, and felt the burn as I attempted to sit up. Fifty thousand volts is enough to ruin anyone's day, but I had things to do and questions that needed answering. As the cobwebs slowly cleared and the buzzing sensation over my skin eased, I collected my thoughts and called out to Chance.

"How about removing these cuffs?"

Chance turned his head and raised a "dad told you to wait" finger. A moment later, one of the state policemen he was conversing with turned and walked over to me. I could see Big Bill watching, his face filled with displeasure, but there was something else—a look of defeat, though I would not bet on that hunch yet. Even in my diluted state, he looked false.

"Come on," the state policeman said. "Can you stand?"

He reached down to help me up.

"I can do it," I replied, my voice sounding like a disgruntled child.

The strain of my muscles and the pounding ache in my head fought me tooth and nail, but I stood on my own. The state policeman walked behind me, keyed the locking mechanism, and the handcuffs restraining me were removed.

"I'd advise you to remain here."

His robotic, monotone voice irritated me like a burning case of poison ivy.

"Would you now?"

I hoped my response was just as caustic.

I rubbed my wrists, already red with irritation from the cuffs. Chance broke away from Big Bill and walked over to me. He did not look happy.

"Let's go, Cass."

"Go? Didn't you see..."

"Shut it, Callahan!"

Chance had only raised his voice one other time at me before today, but this time, it stung almost as bad as the Taser's electrified darts. I should have let it go.

"Come on. We've got to..."

"What *we've* got to do is get the hell outta here. Now."

"What? We're ditching?"

Chance stepped close. Nose to nose, I could feel and smell his breath as he spoke.

"You put us both in a precarious position, Cass. I told you before to keep your cool, but you've gone an' fucked that up. Now, get in the car."

CHAPTER THIRTY-FOUR

I was beaten down emotionally, roughed up physically, yet so damn sure of myself I could scream. But I did not scream. I sat in the passenger seat of Chance's Bronco and looked out the window and remained silent with my thoughts. What moves, if any, did I have to make? I nodded to myself as I considered different plans to find out what was going on at the Bar S and how the Chinese cook ended up dead. Would his wife be next? Her face, her worried, frightened face, splotchy from certain tears, from overwhelming loss, from captivity? I could not shake the image. I made a fist and gently pounded the window, wishing I had done more than stand there when I came across the broken-down Ford yesterday. There was no way to turn back time, so blank you very much Cher! But what was I to do?

The fuzzy, buzzing ache and most of my nausea had passed, but my ears were sensitive, so when Chance's cell phone rang out its cheery *La Bamba* ringtone, I jumped in my seat. Chance pressed a button on the dash, connected the call, and spoke aloud.

"Sheriff Gilbert."

"Yes," a man's voice replied on the other end of the line. "Just the man I was hoping to speak with. This is Octavious Calderón of Horowitz, Lee, and Calderón, attorneys at law. It seems we have a growing problem on our hands." Calderón paused, probably more for dramatic effect than to collect his thoughts. "I have a solution that will solve everything with a simple swipe of the pen."

"I'm listening, Mr. Calderón. Ta what problem are ya referring, and what is yer supposed solution?"

Chance glanced at me.

"I'm glad you asked," Calderón said, sounding almost giddy. "It's really very simple. Fire your special investigator..." Papers rustled over the line as Calderón paused yet again. "Ah, right. Cass Callahan, name him the primary suspect in the murder of one Kang Long, and place him under house arrest for a duration of ninety days while you proceed with the investigation, after which time he will forfeit any opportunities to return to law enforcement in Brewster County, or, frankly, anywhere for that matter, guilty or not. He's a menace and suspected killer, Sheriff Gilbert."

"What's the other side of the coin, Mr. Calderón?"

"Oh, that's a good question, Sheriff Gilbert. Refuse to take action against your employee and face the full weight of our office when we file a massive suit against you, him, and the entirety of the South Brewster County Sheriff's Office."

Calderón's tone became direct. His voice lowered and slowed to a pace that was nearing condescension.

"We have the resources and the manpower behind a multimillion-dollar office to tie you, Callahan, and your entire county up in litigation for years. It won't be long before we own more than just the Bar S in, how do you say it down south, *yer neck a the woods*? Be expecting a courier in the morning with all the proper filings, Sheriff Gilbert."

Octavious Calderón disconnected the call, sending the cab of the Bronco back into silence. Chance pressed a button on the dash, deactivating his cell phone, then reached into his pocket, pulled out the device and powered it off. He tossed it onto the dash and yanked the steering wheel to the left, slamming my face against the window as the Bronco veered onto the opposite shoulder of RR170.

When we came to a complete stop, Chance unbuckled his belt and turned to face me. His eyes were red with fury. His mustache twitched above a sour lip. When he opened his mouth, a flurry of Spanish erupted, spewing forth molten hot words that, contrary to my understanding of the language, resonated deep within my pores. I knew what he was saying. I took it all until he had expelled every thought, frustration, directive, and obscenity at me. I knew he was on the verge of calming down when English worked its way back into his speech.

"*Aye dios,* Cass. You have...we have...*hijo de puta*...What you did wasn't smart. *Ni un poco.* Damn it, *amigo.*"

I started to speak. My mouth opened just a crack, but Chance cut me off with a glare followed by final words of his own.

"The noose has tightened, Cass, which tells me one thing above all else."

I looked on, listening.

"You, *mi amigo,* you and yer gut feeling may be right after all."

CHAPTER THIRTY-FIVE

It was late afternoon when we arrived back at the Brewster County Jail and the inmates were restless for chow. Echoes filled the corridors as prisoners were lined up and directed toward the mess hall. Mealtimes were always dicey inside these fortified walls. Secret meetings were held among the inmates. Plans for action or retaliation of one kind or another were laid out. The fresh meat arrivals were served up as jailbait to the long-timers. Property was staked and claimed, if not by brute force, by psychological intimidation. A few survived on their own, but being a loner only ever panned out in the movies. Even Andy Dufresne had his gang of proclaimed innocents with which to hang. It was during mealtime when Joe Sinclair was murdered.

"'Less you wanna be dinin' with the natives, I suggest ya lay low fer a bit. Head on home, Cass. I'll swing by this evenin' after I finish up a few things here."

"You placing me under house arrest as instructed?"

Chance smiled, but it was not his usual Cheshire grin and slight turn of the head. It was more like a "don't push me on this one...you're on thin ice already" split and curl of the lips.

"I can, if that's what ya'd like, Cass. Even have an ankle bracelet I could fix ya up with. Make it real official." Chance shook his head and placed his hands on his hips. "We got big problems, but we're gonna make the best of 'em. I'll say this, *amigo*, and it shouldn't come as a surprise. Ain't nobody gonna tell me how ta run my county. Not even you, *comprende*?"

I looked down the corridor past Chance to the entrance of the temporary South Brewster County Sheriff's Office, then glanced over my shoulder in the direction of the front security exit.

"Okay, Chance. You win. I'll head home."

For the second time today, Chance stepped close to me.

"Straight home."

I backed away and raised my palms in submission.

"Yeah, yeah. Straight home."

Chance stared at me. I could see the wheels turning in his head. He pointed a finger at me, mouthing the word *home*, then turned and walked down the hall and disappeared into the office.

I stood in the hall for a moment and listened. In jail, in prison, the walls felt alive. Always watching. Always listening. Whispers seemed to echo throughout the halls and ventilation overhead. I closed my eyes and smelled a hint of meatloaf and gravy in the air. It was a torturous smell for sure because the cafeteria did not serve such delicacies to the general population. No, this was homemade deliciousness brought for somebody's late lunch or early dinner. That simple waft of freedom would filter through the jail's cement interior and no doubt reach the olfactory senses of those seated on metal stools, attached to metal tables where Styrofoam trays filled with jail glop surprise was being slurped with plastic spoons. As the scent lingered, let the mind games of regret and animosity begin.

I opened my eyes and walked toward the exit. The aroma thickened when I reached the security checkpoint. One guard saw me through while another sat in a chair and devoured a plateful of meatloaf and mashed potatoes, all smothered with brown gravy. Behind him, an air conditioning return vent whirred. It sucked in particles of dust and floating allergens and the smell of home cooking, sending the mix back into the heart of the jail.

I nodded at the man eating. His face showcased a glop of potatoes stuck to his upper lip as he nodded back.

"Good to go, Mr. Callahan," the assisting guard said.

I retrieved my keys and my gun and made my way to the lobby and out the front door. The sun was low in the sky. Shadows of parked cars and systematically planted trees stretched across the parking lot. When I reached the Explorer, I handled the lock and got in. The backs of my legs burned for an instant before adjusting to the temperature of the black leather seats inside the sunbaked Explorer. I pushed the ignition button and fired up the a/c. At first, a rush of hot air engulfed me, but as the engine warmed up, cool air began to trickle into the cab. I backed out of my parking spot, and headed for the CR.

The city of Brewster was nothing like Houston, especially when considering traffic. Out here, a worst-case scenario was having to wait for two revolutions at a stoplight, and that only occurred within a tight thirty-minute window at the end of the day. In Houston, I fought multiple lanes of bumper-to-bumper cars that lined the freeways from downtown to the Galleria. The nightmare continued for drivers heading to Katy, The Woodlands, Pearland, or Baytown which translated to hours of commuting and daily holdups due to traffic accidents and never-ending construction.

As I drove on, thoughts of Houston reminded me that I owed Ray a call. With everything going on, I wanted to hear his thoughts, and I wanted to revisit our last conversation about Big Bend. Opting to use Siri, I verbalized instructions to "Call Ray Tucker."

Speaking with artificial articulation, Siri responded.

"The closest day trucking company is Bullet Transport in Presidio which is approximately thirty-five miles to your north, and it gets two stars. Is that the right one?"

Typical.

"No, Siri." I slowed my words like I was speaking to someone who did not understand English. "I want you to call Ray Tucker."

"You got it, Ray's Trucking is in Stillwater, Oklahoma, which is approximately seven hundred and thirty-four miles to your north and east, and it gets four stars. Would you like me to call, or get directions?"

"Siri, I'd like you to go to hell!"

"I'm sorry, I don't know that one. There is a Hell's Tattoo in Houston, Texas and is approximately..."

I punched Siri's strobing ball of inadequacy with my thumb and canceled the request.

Freaking tech.

"And fanatics are worried about AI taking over?"

There was nobody in the car to hear me, but saying it out loud made me feel better. Handling the phone, I pressed the phone icon which displayed selections for Favorites, Recents, Contacts, and Keypad. I pressed *Favorites* and found numbers for Raven, Spencer, Chance, Ray, and Flint, the only people I had true cause to call. I tapped Ray's number. A soft hum came over the speakers in the car, and the call went through.

Pick up the phone, Ray.

CHAPTER THIRTY-SIX

"*Well, shit. If it ain't Richard King calling to tell me he's bought another million acres to add to his overcompensating Texas spread.*"

"Can it, Ray."

The crunch of aluminum followed by a wet belch filled my ears as if I were sitting across from my old friend.

"*Panties in a wad, Cass?*"

"No more than usual," I lied.

"*Bullshit. I can hear it in your voice.*"

I was good, really good at picking up people's tells and hearing deficiencies in speech, voice patterns, and diction, but Ray was an expert.

"Fine. I may have angered a hornets' nest, but damn if they don't need extermination."

"*Those days are in the past, Cass. What's going on?*"

The line went quiet. Aside from Raven and Chance coming in a close third, Ray was my most trusted confidant. We fought together, solved crimes together, killed together—experiences like that form unbreakable bonds. That was Ray and me.

I told him everything, starting with the most recent

events with Big Bill, the Bar S, and the dead Chinese cook, and worked my way back to broken down Ford and the battle royale between Raven and Gilly. To my surprise, Ray did not interrupt once. I drove as I laid everything out for him, realizing I had made it to the entrance of the CR on autopilot. Thankful for being home and that I didn't run anyone over during my lack of focus on the road, I turned onto the property.

The cattle guard rumbled and gravel popped the wheel wells as I drove onto the CR. I passed Flint's tiny house and the Six M barracks, pulling to a stop next to Charlotte's older model Toyota Corolla and shifted to *P*. Looking out the side window, I noticed that the yard was empty. Raven and her crew of Six M Ranch hands must still be out on the range. I glanced at the house. No signs of Charlotte or Miguel. Still, nothing was out of the ordinary. Leaving the car idling, I finished my story.

"That's where I'm at, Ray. Hogtied and bent over."

"Yeah." Ray paused. "You're knee-deep in shit and break time is almost over."

"The weird thing is my continued run-ins with Chinese. First, the incident at the park, and now, the couple at the Bar S. And two of the three are dead. It's like *Year of the Dragon* out here. Or has coincidence cursed me yet again?"

"Well, don't feel too bad. You're not the only one having to deal with this shit. Like I told you before, we busted two separate groups of illegals trying to sneak into the port. Two North Africans, smelly bunch, and three Chinese. None of them spoke English. According to the ship's captain, the NAs had stowed away and had been hiding almost a week before they were discovered by a crewman. Nearly starved to death in the shipping container they had hijacked. One of them tried to break into the galley in the middle of the night apparently looking for food and got himself wedged in a porthole. The guy was stuck so bad he hung there all night. Come morning, the crewman who found him said he looked like a limp dick."

"Thanks for the visual, Ray."

"No problem. Anyway, they got him out, found the other guy, held them both until they arrived in Houston, and turned them over to Customs and Border Patrol.

"The rice-eaters were more organized though. They had papers, were employed by, get this, Maersk of all companies—think they'd have better vetting, but help of any kind is hard to find these days, I guess, but they never had a chance either. Chalk it up to coincidence, seeing as how that's on your mind.

"There were two separate ships that arrived in Houston that day, both with illegals trying to get into the country. Obviously, the NAs were never gonna make it. CBP was waiting for them at the docks. Once they were informed about the captives onboard, they initiated Operation Sentinel which screwed the Chinamen's chances."

"Operation Sentinel?"

"It's like an *Alert Delta*, only without the guns."

"When the slant's ship docked later that afternoon, they offloaded and tried to pass through a custom's ware-house using fake security badges but couldn't produce a second set of identification needed as required when OS is initiated."

"And you know all this how?" I asked.

"Got a buddy, Dudley Peters. Goes by Duds. He works security down at the Bayport Container Terminal. Met up with him at Cooter Brown's Place in Pearland."

"I know the place."

"Anyway, after a few drinks, the guy was telling the whole bar how he took down a mob of Chinese trying to invade Texas. Figured it was just another drunk tale. Embellished bullshit and all."

The crack and fizz of an aluminum can opening interrupted his story. After taking a moment to swig and belch, Ray continued.

"But the guy whipped out his phone and showed pics of the Chinese fuckers. Looked like a bunch of kids heading to a karate convention. Messy hair, crooked teeth, tats all over. Real class acts."

I heard Ray gulp another drink, but the last thing he said made my head spin.

"Hey, Ray. Any chance you can send me copies of those pics?"

"I'd have to reach out to Duds. May take a day or two."

"Thanks, Ray."

Out of the corner of my eye, I saw a group of horses making their way past the corral. Raven and the Six M crew were back. At the same time, the front door of the house swung open and Miguel shot out and across the porch with Charlotte close behind.

"Mind telling me what you want with them?" Ray asked.

I watched Miguel as he scampered over to the corral and climbed the railing. I saw Raven, but it was Jesse who was first to notice their little onlooker. He rode over to him, scooped him off the fence, and sat him down in the saddle. Together, they trotted around the perimeter of the corral until they found Raven. I watched as Jesse lifted him up and passed him over to her. Even from a distance, the smiles on both of their faces were apparent.

"Still there, Cass?"

"Yeah, Ray. What were you saying?"

"The pics, Cass. You gonna tell me why you want them?"

"Just curious."

"Bullshit. You're digging for something."

I watched Raven and Miguel ride around the yard, making figure eights before stopping next to Charlotte at the corral fence. Charlotte raised her hands to help him down. Miguel turned and first gave Raven a monstrous hug, then slid out of the saddle and into Charlotte's outstretched arms.

"Cass?"

"Stop busting my balls, Ray."

"Fine. Just looking out for you is all. I'll be in touch."

Our call ended abruptly and with more friction than was due to Ray, but I was tired of having to justify my reasons for what I was doing and how I was going about doing it.

I cut the engine and stepped out of the car to see that Miguel was now barreling my way. His high-speed pursuit did not let up as he crashed into my leg and held on tight.

"Looks like someone is happy to see you," Raven said, having followed him over.

I found a smile deserving of Raven and aimed it at her.

"He the only one?"

Raven tilted her head, the way she does when she studies me. "It's been a long day, Cass. I am happy to see you, but I'd be lying if I didn't admit to be worried."

"Raven. Don't. I'm fine."

Raven stopped within arm's length. "You don't seem fine, but..." She knelt down to Miguel and gently peeled him off my leg. "I love you. If you say you are, you are."

Her words may have sounded sincere, but as she stood, I saw doubt pooling in her eyes.

"I'll prove it to you," I said. "Round up the crew, change your clothes, and let's all run into town for dinner. Rancho Arroyo Steakhouse sound okay? I'm sure the guys wouldn't turn down a good steak."

Raven seemed to perk up at the idea, which was a good sign. I stepped close to her, then leaned forward. She met my lips with a brief kiss, then spoke while our faces were still close.

"Cass, I smell like a horse apple. Do you know what that is?"

I sniffed the air, taking in an aroma that had eluded me until she mentioned it.

"Whatever it is, sounds sweeter than honey."

Raven stepped back as a laugh escaped her lips.

"Never knew you to be fond of horse shit, Cass."

I smiled and shook my head, submitting to having been had.

"If that's what it takes to get back in your good graces, find me a shovel and I'll start digging."

CHAPTER THIRTY-SEVEN

The smell of tasty dead cow filled the room as we sat in a corner of Rancho Arroyo Steakhouse. The crew was eager to take me up on my offer to treat for dinner. Jesse, Pedro, Cody and Gilly sat on one side of the table. Flint, Raven, and Miguel sat next to me on the other side. After such a long day's work, I could see the fatigue on our surrogate rancher's faces, Raven's included, but they hid it well behind their conversation and enthusiasm for being "out on the town."

"Any of you been to Houston?" I asked.

The guys shook their heads but Gilly spoke up clear as day.

"Oh yeah. Been ta the TLSR a few times. It's so big over there. The rodeo is bad ass, but I always like walkin' through the rows of livestock at the convention hall an' seein' the looks on them youngsters faces who are raisin' 'em. You see those kids, yer lookin' at the future of ranchin'."

Gilly raised her bottle of Modelo, toasted herself, and took a swig. It was safe to say that the mood at the table was good. The only thing that made it better was when our food arrived. Two servers delivered T-bones with steamed veggies and baked potatoes for Flint, Jesse, and me, Rib Eyes butted up to mounds of mashed potatoes for Raven and Gilly, a rack of ribs with coleslaw and rolls with garlic butter for Cody, and a man's size serving child's plate of chicken strips and fries for Miguel. The mix of mouth-watering deliciousness served on oversized plates preheated in an oven seemed to chase all our cares and worries away. We sat and laughed and ate in a delectable paradise of steak, beer, and fellowship, and for the first time in as long as I could remember, I thought of nothing else except what was right in front of me.

CHAPTER THIRTY-EIGHT

I waddled out of the steakhouse with a belly full of beef and a feeling of fulfillment that my day had ended on a good note. Horse apples! That feeling vanished when I saw Big Bill and a small crew of Bar S men, including one very familiar-looking Chinese man, walking through the parking lot toward the entrance of Rancho Arroyo Steakhouse.

I stopped in my tracks causing my CR herd to jam up behind me as they tried to exit the restaurant.

"What is it, Cass?" Raven said.

I had a split second to make a choice, a decision that would determine how far down the rabbit hole I was willing to fall.

"Nothing. Just full of food and good times."

Raven slid her arm around mine and pressed her body close.

"I'm glad."

If luck were to have graced me once, it happened in that moment. We had parked on the north side of the parking lot. Big Bill and company were walking from the south side. An errant horn blaring in the street as two cars

filled with local teens sped past drew everyone's attention, which gave me the opportunity to walk on without
being noticed. It took everything I had inside of me to
hold back from confronting Big Bill, but it only took a tiny
hook from Raven to reel me into her thoughts.

"That man over there. The short, Asian-looking guy.
He looks so...familiar."

Now that we were outdoors, the crew walked around
when I stopped and turned to look at Raven. I leaned in as
if to kiss her but bypassed her mouth and went straight
for her ear. Gilly let out a howl and the guys began to hoot
when Flint shut their hoopla down with a sharp word and
a fierce glare before their banter drew anyone else's attention. Miguel walked next to him, bulging his eyes and
covering his mouth with both hands.

"Cass," Raven whispered. "At least wait until we get
home?"

"Listen carefully, Raven. Tell me *why* you think the
Asian man looks familiar."

I turned slowly as if in a dance with my wife, giving
her a clear view of the Bar S men before they reached the
entrance to the restaurant. I felt Raven inch up on her toes
to look over my shoulder, then relax on her feet. She
leaned back and looked at me with eyes filled with a story.

"This may sound crazy, but he looks just like one of
the guys who ran through our campsite in Big Bend."

I pulled her back into me and squeezed. It was the
type of reassuring hug I needed, but a wave of anticipation came with it.

"We have to talk," I said. "Soon as we get home. And I
need you to listen."

"You're scaring me, Cass."

I leaned forward and kissed her forehead. "Everything
will make sense when I explain."

CHAPTER THIRTY-NINE

Three birds, one stone—that was what I faced when we returned to the CR.

As we pulled onto the ranch, I saw something that caused instant regret. Chance leaned against the rear of his red and white two-toned 1985 Ford F-150 pickup. He was dressed in jeans, a button-up plain pocket western style shirt with pearl snaps that seemed to glow, and boots that had seen better years but looked as comfortable as hell. I parked next to his classic ride and hopped out.

"Thought you'd be expectin' me, Cass. Forgit I was comin' out?"

"Damn, Chance. Got sidetracked with..."

"Buenos noches, Raven," Chance interjected, cutting me off and shifting his attention away from me. With two quick steps, he was at the rear car door and holding it open. Raven slid out with Miguel close behind. "And Miguel. ¡Hola, campeón!"

Miguel raised his toy as high as he could. "¡Mira lo que tengo!"

Chance smiled, acting impressed by the display. "Winner, winner, chicken dinner."

"Hey, Chance," Raven said, giving him a sidearm hug. "Missed you tonight."

"No problem, Raven. I'll catch the next one."

Chance closed the rear door behind them. The sound startled Flint, who had fallen asleep in the front seat. He jolted awake, blinked rapidly under the cab's dim light, and muttered, "Shit." Gathering himself, he climbed out and joined us at the tailgate of Chance's truck.

The Six M crew had lagged back on the road and was just now pulling onto the CR. Jesse tapped the horn as they parked in front of the Six M barracks. Truck doors opened, then slammed closed. Twangy voices rose in a wave of "night y'alls" and "thanks agains." Like chickens returning to the henhouse, one followed the other inside. Morning would come soon enough, and from the sounds of it, they had a little after-dinner drinking to do.

Gilly was last in line. Before stepping inside, she turned and let out a shrill, high-pitched whistle that captured everyone's attention. Pointing a playful finger at Raven, Gilly flashed a broad, suggestive smile and gave an enthusiastic thumbs-up over her head. Raven waved back. Gilly nodded, then stepped inside and closed the door.

"I'm gonna hit the sack, folks," Flint said. "Thanks for dinner."

"Glad you joined us," Raven said. "Doesn't happen often enough."

The two shared a brotherly-sisterly bond that I accepted but could not quite understand. In a world opposite and upside down from anything she had previously known, Raven had carved a solid niche in West Texas life, and Flint was there to be her guide.

Before Flint could walk away, I spoke up.

"Hey. You mind hanging for a bit. There are things that

need to be said, and I think we could all benefit from hearing it."

I motioned everyone to the porch. Raven plopped Miguel on her lap in a chair next to me. Chance sat in an old rocker my uncle Stewart had made years before he died. Flint chose to lean against the railing.

"So," Flint said. "What's on yer mind there, Cass?"

I looked at each person in turn. Three intelligent pairs of eyes looked back waiting for what I had to say.

"I'm glad to gather you all at once. Each of you have an insight as to what I have been dealing with since the incident at the campground and in dealing with our neighbors to the north. I know each of you have ideas on how I should move forward, but..." My words hung in the air like Forest Gump's feather caught in an updraft. "I am not wrong about this."

Chance shifted in his seat but remained quiet for the moment.

"There is some shady shit going on at the Bar S, and now I have reason to believe that the incident in Big Bend is connected with them. I felt it more than knew before tonight. The burden of proof is a heavy one, but now I am more sure than ever."

I looked at the woman who had stood by me over the years, redefining what the words "for better, for worse" truly meant.

"Raven confirmed that a short time ago."

Eyes shifted to Raven as if she were the next to hold the conch, but I continued.

"My first run-in with Big Bill was..."

"Big Bill?" Flint interrupted.

"William S. Tankerton, Operator an' lead manager of the Bar S. Big, tall fella," Chance said. "Not from 'round here, that's fer sure.

Raven and Flint nodded.

"Big Bill is what I call him," I said.

"Castin' stones at glass houses again, Cass?"

"Something like that, Flint," I said, half smiling. "Anyway, you all know I tried to help a couple of stranded motorists who turned out to be Chinese folks yesterday and that they were taken away in Big Bill's truck after he magically appeared on scene just after I stopped."

Heads nodded and comments were kept to themselves.

"The last thing I saw as Big Bill's truck pulled away was the reflection of a face in the passenger-side mirror that was neither the man nor woman, but a different man —Chinese, Asian, someone from the far east. It was a glimpse, but I had a feeling I had seen him before. Fast forward past the trespassing and getting caught, past the confrontation at the Bar S this afternoon."

It was Raven's turn to shift in her seat, angling her body so that she faced me rather than sat next to me. I knew what she was thinking, and I commended her for holding back.

"Tonight, walking out of Rancho Arroyo Steakhouse." I stopped and gestured to Raven. "Tell them."

Miguel wriggled off Raven's lap and walked to the front door. His arms sagged and his feet dragged. I got up, unlocked and opened the door, and flipped a light switch on so he could see. He walked inside and headed straight for the couch and laid down.

I returned to my seat and resumed my pursuit of Raven's account in the parking lot.

"Well, it was weird. As we walked to the car after dinner, some teenagers racing and revving their engines caused me to turn and look beyond the parking lot at the street. Once I lost sight of the loud, speeding cars, my eyes drifted to a group of men walking toward the steakhouse entrance. I guess it was this Bill guy you keep mentioning and probably some of his men, but one stood out most of all."

She looked at me, her eyes reeling with worry and understanding. I sensed that while I may be tumbling down a mountainside right now, and hitting every bump along the way, she now knew it was for good reason. I smiled, but she broke eye contact and turned to Chance.

"I think the man I saw tonight was one of the men who attacked us in Big Bend on our camping trip."

Chance slowly sat up. Like a Mexican sloth, he moved with purpose, but at a speed that allowed him time to process what he had just heard and prepare a reply. He laced his fingers together and leaned forward with his elbows on his knees. A perturbed sigh of air whistled from his separated lips.

"Raven." Chance spoke with a low, gentle register. "Tell me again. What makes ya so sure it was him?"

"I just recognized him, Chance. Like Cass. I saw the man and instantly had a gut feeling that I had seen him before."

I jumped back in.

"We know that the men in the park were fighters. Killers. I know that one of the men that wrestled with me took a serious twist to the shoulder. I vividly recall the POP when it dislocated." I raised a hand to keep the floor before anyone could interject. "You may want to ask why our guy isn't wearing his arm in a sling. I wondered that, too. Fact is, if you've ever suffered this type of injury before, it becomes easier to dislocate again. Painful as hell, but not debilitating enough to prevent someone from jamming it back into socket."

Chance remained still, mulling everything over.

"Here," I said. "Let's look at it this way. The fact that Raven recognized the Chinese guy confirms what I have been thinking and who I thought I saw in the truck's mirror. We know he is a killer. Now one of their Chinese cooks turns up dead."

"Hey, Cass." Flint crossed his arms as he spoke. "Remember last night, before yer friend Bill showed up. You remember that sound we heard. Figured it fer an ATV, right?"

"Yeah."

"Remember which direction it was headed?"

"It was pretty far away. You know better than I do how noise travels across the ranch, Flint."

"Yer right. I do. So, I'll tell you. I think it was headin' fer the river."

I locked eyes with Chance.

"What if they'd already killed that Chinaman," Flint continued. "And were haulin' his body out ta dump in the rio. Greenhorns prob'ly figured it wash away fer nothin', but they'd be wrong. With the water levels so low this time of year, there are too many snags ta get caught up in. A nudge this way an' that'll send ya right inta the reeds growin' out from the river bank."

"Right where we found him," Rave added.

"Right where we found him," Flint echoed.

I spoke directly to Chance.

"That should be enough to get us a search warrant. You know the judges. We have probable cause, a dead body, a person of interest identified in two different murders."

"You failed to mention one important thing, Cass," Chance said.

I leaned forward, ready to hear him out and kick some ass.

"I can't do a damned thing with you around. Those same judges I know have already heard from that California law firm. It's part of what I wanted to talk to you about tonight. The fact that Raven can identify the

Chinese man as the one in the park is compelling, which I will follow on up first thing in the morning."

Shit. Here it comes.

"But you, Cass, I'm sorry ta say, have ta sit this one out."

CHAPTER FORTY

Like a team losing to a last-second three-pointer during March Madness, I was out. There was no overtime, no amount of arguing or justifying my way back into the game. Chance made that crystal clear. His hands were tied. I knew it was not what he wanted, but hell, did he not say that no one would tell him how to run his county? His "the buck stops here" mentality was commendable, but with the mounting pressure from threatening lawsuits, the bench of South Brewster County saw my involvement as too high a risk to both the investigation and the looming litigation from Horowitz, Lee, and Calderón.

Being left out was not easy to accept. Chance understood that. So did Raven, but she seemed more relieved than supportive of my position.

"Maybe it's better this way," Raven said.

My only response was bowing and shaking my head in disbelief.

"Seems like this convo just soared over my head," Flint said. "Ms. Raven, I'll see you at sunup. Thanks again for dinner, Cass."

Flint's heavy boots clomped off the porch.

"Cass, let's go inside. Sleep on this. We can talk about it in the morning after your head clears."

Raven's voice was calm. Under different circumstances, it would have been soothing but right now, it felt more condescending.

I raised my head. My temples pulsed. Images of Big Bill, the mysterious Chinese man, the dead cook, his wife, the man from Big Bend with the knife stuck in his chest all flashed in my mind, over and over like a never-ending Facebook reel.

When I did not reply, Raven stood up, wished Chance good night, and walked into the house. The door clanged shut behind her.

"Cass, ya must understand that..."

I stood up, pushing my chair into the porch rail behind me.

"I understand perfectly, Chance. I'm trying to do the right thing here and what do I get for it? I went to battle for this place, risked my life to ensure its safety, and what thanks do I get? I'll tell you. I get the sidelined treatment of a red-headed stepchild at the family reunion, that's what I get."

Chance stood up.

"*We* know, *mi amigo*. *I* know. What ya have done since ya first came ta live on the CR is nothin' short of heroic, Cass. The powers that be are not backward thinkin' though. All they see is what is happenin' now and how it can affect the future. Their future in most cases. It ain't fair. Prob'ly ain't all right, but it's what we're faced with. I promise ya this. Soon as I can, I'll get ya reinstated an' we'll bust this thing down together."

Chance stepped closer, lowering his voice.

"But until I kin make that happen, do not do anything that could jeopardize you or this place. The CR has been in yer family for over a hundred years, but that don't make it immune to the hostilities of a motivated attorney, right or wrong."

"You going to ask for my badge and gun next?"

Chance bit his lower lip and shook his head once.

"Nope. This ain't the movies. But don't go thinkin' of doin' somethin' ya shouldn't. I may not be able ta protect ya if'n ya do. Last thing I want is us ridin' back ta the office together. Me in the front, and you in the rear."

I walked past Chance and stepped off the porch. Lifting my chin, I looked at the salt-sprinkled black abyss. A feeling of insignificance washed over me, but like a wave, was gone in an instant. During that brief moment of calm, I realized what I had to do. Hearing Chance step off the porch, I turned to face him.

"Fine, Chance. I'll play nice. You, the county, the fucking out-of-touch judges won't need to worry about little ol' Special Investigator Cass Callahan on this one. You all get your way."

"It's not my way, *amigo*."

Silence has a way of inviting emotion in to fill the void when thoughts or unspoken words get lost. It happens to incipient lovers, couples on the verge of divorce, people suffering and morning for loss in their own lives and is captured in the quiet gaze shared between a newborn baby and its mother. I heard Chance, and I believed him, but that did not change anything. Swelling in the silence between us, I felt a surge of anticipation. It triggered mixed feelings, but I saw no other way moving forward.

"Yeah, Chance. I get it."

I offered him a handshake, which he accepted.

"Ya may be in the penalty box, but that does not mean ya can't watch the game."

"Hockey, Chance? Really?"

We parted hands. Chance shrugged, emitting a smile more for show than sincerity.

"Hey. Just tryin' ta speak yer language. I'll be in touch, *amigo*."

I watched Chance as he got in and fired up the engine of his old toy of a truck. The classic V8 diesel roared to life, then softened to a lulling chug. Crushed stone crackled under the tires as he gave a wave and pulled away. The truck's bright red taillights looked like deceptive eyes slinking into the night the way a fox's might when searching for prey.

I returned my gaze to the stars and sky above and the feeling of anticipation returned. I reached into my pocket and retrieved my cell phone. With eyes still looking up, I whispered to myself. "Son of a bitch, if it hasn't come to this."

I entered the passcode and tapped the phone icon, then entered the letters B-L-A-D-E in the search bar. Looking at the number, I hesitated. With a sigh, and knowing there would be no going back, I pressed send.

CHAPTER FORTY-ONE

D awn arrived with a red tinge cresting around the outer lining of tall cumulonimbus clouds towering in the east. Building and stretching in all directions, its slow movements across the sky were both beautiful and ominous. I stretched as I watched morning awaken with uncertainty, yet I felt calmer now than I had in weeks.

Hearing the rustling of feet through the open front door, I stepped back inside the house and met Raven as she prepped for a day on the range.

"Morning, Rave. Get you some coffee?"

"Sure, Cass." She sat on the arm of the couch and pulled on one boot while I walked into the kitchen to pour her a fresh cup. "You doing any better this morning?"

When I did not answer right away, I heard the clomp and muffled pad of one booted foot and one sock-covered foot make their way across the house to the linoleum behind me. I turned around holding her coffee and wearing a smile. I handed her the steaming cup.

"Yeah. Actually slept last night. Solid."

Raven raised the cup to her mouth and blew across the opening. Steam wafted away from her face.

"Yeah, I heard you."

"Sorry about that."

"Nah. I'm kinda used to it."

Raven sipped her coffee, rolling her eyes back as the warmth and aroma filled her with caffeinated bliss.

"You out all day today?"

I asked mid-sip, but Raven nodded. Placing her cup on the table, she bent over and pulled on her other boot.

"Moving the herd around to the south this morning," she said, standing back up.

"That's good. You'll be farther away from the Bar S, but closer to the Flyin' H and Floyd Huckabee."

"Floyd." Raven sniggered, then swallowed a longer sip from her cup. "He's like a chihuahua. Obnoxious and ferocious, but harmless. Stroke his ego just right and he might even start kicking his leg."

I laughed aloud, sloshing my coffee at the thought of Huckabee enjoying a belly rub. Raven smiled.

"I'm happy to see you in good spirits this morning, Cass. After how last night ended, I wasn't sure what to expect. You seem...different today."

I shrugged, then used a paper towel from the counter to wipe the drips of coffee running down the outside of my cup.

"It wasn't easy to hear what Chance had to say, but I know the drill. He's backed into a corner. It's clear Big Bill is hiding something and his ace-in-the-hole law firm has it out for me. Maybe I asked for it." I set my cup on the table and reached out to Raven. I wrapped my arms around her and squeezed. "But, I get why I can't be part of Chance's investigation."

Raven squeezed with one arm while holding her coffee away from me. Though brief, I savored her touch. Closing my eyes, I felt her warmth and smelled the floral perfumes of shampoo lingering in her hair, but our embrace ended too soon. She released her grasp of me and finished her cup.

"Charlotte will be out again today around nine. Looks like she'll be regular most days from now on."

"Good. I'm glad that's working out."

"Me, too. Miguel adores her. Who knows, maybe Spencer will come home for a visit and..."

"Will you stop trying to play matchmaker? They have history. Let them figure things out if they want to."

"I'm just sayin'." She trailed that thought with a hopeful smile, which changed when she saw the time on the microwave. "Crap. I'm late."

"The boss is never late."

Raven hustled out of the kitchen, grabbed her gloves off the entry table, and hurried out the door.

"I'm not the boss." Her voice bobbled as she went. "Try and have a good day, Cass."

"I will," I yelled after her.

Halfway to the barn, Raven stopped and whirled around. She blew me a kiss, then yelled back.

"And stay out of trouble."

Two cups of coffee, two bowls of Frosted Flakes with Miguel, and one endless mimic session of the two of us pretending to be Tony the Tiger yelling, "They'rrre Grrrreat," later, there was a knock on the door. I looked at Miguel, who tilted his head with curiosity.

"*Char*-let?" he said.

"*Sí*, Miguel."

His reaction to her arrival rivaled any child's response when finding out Santa Claus had come on Christmas Eve. He bounded out of his chair and scurried through the living room, yelling the whole way.

"*Char*-let, *Char*-let, *Char*-let!"

I called for her to come in, but Miguel was already opening the front door.

"Hey little buddy," Charlotte said, taking a knee and spreading her arms wide for a hug. "Look what I brought."

Miguel stepped back and watched Charlotte reach into her backpack.

"What could it be?" she teased. "¿Qué podría ser?"

"¿Un elefante?"

"What? How could I fit an elephant in here?" Slowly, she removed her hand from the bag holding a small soccer ball.

"¿Para mí?"

"Yes. Yes, Miguel."

Charlotte handed him the ball. He looked over his shoulder at me, spouting streams of excitement in Spanish the likes of which I could not follow.

"Hit a home run with that one, Charlotte."

"Don't you mean scored a goal?" she replied, giggling as she watched Miguel hug his new ball.

"It's not quite nine. Aren't you a bit early?"

"No, sir, Mr. Callahan. My grandma always said, if you're on time, you're late."

I chuckled at the thought.

"Smart lady," I said. "Guess you know where everything is. You have our numbers, just in case. I'm headed out for the day, so I might miss you this evening."

"No problem, Mr. Callahan."

Miguel was already in the hall, kicking the ball into the closed door of his room.

"Hey, mister," Charlotte said, skipping into his view. "Why don't we get you dressed and take that outside?"

Miguel kicked the ball one more time, then opened the door to his room and hopped inside. Charlotte followed him in, and I was free.

Already dressed in jeans, an old *Life is Good* T-shirt

complete with Jake and Rocket lounging on the beach, a pair of well-worn Air Jordan 1 "Chicago" basketball shoes —my go-to day off pair, I grabbed my keys and trusty Astros ball cap and was out the door.

The world was my oyster. My only directive was to stay out of trouble. It should have been easy peasy, but no, I had to go and jack with gray areas and loopholes in the terms of my orders from both Chance and Raven. Truth be told, it should be no surprise. I have always been a bend, sometimes fracture, if necessary, but don't break the rules kind of guy. I said I would stay away from Chance's investigation, and I would. I assured Raven I would stay out of trouble and I would do my best to try.

I hopped into the Explorer and revved the engine. Using the dashboard touchscreen, I navigated through the prompts that led me to driving directions and typed in the location I wished to visit. Two route choices were displayed, both with estimated arrival times. I chose the shorter travel time, even though the distance was eight miles longer.

"Four hours and twenty-five minutes, huh?" I said to the Explorer. "Let's see if I can make it in four flat."

I glanced at the digital clock, taking a mental note of the time, and dropped the gears to *R*. My tires spun and kicked up stone as I reversed away from the house. Sliding to a stop, I donned a pair of Ray-Ban sunglasses, adjusted the Explorer's driving mode to SPORT, shifted into *D*, and hit the gas. Rocks flew again as I shot ahead. The clock was ticking, and I had just a small window in which to get back into the game.

CHAPTER FORTY-TWO

The drab cluster of tan and khaki low-rise buildings centered in downtown El Paso shrank in my rearview mirror as I meandered through the perpetual parking lot of slow-moving cars along Interstate 10E. From the Paso Del Norte Bridge to the Ysleta–Zaragoza International Bridge, people and cargo passed back and forth across the border from Ciudad Juárez, Mexico, like a raid of army ants in relentless, chaotic flux. The distinctive voice of Anthony Kiedis filled the Explorer as I listened to KLAQ 95.5 FM play a countdown of the '90s top hits. I thumbed the steering wheel doing my best bass guitar impression while the Red Hot Chili Peppers' "Give It Away" blared through the speakers.

It was safe to say that my mood was good. Following a visit and a very cringe meeting with the FBI field office's Special Agent in Charge (SAC), Dylan Sharp, I became the newest asset on team TITON. The *Texas Intelligence and Tactical Operations Network* was a covert task force with resources that spread statewide. TITON was charged with one primary goal—locate, investigate, and eliminate

threats that pose a danger to citizens and law enforcement personnel. Though my jurisdiction included the
entire state of Texas, my primary objective as a TITON
Operator was to oversee the safety and security of the
Trans-Pecos region. West Texas, which conveniently
included South Brewster County. When I told Agent Sharp
where I wanted to focus my initial investigation and that
there were some potential legal obstacles in play, he did
not flinch at my request.

"Do what you do best, Callahan," Sharp had said. "I
don't give a shit about some two-bit law firm from California. I know their kind and I've seen it a dozen times.
Their threats of litigation and paperwork puts pressure on
the little guys, like your county. But, with the weight of
the federal government behind you, they'll disappear
quicker than a hot dog on the Fourth of July."

It felt good to have someone, even Sharp, on my side. I
did not expect as much from Raven and Chance once they
found out what I had done. I was supposed to be sepa-
rating myself from this case, not circumventing local
authority to forge my own agenda against Big Bill and the
Bar S. I knew that was how they would see it. Raven did
not like Dylan Sharp at all, and neither did I, but he was a
means to an end for me.

I glanced at the center console and noted the time.

2:47

I had plenty of time to get home before dinner, which
meant I had the whole drive to decide how I was going to
explain myself to Raven and Chance.

As KLAQ paused for a commercial break, my cell
phone rang. Caller ID lit up the Explorer's touch screen,
and Raven's name and number appeared.

"Ears burning, Cass?" I said out loud as I pressed
Accept to connect the call.

"Hey, Rave. Everything okay? Why aren't you..."

"*Where...you? I've been tr... t... ...each ...*"

"You're breaking up, Rave. Say it again."

"*Cass. Did you ear me? Chance ... ...spital.*"

The road dipped and the line went silent.

"Raven. Raven. Did you say hospital?"

Seeing the interstate rise to a peak ahead of me, I stomped on the gas. Communication dead zones were not uncommon in these desolate stretches of highway, especially when the highway rose and fell with the rolling terrain. As I approached the summit, two bars of signal strength popped into view. I slammed on the brakes as I maneuvered to the shoulder. I grabbed my phone and hopped out of the vehicle.

"Can you hear me?"

"Oh, god! There you are." Raven's voice quivered. "Cass, Chance never checked in to work today. When lunch came and he still hadn't been seen or heard from, Deputy Bostwick went by his place, but he wasn't there."

Raven paused to catch her breath.

"Boss came out to the ranch to look for him and found Charlotte playing with Miguel. Boss ended up calling me on the sat phone. I told her I hadn't seen him since last night. While we were talking, she got a call from Deputy Leo."

"Raven," I interrupted. "Have you located him yet?"

"Yes. Yes. He's in the hospital."

Adrenaline surged through me as did wave after wave of helplessness. I squeezed the phone and looked out over the barren, rugged West Texas landscape.

"Do you know what happened? How is he?"

I heard Raven's voice struggle to swallow her emotions.

"Cass, Deputy Leo found Chance's truck overturned in a ditch near the Copperhead Canyon turn-off. It's demolished. Leo said Chance had probably been there all night.

He's in surgery at Brewster Regional, but there's talk of flying him to San Antonio."

"Where are you now, Raven?"

"Sitting in the waiting room with Leo and Boss. I'm scared, Cass. Get here, okay?"

"Soon as I can, Little Bird. I'm on the way."

"Soon as you can?" Raven's voice crackled. She took a deep breath to squash her rising tears. "Where are you?"

I paused. Too damn long, too.

"Cass?"

"I'm on the way. Call me if you get any updates."

Losing the battle of her building emotions, Raven blurted a mix of convulsive tears and concern.

"Hurry, Cass. Hurry."

The sun blazed down on me as I stood frozen on the shoulder of Interstate 10E, nearly three hours from home.

"Chance." My voice rose from a whisper to a yell. "Holy shit!"

I looked at the screen of my cell phone. A picture of Raven and Spencer enjoying ice cream, with Chance photo bombing their pose together, smiled back at me. My entire body felt fuzzy. My ears rang with the chiming of bells and guitar chords from Metallica's "For Whom the Bell Tolls." Over and over, the deep clang and solid riffs echoed through me, penetrating me, cursing me, and the lyrics I loved as a teen now meant something much more. Time marches on.

Move, Cass. Drive!

As if struck by lightning, I whirled around and raced to the Explorer. I slammed the door, ready to launch ahead. I threw the car into gear and screeched away from the shoulder, leaving yards of tire marks along the highway.

I was too far away. Too far to get there as quickly as I wanted to, as quickly as I was expected. The world beyond the windows was a blur. My thoughts accelerated as quickly as my speed, both tearing a path on the pavement and in my soul. I squeezed the steering wheel with the strength and want of a NASCAR driver. With miles to go, I raced toward home not knowing if my friend was going to live or die.

CHAPTER FORTY-THREE

I raced against time, against the sun sinking in the western sky. Streaks of red and orange bled into the white wisps of cirrus clouds hovering like watchful angels overhead. Instead of calls, my phone pinged with text messages from Raven wondering where I was and how soon I was going to arrive at the hospital. Each *ding* sent a sharp jolt of electricity down my spine, a stark reminder that no matter how fast I drove, it was not fast enough.

I covered ground quickly over Interstate 10E to Van Horn and lost little time as I sped down two-lane Highway 90 to Marfa, but once I turned south on Highway 67 to Presidio, I found myself in a scramble to pass commercial vehicles heading for the border and what seemed like an endless string of winter Texans and their fifth wheel trailers lazily cruising and blocking the road ahead of me. I received numerous middle fingers and angry, blaring horns as I blazed dangerously around each of the vehicular obstacles.

It was nearing six p.m. when I turned onto RR170 at Presidio. Having made the drive to this point in record time, I was in the home stretch. Brewster Regional Hospital was a forty-five-minute drive that I was going to make in less than thirty if traffic cooperated. As the mile markers flashed by, their numbers growing smaller by the half minute, I saw a glimpse of civilization on the horizon. My anticipation grew as my worries for Chance's condition heightened. It had been over an hour since receiving my last text message from Raven which had simply been a line of question marks. In all my life, my luck of bad timing had never been worse.

The speed limit dropped to forty-five at the city limits. The digital readout on my speedometer read eighty-seven. *Sue me*, I thought. RR 170 headed straight into town and Brewster Regional was just ahead.

My tires screeched as I made the hairpin turn into the parking lot, my engine roaring like smog preparing to scorch Laketown. I skidded to a stop just before the drop-off point at the Emergency Room and jumped out of the car. My legs felt like rubber as I double-timed it inside. A nurse sitting at the reception desk stood as I entered, her brow furrowing as I rushed through the sliding glass doors.

"Sir. Please slow it down in the building."

I shot her a glare I instantly regretted, but I had neither the time nor the patience to be tactful.

"ICU?" My voice was abrupt.

The nurse deflected my glare but did not answer my question, forcing me to slow my pace and wait.

"Which way?"

"The ICU is down the hall to the right, but I'll need to buzz you in. Who are you looking for?"

I pursed my lips and stepped closer to the counter. A dense heat in my chest grew thicker with each beat of my heart, each moment that I was delayed. Digging deep, I placed my hands on the counter before her, and in my most strenuous and forced of patience of a voice, whispered.

"I am here for Sheriff Chance Gilbert. My name is Cass Callahan, Brewster County Special Investigator."

Is that really who I was?

The nurse's eyes softened, but her command of my attention did not.

"If you can collect yourself, I will lead the way. If you need a minute, I..."

"I don't need a fucking minute."

My voice echoed as my mouth vomited unjust obscenities. The nurse cocked her head. She clenched her jaw as she placed her hands on her hips. The long, red second hand on an industrial clock hung on the wall behind her tick, tick, ticked. Each moment a brick wall that stood between me and my friend, my family. I glanced at the time, then back at the nurse. Her eyes held a look that made her intentions unmistakably clear.

I took a deep breath and swallowed what pride I had left.

"I am sorry. That was uncalled for. Would you please take me to see Sheriff Gilbert."

My apology got the ball rolling but did not change her demeanor or obvious feelings about me.

"This way," she said.

I followed her to a security door, which she used a key card to access, then down a corridor that smelled of fresh rubbing alcohol. Color-coded, arrow-shaped signs pointed down connecting hallways to *Imaging*, *Pathology*, *Pharmacy*, *Cafeteria*, and *Information*. Another sign overhead displayed *Nurse's Station*, *Intensive Care*, and *Waiting Room*.

Saying nothing, she stopped outside the waiting room door and motioned me inside. I nodded, summoned a "thank you" that did not quite escape my lips, and walked through the door.

Out of the frying pan, into the fire—that was what it felt like when my eyes met the looks of Raven and Deputies Bostwick, Leo, Figgs, and Castillo. Raven looked exhausted, worried, and displayed a judgmental frown when I walked into the waiting room. Her face was pale and streaked from dirt and dried tears. She was still dressed in her work clothes, boots and all. Boss and Leo wore street clothes. Deputies Figgs and Castillo were in full uniform. Their expressions showed concern for Chance, but I had to wonder if underneath they shared the same questions Raven had about my whereabouts.

Raven stood up and met me in the middle of the room. She wrapped her arms around me and pressed her forehead into my chest.

"Where have you been?" Her muffled words rose beneath my chin.

"I..."

She leaned back. The red in her eyes spreading like crimson lightning bolts behind an emotional glaze of fear.

"It's been hours, Cass."

"I'm here now. I'll explain everything, but first, what's the latest on Chance?"

"He's alive," she said. "The doctors say he is not out of the woods yet, but that he was very lucky to have survived the crash. Two of his ribs are cracked and he ruptured his spleen. They rushed him into surgery to remove it, but they are worried about infection since he was trapped for so long in the truck with his injuries. He has a pretty bad concussion, and they mentioned his brain is swelling. He has some cuts and other bruises, but it's his head the doctors are most concerned about."

I looked at the circle of deputies across the room.

"Diego, could you tell what caused the accident?"

Deputy Leo separated himself from the others.

"Hard to say. Doesn't appear to be any other cars involved. There was a mangled deer carcass within the truck's skid marks. It's possible he swerved to avoid hitting it and overcorrected into the ditch."

I looked down at Raven.

"Are they letting any visitors in to see him."

Raven shook her head.

"They said it could be hours before he is stable."

I shifted my gaze back to Deputy Leo.

"Diego. Ride with me to the crash site. I want to see for myself."

"Sure, Cass. But it'll be getting dark soon."

"Right. Let's not waste any time."

Raven and I parted. She crossed her arms over her chest in a self-consolable hug. I could tell questions loomed within her, but answers would have to come later.

"Stay here. We'll be back as soon as we can."

"I'll keep her company," Boss said.

I looked at Deputies Figgs and Castillo. Castillo spoke first.

"We've got to get back out on patrol. You need anything, either of you," he said, looking back and forth between Raven and me. "Just call."

As the deputies walked past, each gave Raven an empathetic nod and patted me on the shoulder. The weight of their touch lingered, a silent acknowledgment of the storm brewing within each of us.

Deputy Leo followed them out, his boots echoing into the sterile corridor. The sound seemed to pull me back to reality—a harsh reminder that time was slipping away. I turned to join them when Raven reached out and grabbed my arm.

"I don't know what you've been up to or where you were." Her voice cracked, a mix of fear and frustration bleeding through. "Whatever it is, just make sure you come back to me."

I pulled her into me, wrapping my arms around her, feeling her heartbeat against my own. Her hair brushed against my nose as her cheek buried into my shoulder. She smelled of hard work and hand sanitizer, her grip around me both strong and frail.

"Gotta go, Rave."

I let go, her fingers trailing away from mine, a tangible string of connection breaking as I stepped back. She backed away, turning only to find her seat next to Boss. Diego stood in the hall holding the waiting room door open for me. As the door closed behind me, I saw Raven lean over to Boss, who cradled her as if they were sisters. For all practical purposes, they were.

Whether it was during my military service or my time in law enforcement, those we worked with became family. It was no different here.

My gut twisted as we headed down the corridor and out of the ER, a mix of dread and determination knotting together as the reality of what we might find at the crash site loomed ever larger.

If it turned out that Chance had been injured because of his actions to avoid hitting a deer, I might be able to accept it as a tragic, yet avoidable accident. But, I had too many questions that needed answering. Until I saw the crash site with my own eyes, I was not ready to buy that outcome yet.

CHAPTER FORTY-FOUR

S hades of night crept in with waves of rolling darkness across the road as Deputy Diego Leo and I approached the crash site. What ambient light remained cast a soft hue across the land reminding me of the old John Ford movies I watched on Uncle Stewart's twenty-inch Quasar television when I would visit in the late 1980s.

Diego pointed out the spot where Chance went off the road. Neither of us said a word as I pulled over to the shoulder. In front of us lay a mangled deer carcass buzzing with flies. Its head twisted unnaturally atop its bloodied neck as if looking back to see what had happened in the last seconds of its life. With limbs stretched and broken and innards spattered along the blacktop, it was the dead animal's black eyes that bothered me. They stared ahead, lifeless, frozen, all the while cursing me with heavy, unspoken words.

You're to blame. You're to blame.

I cut off the engine but did not get out. I looked ahead toward the Copperhead Canyon turn off. The switchback road was filled with hairpin turns, most stretches with only room enough for one car to pass at a time. It was a dangerous path that led to a beautiful, secluded entrance to Copperhead Canyon. This off-road hideaway was a popular destination for day hikers venturing into the canyon. However, much like the overlook at El Lobo Vista, it also served as a common rally point where teenagers met to drink and engage in other irresponsible activities. What was Chance doing out here?

Diego opened the passenger door. "You coming?" He looked back, waiting for my reply.

I squeezed the steering wheel with both hands, then released my grip as the tension in my knuckles broke my focus on the mangled deer.

"Yeah."

Stepping out of the Explorer, I walked along the fresh stripes of peeled rubber from Chance's truck tires. Closing my eyes, I envisioned what I thought may have happened —Chance cruising along. The deer jumping onto the road in front of him. His quick, possibly overreaction to the animal. The swerving path of his tire marks. On the surface, it looked just as everyone had thought, a one-car accident.

I followed the black streaks to the edge of the shoulder where they disappeared. Earthen tire imprints took over at the road's edge where gravel and dirt led to a sharp decline away from the road. I saw broken glass spread over a twenty-foot-wide area, deep gouges in the earth and crushed brush where the truck rolled over and over, metallic fragments strewn out as if shot from a centrifuge, a Texas license plate sticking in the ground as if tossed like a dart, and the deep drag marks and parallel tire treads from what was most likely Hector Chavez's wrecker pulling Chance's truck from the scene.

I walked head facing down, scanning the ground for anything that might suggest that this was not a single car accident as originally reported. With each step, my chances of finding something were getting sucked into the darkness that follows twilight. I circled the entire scene, stopping once to pick up the license plate. Maybe this was the miracle connection I was looking for. I held it up and read its face: 85AMIGO. It was from Chance's truck. As the last light of day faded and dusk became night, my hopes for finding anything to support my line of thinking went with it.

"How the hell did he let that deer get the best of him?"

I spoke aloud more for myself than anything else, but Diego answered.

"It happens more often than you'd think."

"But not to Chance." I paced back and forth, responding to Diego but continuing to think aloud. "Not to a guy who has lived out here his entire life. He knows, probably better than the rest of us, to take out the animal before putting himself or others in jeopardy. And what was he doing out here?"

"Maybe..."

I held up a finger, cutting Diego off before his words could interrupt my thought process.

"He was with me and Raven last night. When he left, he would have taken the main road back to town, but instead, he drove out here."

I considered the possibility that maybe he had taken his truck out this morning for a drive, but according to one of the text messages Raven had sent me, she led me to believe he was still wearing the same clothes as last night. My heart sank at the thought of him trapped and injured out here for so long.

"It's getting hard to see. We should come back in the morning. No one will disturb this area overnight. A few coyotes looking for deer scraps, maybe. But that's about it."

Diego turned around and walked toward the Explorer. I looked to the horizon, then down the road in both directions.

"You know. We aren't that far from the CR, which means we're even closer to the Bar S. How far out does Copperhead Canyon run, Diego?"

Diego stopped and looked west, then shifted his gaze southward.

"The land evens out closer to the river. Butts right up to the northernmost edge of the Bar S. Why?"

My cheeks puffed out as I blew a hot and bothered breath of air from my mouth.

"Did Hector take the truck to impound?"

"No. The truck is totaled. It's sitting on a flatbed behind his shop, but he's gone for the day."

"Get him on the phone, Diego. I want to have a look at the damage. Tonight."

"You know Hector. Soon as he shuts down, he heads over to Tio Andres, and it's two-dollar well drinks."

"Call him."

"He ain't gonna like it, Cass."

"I don't give a shit. Get him back out there to let us in. If he puts up a fight, remind him that I can make every tow a nightmare. No more warnings. First sign of trouble, and I'll have his license and his truck. He won't be able to tow a tricycle when I'm through with him."

Diego made the call.

I stood looking out into a sea of darkness. What had been clear as day moments ago, was now black. I walked back to the Explorer, opened the driver's side door, and reached in to turn on the headlights. Two bright xenon beams cut through the blackness, lighting the road while blinding Diego who stood in their direct path. He held the phone away from his ear and turned his back to the flood of light. As I walked back to the edge of the road I could hear Hector's agitated voice over the line. I thought about taking over the call, but Diego was right to let Hector rant. In the end, it would not matter what he said, he would still be meeting us later this evening, like it or not.

I reached the point on the shoulder where Chance had careened off the road. Even with the Explorer's headlights burning a hole in the night, their beams did not light up the spot where Chance's truck had overturned.

"Let's head back into town, Diego," I said, folding this hand to the West Texas night. "Go see our good friend, Hector."

"He said he'd be there, but I wouldn't repeat what he called us to my mother. I think the term *friend* may be off the table."

With my eyes glued to the blackness, I stepped backward, one foot behind the other as if carefully retreating from a threat. One step. Two steps. Three. My fourth step landed on something spongy, causing me to stumble and turn. I leaned over, letting the license plate fall with a clang onto the pavement, my palms hitting the sticky ground to catch myself before I took a hardcore Hulk Hogan-style splash onto the dead deer.

I was face to bloody face with the poor animal. The smell of rotting meat wafted into my nose. Its warmth radiated over my exposed skin as if I were standing on a crowded Houston city bus in the middle of August. I pushed my body up and away, but the stench lingered, having slipped through my nasal passages and into my mouth.

"Damn, Cass. You okay?" Diego jogged toward me, offering me a hand.

I stood up on my own. I nodded, then summoned all the saliva I could muster and spat.

"Don't think I'll be eating jerky any time soon," I said, then spat a second time.

"Hector will be waiting for us at this garage. We should get rolling," Diego said.

I picked up Chance's license plate and tucked it under my arm.

"Good. The sooner we can take a look at the truck, the better."

Stopping at the Explorer's doors, Diego spoke before getting in.

"What are you hoping to find, Cass?"

I looked back at him, my head reeling with hypothetical scenarios that challenged every aspect of the accident scene.

"I'll know when I find it," I said, ducking my head and getting into the car.

Once Diego was in, I pushed the ignition button, and the engine roared to life. Pulling the wheel hard left, we rolled away from the shoulder and turned for town. As we accelerated, I rolled down my window and spat again, but that damn frothy taste of dead deer stink clung to my tongue. I smacked my lips and rolled up the window.

Just like that dead deer, I thought. *This whole thing reeks of something rotten.*

CHAPTER FORTY-FIVE

Had I not known Hector, I would have felt threatened by his scowl and display of bared teeth, his hands balled into fists at his sides, and the menacing, deliberate steps he took toward me.

"What the hell, Cass? You think you can just pull me outta whatever I am doing just because you wear a badge, *ese*?"

"Well," I said, pointing out the gold-painted lettering on his garage office window: *Proud partner of the South Brester County Sheriff's Office.* "The way I see it, we're on the same team, and it's your turn to get in the game, Hector."

"My turn." Hector's voice sagged with disgruntled sarcasm. "*Ese*, we ain't teammates. I'm more like the janitor who cleans up the gym."

I walked up to Hector, stopping inches from his chest.

"Can't help if that's the way you feel, so let me put it this way...grab a mop 'cause we have some shit to clean up."

I brushed past him with Diego close behind. I could hear Hector mumble in angry Spanish bursts, but he fell in line. I walked around the building to a closed chain-link security fence. Hector tapped the keys of a numerical security box that looked like an old payphone, and the access gate clicked open.

Once through the gate, Hector walked to the edge of the building and raised a power switch that activated a system of bright floodlights mounted on posts throughout the holding yard. Night became day with the flip of a wrist. Hector had cars of all makes and models lined in rows, each in various stages of decay. Near the rear of the yard, flattened cars lay piled on top of one another. "Project for a rainy day, Hector?" I said, pointing to the stacks. He sneered and lifted his chin in reply. I saw no value in vehicles that were in such bad a' shape, but one man's junk was another man's treasure. Toward the front, newer cars, most likely recent tow-a-ways, waited for their owners to pay a fine and collect them. If Hector was lucky and the owners did not claim the vehicles within thirty days, he could file the appropriate paperwork, claim ownership, and then put the cars up for sale. I felt it was a sleazy way to make a buck, but it was well within Hector's rights as the business owner.

Hector's flatbed hauler was parked under a floodlight that illuminated the steel corpse of Chance's classic 1985 Ford F-150. It lay uncovered, like a cadaver awaiting embalming in a funeral home basement.

"Damn."

I heard myself whisper and felt the gravity of my emotions rise with each step as I approached the truck.

"He's lucky to be alive," Diego said behind me.

I placed a hand on the front wheel. It felt cool, lifeless. Looking at what was left of the truck, I could not agree more with Diego. The roof was smashed in at an angle from the driver's side to the passenger's side. Broken shards of glass held onto the frame, dangling like jagged teeth in a villain's mouth. The steering wheel was bent ninety degrees toward the dashboard, probably as a result of Chance's body ramming it as he held on during the crash. I walked along the exterior of the driver's side. The bed of the truck was twisted. The rear axle had dislocated from the main frame, causing the rear wheel to tilt inward, as if the face of the wheel were looking up for help. I ran my hand along the damaged metal, my fingers finding patches of perfect paint mixed in the ragged carnage of scrapes, dents, and twisted metal.

Standing at the rear of the truck, I saw the cracked and empty bracket on the bumper where the license plate I found should have been. I circled around to the passenger side, eyeing the truck and taking mental photos of the damage, then made my way to the front. I stared at the grille, at the hood, at the license plate that remained intact on the bumper. I took a step backward to widen my view.

"Find something?" Diego asked, joining me at the front of the truck.

"Not exactly, Diego."

I stepped forward and leaned close to the grille and sniffed. Engine oil, coolant, a hint of gas, nothing irregular caught my attention. I ran my fingers along the metal, inside the grille's cross patterns, felt the smooth layer of unbroken glass of the headlights, then reached underneath the bumper and pulled myself onto the bed of Hector's hauler for a look at the underside of the truck chassis. After a moment, I slid out again, hopped down, and stepped back again to take in the entire view of the front of Chance's truck.

"Satisfied?" Diego said.

"Not even a little bit," I said. My voice firm and growling.

"Come on. How much longer, *ese*?"

I ignored Hector's impatience and made a second pass along the driver's side of the truck. As if reading by Braille, I followed my fingers along every inch from the front panel to the rear wheel well.

"Son of a bitch," I said to myself. "Son of a bitch!" My voice rose in volume as did a surge of adrenaline.

"What is it?" Diego said, hurrying over.

Facing the truck, I ran my finger along a short streak of blue that, from a distance looked more like bare metal than anything else. Disguised in the shadow of a massive dent, it now stuck out as clear as day.

"Two things, Diego. One, the front of Chance's truck showed no signs of hitting a deer, or anything head-on at all. No tufts of fur. No blood stains. No meaty animal chunks ripped into the underbelly of the frame. And here." I pointed to the small, blue streak of paint. "I think we both know that Chance treats this truck as his baby. There is no way in hell he'd stand for a scratch to invade his original red and white paint job. Look at the indentation of the metal. It doesn't match the flow of damage to the surrounding section of the panel."

Diego leaned in for a look.

"If I am hearing you, you're thinking this was no one car accident."

"You broke the code, Diego. I think Chance was run off the road. The position of this marking is at the vehicle's most vulnerable point. Hell, we both know the PIT maneuver—just a nudge in the right spot can make a driver lose control."

"You have any idea who may have done this? Being a sheriff isn't all bells and whistles. Chance has enemies on both sides of the border. You said it before, he's lived out here his whole life. There's no telling who may have gotten to him." Diego paced. I could sense his growing frustration. "If all we have to go on is a little scratch of paint, we may as well look at every blue vehicle in the state."

Staring at the truck, I felt the weight of how Diego was feeling, but I had an ace in the hole.

"No, Diego. Not the whole state. Just one truck in particular."

I whirled around and headed for the exit.

"Hector, don't let anyone touch this truck until you hear from me," I said as I stormed past. "Tell Andres your drinks tonight are on Cass Callahan. He owes me one."

I picked up the pace as I pushed through the gate with Diego following close behind. It was late, and I had a few things to see to before the night was through.

CHAPTER FORTY-SIX

I arrived back at the hospital to find Raven and Boss walking down the corridor from the ICU waiting room where I had left them. Raven looked exhausted. She slouched, dragging her feet with each step down the hall as if her boots were filled with cement. When she saw me, her eyes lit up, then retreated to their dazed and tired state. Coming together, she gave me a halfhearted hug, then stepped back next to Boss.

"How is he?" I asked.

"Resting now. Still in ICU but doing better. The swelling in his head is improving, but he hasn't regained consciousness yet. They told us his surgery was a success and that he is on a heavy dose of antibiotics and painkillers. Don't ask me what kind. I couldn't pronounce them. Anyway, the doctors are optimistic, saying that if his condition continues to improve, he may be moved out of ICU by morning."

I looked at Boss. She wore a similar veil of concern but was not one to share her emotions.

"And you, Raven?"

"I'm okay. Worried about Chance." She paused and looked at me. "And about you."

"Let's focus on Chance for now, okay?"

Boss motioned at the door.

"Hey, you don't need to go," I said.

Raven turned to Boss.

"He's right. Why don't we—"

"Thanks," Boss interrupted. "I have an early shift. And with Chance in the hospital, there's going to be a lot to do around the office." She stepped closer and spoke into my ear. "I know that you're supposed to be on some kind of leave, Cass. I don't have all the details, and it's not my position to tell you what to do. What I will say is, I won't blame you if you disregard whatever orders you've been given, under the circumstances, but I may not be able to protect you, either."

When she stepped back, we shared a moment that transcended the badge—a moment of friendship and loyalty, a solemn look of understanding, yet one where boundaries were still expected to be respected.

"You're the boss, Boss. You don't need to worry."

Boss's mouth curled to one corner.

"Heard something like that before, Callahan."

Boss walked away leaving me standing with Raven. She grabbed my arm and tugged at me.

"Are you going to tell me where you were today? Don't forget, I know you better than anyone, Cass. The more you keep things from me, the more I know it. What are you planning?"

In the past, I have always been forthright with Raven. I have told her when I am unable to share details about my missions or investigations, and I have included her on many cases with the hopes of gaining a new perspective on the situations with which I was faced. I had already bent the truth over my current investigation more than once, which I knew had begun to fracture trust between us, but could I afford to tell her everything now?

"Come on," I said, sliding my hand down her arm. I laced my fingers into hers and squeezed three times. "Let's talk on the way home."

The ride became more tense with each passing mile. The more I shared about what I had done and about what I was going to do, the more Raven became visibly uncomfortable in her seat.

"Behind our backs? Really, Cass. Is that what this has come to? Is that why you lied about what you and Flint were up to?"

We had arguments in the past—doozies that rattled the walls and echoed down the halls, but most of those had been trivial misunderstandings. What hurt most tonight was the trust I had broken. I saw it in her eyes, on her face, in her quiet tone beyond her insinuating tones and judgmental voice.

"And now you're teaming up with agent asshole? What were you thinking? You're not even on Chance's side."

I slammed on the brakes, coming to a complete stop in the middle of RR170.

"I am doing this because no one seems to be on my side. I know what I feel. I know what I saw. I know what to do. Everyone has said, 'Oh, Cass. You've been through so much these past few months. We understand what you must have gone through. Maybe you should just take a break. You've earned it, you know.'"

My heart raced.

"Nobody knows what I went through, so don't sit there and say that you do."

"I am not the enemy, Cass."

"No. You're not the enemy. But you might as well be fucking Switzerland this time because it sure as hell seems like you don't have my back. All I am trying to do, all I've ever done was to make sure those around me were safe. You. Spencer. The ranch. The people that trust me to wear a badge, which means everyone. Everyone."

"Everyone?" Raven's voice spiked pitches higher than I had ever heard. "Everyone, Cass. What are you supposed to be? The savior of the world now?"

Raven unbuckled her seat belt and twisted to look at me head-on.

"You're one and only objective, to use your goddamn institutional words, was to take care of your family, Cass. That's it! I have stood by your side for years. Years! Wondering if you were going to come home from war, from your shift. I prayed every time you left me alone that you would return to me. When you deployed to god-knows-where, we never said goodbye, remember? Same with the job. It was always me walking on pins and needles until our return embrace. Do you know what I've been through? The not knowing is torture." Tears streamed down her face. "You say no one understands. Maybe the truth is you're so focused on what you need to do, you forget that there is more at stake that just your survival, Cass!"

Her emotions boiled over. Angry, fearful hurt poured out of her.

"Rave, how can you..."

"How can I what, Cass? Huh? How can I what!"

Raven whirled around, pulled the door handle, and got out of the Explorer. Slamming the door, she stomped up the highway toward home. As she passed into the beam of the headlights, her body cast a long, dark shadow on the road in front of her.

RR170 was empty in both directions. I waited for

Raven to be clear of the front of the Explorer, then pulled to the shoulder and hopped out with the engine still idling. I ran ahead, trying to reach out to her, but she kept pulling away.

One last futile attempt was all it took. I stopped chasing after her and yelled.

"What do you want from me? What am I supposed to do, Raven? Ignore the fact that we were attacked. Forget about who I saw, who I know is right next door to us? Forget about the dead man? And Chance...it was not a one car accident. He was forced off the road. There is more going on here, Raven. It's bigger than you and me."

Shit. That did it.

Raven stopped marching. Slowly, she turned around. Her face was just out of reach of the headlights, but I could see her hands. They moved together in nervous twitches like she was manipulating a ball of clay. Her steps were short. Reserved. I looked on as she moved closer, the headlights drifting up her body like a sunrise.

God, how has everything gone so wrong, gotten so twisted upside down and inside out? Disbelief rained down her face. Her puffy eyes, her sheltered hands, it brought me back to the days in Houston following the home invasion. She was a victim then, living out the guilty, stress-filled depressive role of a person dealing with real trauma. Had my actions, my words sent her spiraling back to how things were then?

She did not stop walking until she stood within arm's reach of me. Her bottom lip quivered.

"Do you mean that?" She wiped her mouth and nose with her sleeve. "Is whatever this is really bigger than you and me?"

When I did not answer right away, Raven stepped past me, saying one thing before getting back in the car.

"Just...take me home."

There was no right answer I could give that would reverse the damage I had done. And there was no way I was going to give up and let things go, either. Danger surrounded us, and I was the only one who could bring it to an end. But in doing so, I might just lose the ones I was trying to protect.

CHAPTER FORTY-SEVEN

The cab of the Explorer felt like the inside of a Yeti cooler filled with ice—cold with no chance of thawing for days. The drive home was reminiscent of our first leg out of Houston last year. Raven stared silently out the window. I drove wondering if I would ever again find the woman I had married, even though she sat right next to me. It was hard then. It was blistering now.

My foot felt like a sponge on the accelerator, our speed rising and falling between five to ten miles an hour under the posted limits. The mental and physical challenges of what turned out to be an excruciatingly long day were tightening its grip around me, but I still had more to do.

With ease, I turned onto the ranch. The slow bump of the cattle guard rattled the Explorer with deep thuds, each rung gonging like a bonshō bell. I rolled past Flint's tiny house and the Six M barracks, then braked hard. The thrust of our immediate stop jolted both of us into our seat belts.

"What the hell, Cass?"

"Shhh," I said.

Following the outdoor lighting, I scanned the yard,

the corral, the barn, and finally rested my gaze on the wide-open door at the front of our darkened house. I turned off the headlights and, with gentle precision, reversed the Explorer, parking it in the shadows near the side wall of Flint's house.

"What are you doing?"

"Raven." I kept my voice low, calm, professional. "Something isn't right."

Peering over the dash, Raven looked out the front window.

"I don't see anything." Her head swiveled left to right. "Wait. There. Leaning against the barn. Isn't that Cody?"

Following Raven's gaze, I saw what she saw. Opening the boot between us, I removed a panel inside revealing a sub-compartment that housed an old friend of mine. I removed my battlefield green Glock 17 from its secret hold in the Explorer's belly, pulled the slide back enough to confirm I had one round already seated in the chamber, and closed the boot again.

Raven watched with concern.

"What are you doing? Cass? What's going on?"

I turned to face her. Disheveled and exhausted but energized with uncertainty, Raven stared back at me. Regardless of things said or tensions raised to the point of snapping, I loved her and would do anything, *any...thing* to protect her.

"Slide over to the back seat and get on the floor." I looked out the window again. The grounds were silent. The darkness concealing. "Stay in the car, Rave."

"Miguel? Charlotte? You're scaring me, Cass."

"Everything will be all right. Just keep out of sight. As soon as I know everything is safe, I'll come get you."

Raven opened her mouth to speak but caught herself before saying anything. I could see in her eyes she did not want to hide. Add that to the laundry list of emotions and pent-up frustrations she had, all of which were my fault, but still, she did not put up a fight. I leaned my left shoulder on the driver's side door and Raven slipped into the back seat.

"I'll be right back," I whispered.

Before opening the door, I toggled a switch that disabled the interior dome light. Glancing around the property once more, and deciding to proceed, I pulled the handle and opened the door.

Warm air met my air-conditioned face. Easing the car door closed, I held my gun at the ready and moved to cover behind the rear of the Explorer. Through the back window, I looked inside. Raven was crouched low between the seat and the floorboard.

Safe, I thought. *For now.*

The yard was a mix of light and dark, a Chiaroscuro effect straight out of the movies. A lull of quiet hovered in the air. I looked at Cody. He was propped against the exterior wall of the barn. His head lagged to one side. Was he drunk and had passed out, or had something much worse happened to him?

Backing away from the Explorer, I slunk along the edge of Flint's house to the nearest window and looked inside. It was dark and empty. I returned to the rear of the Explorer, then made a dash across the yard toward the house.

My strides drew long, eerie shadows that, with each step, looked like black wraiths biting at my heels. I leaped onto the porch and took cover behind the outer wall. The front door hung open ninety degrees from the house. I pressed my ear against the old wood slats, desperate for a fresh coat of paint, and listened.

The CR had been in existence for over a century, and this house had stood more than seventy of those years in this very spot. It had housed family and friends and experienced more under its roof than most from its era. If walls could talk, this house would have stories to share for ages, but tonight, when I needed a sign, a story, a single breath of fresh air, it had nothing to offer me.

I peered around the doorframe into the house. All remained still. The soft click of Uncle Stewart's old cuckoo clock hanging near the entrance to the kitchen found its way to my ears. The rhythmic *tick, tock, tick* was polarizing. Led by my weapon, I slipped through the door and into the living room. The room was empty. Not wasting any time, I moved to the hallway. Miguel's room was on the right. Our bedroom was at the end of the hall. Both doors were closed.

With gun raised and my back sliding against the wall, I stopped outside Miguel's door. My heart pounded. My breath felt short. I paused to listen, then reached for the doorknob. With one swift movement, I opened the door and lunged inside, sweeping the room with the barrel of my Glock.

Clear.

Miguel's bed was neatly made and his toys were placed in the appropriate bins. I stepped back to the door and continued to our bedroom.

Once again, I paused to listen. All I heard was the kitchen clock, its agitating click painful growing in my ears as if I was experiencing a deranged torture, each tick a hammer pounding my sanity. I opened the bedroom door and swept the room.

Clear.

Where is everyone?

On light feet, I moved down the hall and across the living room to the kitchen. The clang of the clock now rang in my head, gonging, gonging, clanging. Standing just below the ancient menace, I reached up and grabbed the pendulum, stopping its momentum. The room was quiet once again, but a residual silent pounding of ticks and tocks echoed through me.

From just beyond the kitchen, a solid bump sounded out sending electrified tendrils of adrenaline to shoot through my veins. With two hands on the grip, I followed the barrel of my gun through the laundry room to my uncle's office. The door was ajar, but only wide enough to slip a hand through its opening. Another bump, slight as it may have been, sounded out in the room.

I took a deep breath, closed my eyes for a second to focus my energy, and prepared myself to charge inside.

On three...two...one...

Using my shoulder, I rammed the door open. The room was pitch black. Releasing one hand from my gun, I flipped the wall switch. Instant light, blinding and bright filled the room. Frantic rustling sounded out beneath my desk.

"Out! Hands where I can see them. NOW!"

Whimpers rose from the desk. With my gun poised and ready, I moved around the desk. Huddled beneath and clutching my old Louis L'Amour paperback copy of Hondo, was Miguel. Tears streamed down his face. Mucus coated his upper lip. His eyes grew large as black saucers and a slight shriek escaped his lips.

Tucking my gun into the small of my back, I knelt next to the frightened child.

"Whoa there, Miguel." I reached my arms out to him. "*Todo bien. Todo bien.*"

Miguel looked at me, a draining helplessness pouring out from him. With book in hand, he raised his arms.

"*Papi Cass.*"

His voice wavered through sniffles as I lifted him out from his hiding place.

"You're okay."

Miguel buried his face in my neck. The warmth of his

grasp, the moisture of his tears and sticky residue from his face spread over my bare skin. He was safe. That was all that mattered. With gentle hands, I pulled him out of his clutched position to look him in the face. Pulling a tissue from the shelf, I wiped his eyes.

"Where is Charlotte?" I asked.

"Char-let?"

"Yes, Miguel. *¿Dónde está Charlotte?*"

He took a moment to look around the room, then turned his deep, hound-dog eyes to me.

"*El Cucuy. El Cucuy.*"

Tears returned in floods of fright. I lifted Miguel and cradled him against me.

"Shhh."

"*Mami Raven. Mami Raven.*"

"Quiet now," I whispered. "We'll go see her now."

With Miguel curled up on one arm, I pulled my gun out with my free hand and stepped to the doorway. Peering out, we moved through the laundry room and kitchen, past the silent cuckoo clock and into the living room. Before heading out the front door, I peeled the window curtain back enough to peek outside.

The yard looked calm. The black and white stripes of light and shadow, masked by the glowing gray backdrops of the barn and the tiny houses soaking in the stretching gleam, gave the scene a ghostly appearance. I flashed a glance back to the barn wall. Cody was gone. Scanning the yard again, I stopped on the Explorer. An odd flicker danced on the wall of Flint's house.

What is she doing? I thought. With caution, and eyes fixed on the car and getting back to Raven, I stepped outside. Before I reached the first steps at the edge of the porch, the flicker on Flint's house disappeared. Chalk it up to experience and a terrifying instant realization, I twisted my body in time to shield Miguel as the Explorer exploded in a ball of flame and burning metal. The shock wave knocked us down. Miguel cried out. I covered his face with my hands as my body shielded him from the brunt of the blast.

Dear God.

The deafening roar and brilliant light of fire twisting in and out of the Explorer's shattered windows and scorched frame, and the popping and charring of burning wood as Flint's tiny house caught fire from the blast was nothing compared to the scream that rose in me as I struggled to my feet.

Clutching Miguel, I stood frozen in disbelief.

"Raven!"

CHAPTER FORTY-EIGHT

Heat from the fire radiated over my face as electric bursts of painful numbness shot through my body. I held Miguel close, afraid that if I let him go, I might not be able to keep myself together. The world in front of me spun, drifting in and out of focus, like a bad reel-to-reel video in middle school science class. My head rang with a mix of bells and gongs, muffling the roar of the fire, of Miguel's sobs, and the sound of distant voices too far away to recognize. I did not care. What did I have left? My whole world had just gone up in flames, and there was nothing I could do to stop it.

CHAPTER FORTY-NINE

"Cass."

That was my name. Four short letters stretched to one long, drawn-out call as if hailed through a megaphone planted firmly on the ground. Again, the muffled "C...A...S...S..." echoed like I was part of a dream, a nightmare where the killer stood right behind me, machete raised and ready to slice. Should I run? My eyes were fixated on the hell that swirled through my burning car, through my charring life.

"Cass."

Now, crying. Wriggling. And then small words pierced the void. Sharp and undeniable, its message stabbed at me like I was Caesar and all of Rome fell on my shoulders.

"*Mami Raven. Mami Raven. Mami Raven.*"

Over and over and over. Tiny arms reached out, then tiny fingers grabbed hold of my shirt, clutching the sweat soaked cloth.

A large bulge, out of focus and dark like the fiends of a childhood fairy tale, blocked my view. Every breath I drew became hotter, dryer. I had no strength to scream, to move. Kill me now, whatever you are.

"Cass!"

My shoulders shook as two large hands rocked me back and forth.

"C'mon, goddamn it!"

I closed my drooping mouth. A cacophony of voices erupted in my mind. It was as if every person I had ever known, ever saved, ever killed, pushed me, demanding that I rise from the fiery pit into which I descended like a deflating balloon. With a sudden jolt, all the voices stopped except for the one that kept shouting my name. My eyes focused on the furrowed brow and hardened face before me.

"Flint?"

"Jesus, Cass. Hold onta Miguel. We gotta move."

With arms built for bulldogging, Flint pulled me off the porch. I held Miguel tightly in my arms as he led us straight for the barn. Each footfall was jarring. Each step widened the distance between me and misery, although I knew that I would never be able to fully escape.

Stepping into the barn, its musty smell filled my nose. The main hall was illuminated by two fluorescent tube lights over the workbench on the far wall. I saw Cody on the floor, his back propped up against a stack of hay bales. Blood covered the lower right portion of his shirt. Gilly knelt next to him. Pedro and Jesse hovered close by. As we approached, Flint whistled.

"Let's go! Head for the pump on the side of the barn and grab the hoses. If we don't get that fire under control, the whole ranch'll burn."

Pedro and Jesse jumped into action. Gilly bore me a look of ferocity, reprising the battle-ready glare she wore prior to her fight with Raven.

"C'mon, Cass. You, too. I need every able body. Leave Miguel with Gilly and Cody, and let's get to work."

Gilly stood and hurried over to us with outstretched

arms. Miguel held tight, but Gilly's hands, hardened and calloused from a lifetime of ranch work, peeled him away with the touch of a mother's grace.

With empty arms, I stood motionless, my head spinning in disbelief. Flint had started for the exit, then whirled around and marched right up to me. He leaned close, his nose inches from mine.

"This shit has hit our home, Cass. Wake up that goddamn soldier inside of you. Standin' here ain't gonna change what happened." Amid his drilling, he placed a gentle palm on my shoulder. "Let's put this fire out, then we can go light one of our own."

I focused my gaze, fighting away the blurry haze of unjust grief, and locked eyes with Flint. Even in the shadows, I saw a flicker rise within him. That tiny spark, the tipping point between desolation and ground zero, found a way to burn through the bonds of anguish that consumed me. With one thunderous, internal explosion of anger and desperation, I felt myself awaken.

Adrenaline surged through my veins. My muscles flexed. My jaw clenched.

I glanced past Flint and saw Miguel sitting on the ground next to Cody. His body shuddered with frightened tremors, and yet, he laid a hand on Cody's arm as if to console him. I knew, in an instant, it's what Raven would have done. Watching Miguel emulate her was the last jolt I needed to get my ass in gear.

"Let's go," I said.

I followed Flint as he hurried to catch up to Jesse and Pedro. As I passed Cody and Gilly, I heard him tell her, "You go too. The little man and I are fine."

The Six M crew were more than ranchers. They were a tight-knit bunch. A family. Trust in words meant just as much as action behind muscle. Gilly did not hesitate. She fell in line behind me, her stride marked by long, determined steps.

We each passed through an exit door on the far side of the barn that opened into a small drive between the tiny houses and the garage at the rear of the structure. Pedro and Cody were already dragging two large hoses toward the center of the yard.

"Gilly, yer with Pedro. Cass, with Jesse. Hurry the hell up. I'm gonna cut on the water and those boys'll need ya."

Gilly rushed ahead, her silhouette outlined by orange and black. I ran to join Jesse, who had stretched his hose to its furthest reach. A swarming heat replaced the numbness in my legs and arms. The yard felt thick. A metallic tinge of burning fuel and scorched metal made it difficult to breathe. Flames rose and danced with twists and swirls, propelling smoke and toxic ash particles into the air from what was once the lux interior of my Explorer. Fire eating through the pine clapboards of Flint's tiny house crackled and popped with each terrific gnash of flaming teeth.

A shrill whistle pierced the roaring fire, followed by a warning yell from Flint.

"Yo! Water's comin'."

No sooner had he spoken than the water pulsed through the hoses, the pressure in each causing the lines to stretch and straighten. Flint had opened the lines up to their fullest, challenging the water pump's limits and capacity, which caused a massive burst of shooting water to blast the growing inferno. I held on with Jesse in the lead, helping to aim the nozzle at the center of the burning Explorer. Pedro and Gilly were positioned to our right, angling their attack on the flames in a crossing pattern from ours. They swept their spray back and forth between the car and the side wall of Flint's house, but the fire fought back.

With total disregard for his own safety, Flint charged ahead carrying a pickaxe in his hands like a soldier advancing on an enemy in battle. I watched as he ran toward his home. The bright flames illuminated the misting extremities of the streaming jets of water creating a lighting effect that looked as if it were raining fire on the CR. As he approached the house, he raised the pickaxe above his head, then chopped at the siding of his house just beyond where the flames were burning. His strength and speed were remarkable, and his resolve to win this hellish fight unmatched.

Wood splinted with each hack and pull. Pedro and Gilly maintained their aim on the side of the house, pushing back the flames and soaking Flint beneath. *Hack.* Boards splintered. *Crack.* More planks were ripped away from their nail heads. He made quick work of the siding, punching through the aged pine.

Fresh air from inside the house fanned the flames. Like a living beast, they seemed to turn and roar with excitement and fury, as if a new opportunity for fresh meat had appeared, only to find it already claimed by another. Seconds stretched into minutes. Minutes felt like hours. Gallon after gallon of water pumped through the hoses, spewing over the fire, sizzling on impact. Sloshing mud puddles formed around the melted tires and scorched frame of the Explorer with each drop of liquid fight. I could see water pouring into the open section of wall that Flint had pulled away as he fought to keep the fire from spreading.

Sweat and water, heartache and rage dripped from my body. I could feel each wrenching thump of my pulse, from my hands gripping the hose to the empty cavity inside my chest. The very thought of Raven's burned body hiding in the back seat made me sick to my stomach.

There would be no saving her tonight—just recovery, and then revenge.

CHAPTER FIFTY

We wrangled the flames like scattered cattle on the prairie, tending to each in turn until the herd had been rounded up. The roar of flame sounded more like a plea for mercy as we drowned the fire. What once was bright and overwhelming to look at was now but a smoldering flicker. Steam rose where flames once danced. The wet, hot stench of scorched wood and melted pieces of Ford Explorer replaced the thick wafts of burning fuel. Flint continued to whack away at the siding of his house, ensuring that no pieces that had burned or that were still smoking remained attached.

Out of the corner of my eye, I saw Gilly leave Pedro and run toward the barn. A moment later, I felt the pressure in our hose begin to dwindle from a powerful blast to a manageable flow. A feeling of dread was quick to sweep in. I released my grip on the line and tapped Jesse on the shoulder.

"I gotta..."

I paused, unable to find the words to complete my thought. *Gotta what?* Go look for my dead wife? There were steps I must take. Engrained procedures to follow. As natural as fear is a part of life, even for the most battled-hardened warrior, it showed no prejudice, and I was scared shitless.

Jesse looked over his shoulder at me. I could see the concern on his face. He knew what I was going to say. He nodded, then turned away, raising the hose and repositioning its stream.

I stepped ahead, forcing my cinderblock feet to move forward. Inching toward the smoldering mass of jet-black metal and broken glass, images of Raven swirled in my mind. Her young face when we first met, the curves of her smile, the bounce of her hair, the look in her eyes beneath her wedding veil, and the disgust of my final words to her. "*This is bigger than us.*"

I stopped and closed my eyes. Nothing was bigger than us, but I said it, nonetheless.

"Keep away, Cass. It's hotter than hell. Steam'll burn ya just as quick as a flame."

I opened my eyes to see Flint, drenched from head to toe, resting the handle of the pickaxe over his shoulder.

"I gotta see," I said.

Flint shot me a questioning glance.

"Ain't nothin to see." He walked away from the gaping hole in the side of his house, stopping a few feet in front of the smoldering car. "It's a total loss."

"Ra..." I couldn't finish saying her name. "She. She was in the..."

My voice carried across the yard, tinged with palpable desperation. Flint cocked his head. It took a second for him to catch on, but when he did, his eyes bulged and he whirled around and stared at the burned-out car.

As if hit in the back by a gust of wind, I surged ahead, reaching out for the rear door handle with my left hand. Flint met me at the door and tried to restrain me, but he was not fast enough. I grabbed the handle. The skin of my palm seared as I pulled, but the door would not open. Flint grabbed me around my waist and lifted me off the ground, but still, my grip held firm.

"Let go, Cass. You don't wanna see that."

Before I knew what was happening, I felt more hands latch onto me, pulling me away. When the force was too much and my strength gave out, I let go. The sudden loss of grip caused me and Flint to topple onto the ground in a tangled pile that included Jesse and Pedro.

Flint was the first to recover. He wrapped me in his arms from behind and squeezed as I fought to regain my footing. Trapped in his grasp, I yelled out.

Pedro and Jesse grabbed hold of my legs, but Flint stopped them.

"Let 'im be. I got this."

My legs flailed once as the two backed off.

"Ease down, Cass."

Flint's words were both calm and sharp as blades.

Gilly had rushed over as well but had not been pulled to the ground when we fell. Instead, she stepped toward the burned shell, the charred hiding place where I told Raven to stay put and out of sight, stopping close enough to peer into the broken rear window.

My body ached. My head spun, reinviting the grief that I had suppressed to fight the fire. Now, reality was upon me and it was becoming too much to bear.

I watched as Gilly slowly backed away from the car. When she turned to look at me, I could not read her emotions. Her face was blank. She took three tentative steps, then knelt in front of me. My face twisted. My lips quivered as I waited for whatever came next. Placing a hand on my leg, she looked deep into eyes and spoke.

"Cass, the car is empty."

CHAPTER FIFTY-ONE

Gilly's words hit me hard. I must have looked confused because she repeated herself, this time with a cautious smile.

"The car is empty."

I could feel the tension in Flint's grip around my chest loosen. Numbness returned to my hands and cheeks. I leaned forward, freeing myself enough to crawl on my hands and knees across the mud-puddled ground, stopping right next to Gilly. Propping myself on my knees, I looked at her with pleading eyes, wanting, needing her to say those magic words one more time.

"Gilly...please."

"Where is Raven?" she asked.

I reached out and placed my left hand on her shoulder, then yanked it back as an intense shot of pain raced up my arm. Recoiling, I looked at my hand. Bubbles of growing blisters spread across the base of my fingers, with another long, crescent-shaped one forming across the top portion of my palm. Redness flared out from each blister with a surrounding wetness that gave my hand a very raw appearance. Gilly grabbed my wrist and pulled my hand into her view.

"That door handle was hotter 'n' shit. You need a doctor, Cass. This don't look good."

I pulled away from her. As things calmed down, my adrenaline subsided leaving me to feel the full brunt of throb and burn in my hand.

"Later," I said.

The two of us rose to our feet and turned to face the car.

"Where are you, Little Bird?" I whispered to myself. The realization that she was not inside the car when it exploded was relieving, but a new question remained, the answer to which I was certain I knew. I turned and faced Flint and the Six M bunch. "I need to find her, and fast. Tell me quickly, what did you see? What happened to Cody? Has anyone seen Charlotte?"

My questions flooded the space between us. Jesse and Pedro shared an unknowing look. Gilly bowed and shook her head. Flint finally spoke up.

"Damn, Cass. None of us"—Flint circled his finger at himself and the Six M crew—"saw a thing. We was ridin' in fer the day. Cody was leadin' us all by a stretch when the three of us reined up 'bout five, maybe ten minutes out from the barn. Heard some ki-yotes, but after a listen, figured them ta be callin' to the north on the Bar S. It wasn't 'til we was halfway in when we heard a gunshot. The three of us ran the horses the rest of the way, tied up at the rear of the barn, an' took cover inside before we found Cody propped up against the outer wall."

"Yeah," Gilly added. "Pedro and Jesse dragged him inside. When we saw he'd taken a shot to the waist, we was gonna run 'im inta town but..."

She paused and motioned to the demolished car. Flint jumped back into the conversation.

"I told 'em ta hold up. Wanted a look first. Make sure it was safe. I stepped inta the yard just as yer car blew. That's when I saw ya standin' on the porch with Miguel. Ya know the rest."

I rubbed the top of my head.

"Son of a bitch." I stood in disbelief, then walked toward the rear of Flint's house.

"We gotta get Cody ta the doc. You, too, Cass," Gilly said again.

I looked back.

"Go on. Jesse, bring your truck around. Gilly, take Miguel with you. Pedro, get Cody. I'll be right behind you to help load up. Run with hazards flashing. I'll call it in and have one of the deputies meet you en route to lead you the rest of the way to Brewster General." I waved Flint over as the others hustled back to Cody and Miguel. "I need your eyes. Grab a flashlight and look for anything out of place—footprints, tire treads you don't recognize, anything at all."

Flint nodded, then turned to leave when I caught his arm. "You carrying?"

"Does yer pecker help ya piss?"

"Good. Be careful." I lowered my voice. "This is far from over, Flint. I wouldn't be surprised if we had eyes on us right now. Get to it. I've got to speak with Cody before they leave."

I heard Jesse fire up his truck and ran over to help load Cody while Flint retrieved a flashlight from his smoke-filled, water-soaked house and began his search.

The Six M crew were fast workers. Pedro and Gilly had arms wrapped around Cody and were already out the barn door by the time I reached the truck. Miguel followed behind still clutching the old paperback book. Jesse jumped out to help Cody while I opened the rear passenger-side door.

"C'mon, man," Jesse said. "In ya go."

Cody winced as his three friends lifted him.

"Shit, Cody," Gilly said, her voice masked with sarcasm. "Ain't half as bad as when ya got throwed off ol' Nellie."

Jesse and Pedro smirked. Cody coughed a painful laugh.

"Nellie one of your bulls?" I asked.

Jesse ran around to the opposite side of the truck and pulled Cody by his armpits until he was laid out flat on the back seat. Gilly climbed in and sat next to him.

"Nope," Pedro replied. "Nellie was a gal he'd followed home from a dance hall up north."

"Dancin' Diamonds," Gilly added.

"Yeah, that's the place," Pedro said.

Cody groaned as he held a red-soaked rag to his wound. "Damn, y'all."

Ignoring Cody, Pedro continued. "Whelp, ain't no gettin' around it. Nellie was a biggun, but Cody had enough alcohol in 'im to serve an entire county. We found 'im staggerin alongside the road near the entrance to the Six M Ranch. Naked."

"Butt-ass naked," Gilly echoed, laughing.

Smiling, Pedro nodded. "He had bruises all over 'im an' he was chaffed worse than if he'd been ridin' drag all day on the range."

"Enough," Jesse said, a hint of laughter still hanging onto his voice. "We gotta hit the road."

I leaned into the cab of the truck and looked at Cody from the front seat, blocking Pedro's path to get in.

"Cody, fun and games aside, who did this to you? What did you see?"

Cody took a shallow breath, then turned his head to look me in the eyes. His forehead was drenched with sweat.

"I beat everyone back and was in the barn when I heard someone screamin', like they was arguin'. I ran ta the barn door to see what was goin' on and saw two men pullin' Charlotte outta the house. They wore all black. I didn't get a look at their faces, 'cept fer one other guy. He stood in the center of the yard, like a lookout. Or maybe their boss. I don't know. I yelled for them to stop but before I could take a step, the man in the yard drew a gun an' fired. I went down, hard an' fast. Didn't hear anythin' else."

"The man who shot you, was he in black too? Did he wear a mask?"

With his foot on the brake, Jesse shifted the truck into gear. "Cass, we gotta..."

"I know. I know." Time was running out. "Cody, could you recognize him if you saw him again."

"Hell yeah. Dude looked like he was straight outta one of them karate movies with Jet Li or Jackie Chan."

Miguel climbed past me, then wiggled over the boot and joined Gilly in the back with Cody. Cody laid his head back on the seat and closed his eyes. I backed out of the truck so Pedro could load up and they could get on their way. I closed the door behind Pedro and caught a final look from Jesse.

"Be on the lookout for your escort. I'm calling it in right now," I said.

Tires spun and dust flew as Jesse's truck tore out of the yard. Its loud, rumbling diesel exhaust roared as the Six M crew and Miguel sped on to the hospital.

I pulled out my cell and contacted dispatch, who then connected me with the nearest deputy on duty, AC Castillo. I explained the situation to Deputy Castillo but cut the call short when I caught up with Flint. I could see on his face that he had found something.

"Couple set of tracks lead behind the Six M barracks

and over the front pasture. We get ta the road, I'd bet my hat we'll find fresh tire marks." He motioned to the front of the CR, his flashlight slicing through the darkness to illuminate the fence and the road running parallel beyond. "And I found this in the yard."

Flint held up a single spent shell casing. I took it and held it in the light.

9mm Luger.

Having handled the evidence with bare fingers, I slid it into my pocket.

"You got a plan, Cass?"

"Bet your ass I do." I stepped into the beam, catching the brunt of its brightness on my chest. My mind raced as fragmented images of the person I knew was behind the escalating crisis in my county, and in my life, pieced themselves together. "Bring your truck around. It's time we light a fire of our own."

CHAPTER FIFTY-TWO

My heart throbbed against the swelling of my burned left hand but the pain would have to wait as I had yet to fight. All evidence, circumstantial as it may be, pointed directly at the men occupying the Bar S ranch. Aside from the shell casing in my pocket, there was no definitive certainty that I would find something tangible to present to a court, but that was not going to stop me from paying them another visit. I knew in my bones that Big Bill, the Chinese mystery man, and their high-dollar, California law firm were all involved. Assault, attempted murder, first degree murder, kidnapping, the list goes on and on. And now, with Raven and Charlotte missing and Cody shot and being rushed to the hospital, I was ready to enact war.

It seemed I always found a way to involve myself with the most vile criminals. Maybe I was cursed. Perhaps I was destined to hunt down men, case after case, like the ghost riders who blaze a hellish trail behind the devil's herd across the sky. If all that were true, God help anyone who gets in my way.

I pushed through the front door of the house and

headed straight for my uncle's office. In the office where Miguel had been hiding, was one of two cases I needed. I reached into the kneehole and removed a chrome cast reinforced aluminum tactical case and placed it on the desktop. I dialed the combination code until a metallic click signaled that the case was unlocked. I flipped the clasps and opened the case.

A custom cut, foam inlay revealed an empty space that housed the Glock 17 I currently carried. Next to that and resting securely in another form-fitting cutout were two polymer-coated magazines fully loaded with 9mm NATO, 124-grain FMJ bullets. On the opposite side of the case were two rectangular cutouts. One held my Nitecore P20 tactical flashlight while the other cradled a Holosun HS507C red-dot sight. Two larger custom cutouts below the Glock 17 held the upper and lower receivers of my Colt AR-15.

I reached for the two halves of the rifle and removed them from the case. My right hand managed the weight, but my burned left hand screamed under the pressure. I set the upper and lower receivers on the table, then used my good hand to assemble the weapon. I aligned the upper and lower receivers of the Colt AR-15, deftly securing them with the front pivot pin using my right thumb. Using my left forearm to stabilize the setup due to my injured hand, I snapped the rear takedown pin into place. Next, I placed the bolt carrier and charging handle on the table, sliding them into the upper receiver and locking them with a firm push. After a swift visual check to ensure everything was correctly assembled, I lifted the rifle, feeling its balanced weight. I cocked it with a sharp pull on the charging handle, readying the rifle for action. After ensuring the rifle was clear and engaging the safety, I gripped the charging handle and depressed the trigger, allowing the hammer to ease down gently without striking.

I set the battle-ready rifle on the table, then turned to a cabinet on the wall behind me. Opening one of the doors, I removed a smaller, locked case and set it on the seat of the desk's leather wingback chair. I turned back to the cabinet and removed a small key taped to the under-side of the cabinet's bottom shelf, using it to unlock the case.

This was a toy box of destruction. Carefully placed in custom cutouts, I looked over a series of flashbangs, smoke grenades, and one cylindrical canister that housed the deadliest item in the case. I removed the canister from the box and unwound a length of tape covering a seal along its middle, then slid the top portion off to open and expose one very real, blow your ass to hell, M67 fragmen-tation grenade. The small baseball-sized device seemed to look up and say, "Is it my turn to play?" I removed it from the canister and held it in front of me, admiring it like I was Indiana Jones holding the golden Chachapoyan fertility idol that he discovered in the beginning of *Raiders of the Lost Ark*.

"You'll do," I whispered as I set it on the desk next to the AR-15.

I pulled a black canvas backpack from a lower desk drawer and unzipped the main compartment. One at a time, I removed four flashbangs and two smoke grenades from the case and placed them inside the backpack. I then pulled a handful of heavy-duty zip-ties from the cabinet and slid them into an exterior pouch on the pack, securing them under a Velcro flap.

Turning my attention back to the fragmentation grenade, I contemplated my need for such a destructive weapon, then fell back to advice my father had told me when I was younger—*Better to have it and not need it, then need it and not have it.*

It was great advice for life when making decisions about everyday items. My guess was that he never considered I would take his words of wisdom and apply them for destructive purposes. Still, he was right. I lifted the grenade off the desk and placed it in a separate exterior pocket, securing it with a quick zip of the pouch's zipper. I slung the pack over my shoulder, grabbed the AR-15, and headed out of the office.

Mindful of my need for expediency, I forced myself to detour to the bathroom and tend to my burns. I ran water over my hand, gritting my teeth as the coolness washed over the newly formed blisters and red, raw skin. I should have let the water run for much longer than a minute, but I had to get moving. Satisfied with my palm's initial cleanliness, I patted it dry, applied a smattering of burn ointment from Raven's favorite holistic shop, *La Mariposa Mística*—The Mystical Butterfly—and then wound it with a gauze wrap to keep it covered. Living a life surrounded by two daredevil boys, Raven had amassed plenty of first aid supplies, and with her frequent visits to see her friend Señora Cruzita Vasquez, the quirky owner of *La Mariposa Mística*, it was easy for me to find everything I needed to treat my injuries.

Before exiting the house, I threw on a black, long-sleeved, lightweight pullover, and changed into a pair of tactical boots. When I stepped onto the porch, armed, bandaged, and ready for a fight, I was met by Flint and one other person I had not seen in weeks.

CHAPTER FIFTY-THREE

"Ramón? What the hell are you doing here?"

Ramón López stood next to Flint, armed with a silver-plated Benelli M4 Super 90 shotgun, his eyes squinting with a battle-hardened glare. Once a former Sinaloa gang member and ex-employee of Roy Sinclair on the Double SS, Ramón had been my own personal undercover operative helping me track down and kill the cartel sicario, El Despiadado, in Mexico. He disappeared shortly after the mission, so seeing him now standing at my door was a surprise.

"I hear things, even south of the border. When the sheriff ended up in the hospital, I figured you would be planning something dangerous. It's why I'm here, Callahan."

I reached out, and we shook hands. Flint glanced back and forth between us, his look less inviting.

"I see you got started without me," Ramón said, gesturing to my fresh bandages.

"You could say that," I said. "But now that you are here, I have an even better idea of what we are going to do."

I reached behind me, ensuring the front door of the house was closed and locked, then stepped off the porch with Flint and Ramón in tow. Flint's truck, a blue 2016 Chevrolet Silverado 2500HD LTZ 4x4 growled in the yard like a wolf protecting its kill. Parked next to the house was an old 1970s El Camino. I stopped and looked at both vehicles.

"That what you're driving these days, Ramón?"

"Yeah." His reply was tentative. "Why?"

I looked at Flint, then back at the classic near the house. "They'll hear us a mile away in Flint's truck. My guess is they'll be expecting me, but they won't be expecting you, Ramón."

"Shit. Anything happens to my car, Callahan."

"Nothing will. Come on. It'll be a tight fit, but it's a short drive."

I led the way past Flint and Ramón and set my backpack in the bed of the El Camino closest to the cab. Looking back, Ramón shook his head, whispering something to himself in Spanish. Flint reached into his pocket and removed a key fob. With a single click of a button, the monster-sized Chevy's engine turned off. He locked it with a click of another button, then placed the fob at the base of a clay planter that stood at the foot of the porch and walked over to join me next to the car.

"If the shit goes south, you trust 'im?" Flint whispered.

"About as much as anyone."

"Then let's load up. Longer we stick 'round here, the worse off fer Raven an' Charlotte."

I nodded, then called out to Ramón, "Vamos, amigo."

As he walked to the car, my pocket buzzed with an incoming text. I pulled my phone out, held it to my face to unlock it, and then pressed the messages icon.

THURSDAY: 7:44 P.M.:

Cass, I've completed the examination and analysis of our suspected drowning victim, confirmed of Chinese origin. Interestingly, there were only trace amounts of water in his lungs, indicating he did NOT die from drowning. The X-ray results confirm a crushed Hyoid bone, aligning with our initial hypothesis.

Further examination revealed fractures and dislocations at the C3 and C4 levels of the cervical spine. Additionally, there is evidence of extensive strain, sprain, and tearing in the soft tissues of the neck, particularly those connected to the Hyoid bone. The severity of these injuries would have rapidly deteriorated his respiratory and neurological functions, leading to his death.

Also, I found trace amounts of manure on his skin just below his chin.

My official diagnosis is that the victim died from blunt force trauma to the neck resulting in acute asphyxiation.

Unofficially, it seems that someone kicked him in the fucking throat and let him die while they watched. His body is now on ice in the morgue. Please relay this message to Chance as he's not responding to his phone.

~Frannie

I hate it when I am right. What's worse is that Frannie has no idea Chance is in the hospital.

"Hey!" Ramón's voice sounded out over the roof of the car. "You gonna tell us the plan, or we just winging it?"

I looked at Flint who had yet to get it. I could tell he was ready for a fight, but more so, I felt that his concern for Raven outweighed my objective to bring the Bar S to its knees.

I laid out my plan, revised a bit now that Ramón was joining us, and waited for resistance.

"So, you want me to drive up to the security gate. Alone. Pretend to be looking for work at this time of night and expect what exactly?"

Ramón sounded skeptical, but I knew him well enough to understand he operated better after he had the chance to repeat and process instructions. It was his way of clarifying actions; however, I've known plenty of brass over the years who would take offense and see it as questioning a tactical plan.

"Right. With everything going on tonight, the last thing they'll be expecting is a quick response. They've been able to avoid attention this whole time. Why would they think their actions tonight would be any different. Shock and awe are usually debilitating for a victim. The explosion, the missing girls, any rational person would have no idea what to do next except call the authorities, but with Chance in the hospital, me on the sidelines, and the rest of the county stretched thin, my guess is they are not concerned about any response at all. Whoever is pulling the strings has been one step ahead of me this whole time, until now. You get the guard away from the shack, Ramón. Take him out quietly, then disable their exterior surveillance. Can you do that?"

"Shouldn't be a problem. I have just one question—how big is the guard?

"You worried ya won't be able ta handle 'im?" Flint said.

Ramón dipped his head and smiled. "No, *ese*. I just like to know if I should use these or not." Slowly, he showed his fist draped with a set of brass knuckles.

"Damn, Ramón. That should take care of about anyone. Just be careful and do it quietly."

"This is what I do," he said.

He gave a chin lift, then disappeared into the car. Looking at Flint, I saw him staring back at his burned-out house.

"You sure you're up for this?" I said.

Turning to me, his face looked like chiseled stone.

Saying nothing, he pulled his Colt 1911 and hopped into the bed of the El Camino. I jumped in back next to him as Ramón fired up the engine.

Darkness consumed us as we pulled off the CR. The ground crackled beneath the El Camino's tires as we drove north toward the Bar S. As the wind whipped by, I leaned over and explained to Flint what I needed him to do. He remained silent, more focused than I had ever seen him before. When I had finished, neither of us spoke a word. Finding Raven and Charlotte and bringing down a murderer were all that mattered. He knew it. I knew it. And we all knew the price we would pay if anything went wrong.

I squeezed the handguard on my AR-15 with my right hand and took a brief second to close my eyes.

Hang on, Little Bird. I will find you. If it's the last thing I do, I'll get you and Charlotte home.

CHAPTER FIFTY-FOUR

amón slowed our speed to a crawl, allowing Flint and I to jump out of the bed of the El Camino without giving an appearance to anyone who might be watching that a car had stopped along the dark road leading to the Bar S. With my backpack slung over my shoulders, and my rifle at the low ready, Flint and I crouched along the edge of the road where the gravel met the chalky West Texas dirt. The El Camino's taillights cast a momentary red glow on our faces as Ramón continued to drive toward the Bar S entrance.

Only a half mile separated us from our target. Getting past the guard shack unnoticed would be a feat that would make Harry Houdini proud, but remaining undetected once we breached the outlying buildings would take a miracle. Under a heavy blanket of star-studded darkness, the Bar S ranch looked like a small city basking in the glow of after-hours activities. The whole compound was painted as clear as day with lights dotting the landscape from the entrance road to the compound beyond the security gate. Shadows stretched from the main build-

ings in all directions, indicating additional lighting in
multiple spots inside the perimeter.

Once we made it that far, finding Raven and Charlotte
was our first priority. Apprehending and arresting Big Bill
and the Chinaman would come next, if circumstances saw
it that way. It would be good for everyone if they were to
go quietly, but something told me that just would never
happen. I prefer quiet. I can handle quiet. But, if loud was
what they wanted, I had a backpack full of boom and an
arm full of bang waiting to greet them.

As these thoughts swirled in my mind, I had to remind
myself that this mission was far different than my last
one. The assault on the cartel compound in Mexico was
secretive, with a clear mission objective to seek and
destroy. Tonight, on American soil, there were procedures
to follow, but acting under my authority as a TITON
agent, I had plenty of leeway in which to uphold justice.

I was familiar with the layout of buildings from my
prior visits to the Double SS, but a lack of viable intel with
regard to personnel on the Bar S weighed heavily on me.
That reason alone should have made me pause and recon-
sider, but with Raven and Charlotte's lives at stake, all
bets were off.

"Stay low. Let's move out," I said in a whisper.

The road was minimally developed, which was to say
that there was a layer of gravel that lined the main
roadway that was bordered by a slight drop off on either
side to accommodate runoff. There was no money nor no
need for pavement way out here in the sticks.

I led the way with Flint on my six. We moved with
swift, careful steps, avoiding the ditch and any sinkholes
or venomous creatures that might want to take our feet
out from under us. West Texas dangers came in all forms
and held no prejudice over their victims.

I kept my eyes fixed on the El Camino as Ramón

turned left up the entrance road and headed straight for the security gate.

"This is it," I said.

"Hope he knows what he's doing," Flint replied.

Sweat dripped down my neck as I increased our pace. My thighs burned from moving at such a low, crouched position, but we covered the distance from where Ramón had dropped us to the head of the entrance road just as the El Camino's brake lights cut through the night.

"He's there."

Come on, Ramón, mess this up, and it's all over before we get started.

I raised my rifle and peered through the red-dot scope and watched as the security guard approached the driver's side of the car. I saw a clipboard in his hand, a radio on his shoulder, and a sidearm strapped to his right leg. I watched his head bob as he talked, then nodded as if he were listening.

Come on. Come on.

Every second Ramón was parked at the entrance was a second too long. When the driver's side door opened and Ramón stepped out of the car, a shot of adrenaline surged through me. He was close. Any second now, he would make his move and we could advance up the drive. The guard looked down at his clipboard, used a pen to write something, and then...*shit!* He reached for his radio and spoke into the receiver. Ramón stood by, inactive. His demeanor was calm. The guard returned the radio to his shoulder holster, then motioned toward the compound.

"What the hell is he doin'?"

Flint sounded impatient. Untrusting. By all accounts, he had known Ramón longer than me. They had a long history of working on opposite fence lines, and from what I had learned since arriving at the CR, most of the time, their familiarity with one another was questionable. All that ended when Ramón had been shot and I ended up being the one to save his life. The shooter had never been identified, but at the time, while most of the speculation fell on Joe Sinclair, a handful pointed in Flint's direction. I never considered it myself, nor do I think Flint had a hand in the shooting, but then again, I dismissed the thought as soon as it entered my mind and focused on Ramón and the guard.

I watched as the two men approached one another. Then the guard extended a hand, which Ramón accepted. They shook, then released. The gates opened, and Ramón got back into the car and the guard returned to his perch inside the guard shack.

I looked on in disbelief.

"Something's wrong," I said.

"I asked ya at the house, an' now I'm gonna ask ya again. Do you trust 'im?"

I watched as Ramón pulled ahead, passing beyond the barrier meant to keep others out. I lowered the rifle and tucked it by my side.

Shit.

CHAPTER FIFTY-FIVE

The security gate lowered behind Ramón's El Camino and all I could think was, *why would he betray me?* I lifted my rifle to peer through the scope again and saw that the car had stopped and all the lights had cut off. As I swept back to the shack, I noticed the guard was still visible through the security window, focused on something in his hands. A phone? The clipboard? I had no idea, but he seemed oblivious to the fact that Ramón had stopped. Turning my attention back to the El Camino, I saw Ramón had exited the car and was moving back toward the security entrance on foot. I tracked him as he drew nearer, then lost sight of him when he disappeared behind the shack.

One Mississippi, two Mississippi—a stupid childhood counting game, but that's what popped into my head, and that was all the time it took for Ramón to enter the shack through a rear door, slip his forearm around the guard's neck, and punch him in the side of the head. His attack was quick and precise. I could see the guard's body go limp in Ramón's grasp. He lowered him to the floor, then looked out the front security window and pointed to his fist and the polished brass wrapped around his knuckles.

"We're in," I said.

"Not how I woulda handled it."

"We can debate assault technique later, Flint. Let's go."

I lowered my rifle and ran ahead along the entrance road. The twenty seconds it took to cover the ground felt like slow-motion minutes where each step I made was another moment to be spotted by somebody on the inside. With Flint close behind, we did not stop until we stood in the security shack.

"What the hell, Ramón?" Flint started in before I had a chance to speak. "What was that?"

Ramón kept his cool, ignoring Flint until he had made a final keystroke and hit enter on a keyboard attached to a networked computer.

"Callahan wanted us to get in unnoticed. That's what I did."

"Sure have a funny way of goin' about it."

Ramón faced Flint.

"Look, *ese*. I pulled up and the guy walked over like he was expecting me. I barely had to say anything. Just went along with what he said."

"Which was?" I asked, now intrigued.

"He thought I was the driver for some overnight haul to Mexico. So, I went along with it."

"Guess bein' a wetback has its privileges," Flint said.

"Flint, we don't have time for that," I said. "This was step one. Now comes the fun part. Getting the rest of the way in and finding the girls."

I peered out the door, sizing up our approach over the fifty yards that separated us from the nearest building.

"You didn't let me finish," Ramón said.

I turned back around to hear him out.

"The guard also let it slip that he was shutting things down out here at nine o'clock and was going in to take over the surveillance operator position. That's only seven minutes from now."

"Surveillance operator?" Flint repeated.

"It's the guy who monitors the security cameras, *ese*." Ramón turned his focus to me. "Here's the best part. The guy he is replacing has already left his post."

"An' yer friend here told ya all that? Seems like a stretch, if ya ask me." Flint rained skepticism.

"No," I said, pausing to look down at the unconscious guard. "Security guards are a dime a dozen. If he felt even the slightest bit comfortable with Ramón, it would be easy to share information without a second thought, especially if he had things to do."

"Yep." Ramón nodded. "Said he was in a hurry and that I should report immediately to the barn where the rig was parked. Cass, the truck is scheduled to leave at ten."

I looked at the clock. *Five minutes to nine.*

"Listen, I've already disabled the gate alarm and activated a countdown timer that will disable network cameras throughout the whole ranch. They'll be down only as long as it takes the main surveillance hub to power off and then reboot. A minute, maybe more. After that, it's back to live TV at the Bar S."

"Yeah, but with nobody to watch the show," I added.

"Right, that's why the timer is counting down for ten minutes from now. With our guard here out of commission, we should be able to make it to the main house unseen and have a look around. If somebody ends up noticing that he hasn't made it to his post, the timer will most likely expire by the time they get the position covered. The code will activate and take down the whole network of cameras. They'll think it was a glitch due to a power surge. With all these lights, they are sucking all the energy they can outta the West Texas power grid."

Enough explanations. The clock was ticking and it was time to move.

"Ramón, hop back in the car, drive ahead, and play the truck driver part. If he's already announced your arrival, they'll be expecting you. Flint, you and I will start at the main house, then work our way to the barn. Take out anyone you come across, but do it quietly. We're not here to kill anyone." I paused to catch two questionable looks. "Not unless your life or the girls' lives are in imminent danger."

"So, dance to the music that's playing?" Ramón shrugged, then gestured his fist to Flint. "Wanna borrow my knuckles, *ese*?"

Flint snarled, cracking his own by balling his hands into a tight fist.

"Get moving, Ramón," I said, ushering him out the door.

The drive was lined with track lighting that stretched the length of the entrance road. Looking both ways, I prepared myself for the sprint to the main building. As I was about to lunge ahead, Flint grabbed me from behind.

"We got another problem." Flint pointed out the window to a pair of headlights coming down the road toward the ranch. "How much you wanna bet that's the real truck driver?"

Tick. Tick. Tick.

"Deal with him," I said. "I'll head to the house and begin the search."

Flint huffed. "Deal with 'im. Okay, Cass. Don't get caught er killed before I get there."

I nodded, then shot out of the guard shack at top speed. The backpack bounced on my back and the weight of the rifle swung back and forth in my arms with each stride. Running across the road, I cut a path between two track lights into the rough and found cover behind a storage building adjacent to the main house. With my back against the wall, I crept to the corner and peered around the edge into a small passage that ran between the two buildings. Bathed in shadow, it was a perfect spot to pass through.

As I stepped into the passage, I glanced back and saw an old 1980s Monte Carlo approach Flint at the guard shack. Compared to Ramón's El Camino, this car was a true POS—its clanky motor and patchy paint job approaching the end of the road.

"You got this, Flint," I whispered to myself, then turned around and slipped through the thin sheen of gray.

I stopped and crouched at the front of the building, my rifle at the low ready. Looking out from my concealed position, I watched Ramón park along the far side of the yard near the barn. Two men met him as he got out. They were both dressed in jeans and boots. One wore a straw hat and had a sidearm strapped to his leg. Neither had the swagger of a true rancher, which was no surprise considering what I already knew about the Bar S. They talked for a moment, shared agreeable nods, then the man with the hat led Ramón away from his car. The other man followed behind as they sauntered toward a large barn door. The man with the hat slid the large door open just enough for the three of them to pass through.

"Okay, Ramón. Keep your cover story intact, and you'll be safe."

My lips moved, and the words were there, but no sound fell from my mouth.

As I was scoping out my next cover point, three different men walked out of the barn. They stopped in the center of the yard, huddled together in conversation. Only one man was dressed in ranch wear. The others looked more like businessmen in casual attire. One pulled a pack of cigarettes from his back pocket, fished out a stick, and then held up the pack, offering one to the others. Upon their refusal, he returned the pack to his pocket, produced a lighter from another pocket, and fired up for a smoke.

That makes five, not counting the guard Ramón knocked out or the surveillance operator. And where are you, Big Bill? And your Chinese friend?

With no way to advance unseen, I backed down the passage to the rear of the building. Before stepping out, I noticed that the Monte Carlo I left Flint to deal with was driving away from the ranch. *Good.* I glanced at the guard shack, expecting to see him inside. It was empty.

CHAPTER FIFTY-SIX

A lazy breeze picked up, whistling through the passage as I stepped behind the main house and slinked along the outer wall. The moon hung low on the horizon. Its crescent shape smiled at me as if in approval of my mission. Or was it a more sinister grin hiding secrets of which I was unaware?

I moved past windows, ducking beneath the glow cast out by each. I was quick to pause and peek but saw nobody inside. At the corner of the main house, I had a choice of proceeding along the perimeter to the front of the building or slipping behind a third structure that looked like a detached garage. There were no windows between the two buildings, save one door on each. The space between was well lit with a short canopy covering a wooden boardwalk that ran to the doors of each building.

I opted to continue along the backside of the garage. It was a smaller structure and would be easier to sweep and clear. I slowed my advance and tightened my grip around my rifle as I approached a rear access door leading into the garage. Two trashcans stood guard along either side of the entrance like smelly sentinels assigned the lowest duty on the ranch. As I drew near, I noticed that the door had been left ajar. Even more noticeable was that, unlike the other building's windows which pulsed with interior lighting, the garage itself was cloaked in darkness. Inside I would gain another moment or two of invisibility, but my options to remain undetected were running out.

I eased the door open with my left hand, catching my bandage on a nail head sticking just above the smooth, creamy paint. Pulling away, a shot of frustration jolted me as I stood in the open doorway, ensnared by the tiniest enemy. Gauze was meant to be tough, its fibers woven in tight patterns created a protective seal that was both soft as cotton and strong as a spider's webbing. I yanked my hand, but the nail held firm and the door swung at me. I slung my rifle over my shoulder and used my right hand to work the tangle. Each attempt to free the strands of gauze from the nail only knotted them further, tightening the grip on my hand. Making matters worse, I heard a door around the corner from me open and two voices sounded out as their feet clomped on the solid wood boardwalk. One voice sounded angry, the other choppy and reserved, belonging to a woman. Even more telling was that they were not speaking English. It sounded Chinese.

Bracing the door with my right hand, I pulled down hard with my left.

I don't have time for this shit!

The voices carried as if they were getting closer. I gritted my teeth.

C'mon you son of a...

Ripping into the rigid wrap, I felt the gauze stretch and finally tear, freeing me from the nail. What remained of the bandage dangled from my hand and fingers.

More angry words continued only feet around the corner from me. The woman spoke back. Though I could not understand the words, I did understand the tone of her voice. She pleaded with the man until he cut her off. I heard the male voice give a sharp-sounding order, then all was quiet between them. Breaking the silence, a door opened, then slammed closed, causing a window on the house to shudder. The man had returned inside, leaving the woman outside by herself.

Soft whimpering filled the void between the buildings. I wanted to have a look, to see who remained, but that was not my mission. A moment later, footsteps moved along the wooden boardwalk. I heard the creak of a door swing open, then close again, but so softly that I was unsure of which building the sad woman had entered.

Not wanting to waste any more time and feeling as if I was clear for now, I unwound the remaining strands of gauze, balled them up, and tossed them into one of the trash cans by the door.

"Shhh, payment for your silence," I whispered as I stepped into the garage.

Before closing the door, I glanced at my hand under the pale glow of security lighting. It was raw and swollen, with a burst blister at the base of my middle finger. The cool night air brushed against my skin, reviving the burning sensation as if my palm were still clenched around the scalding car door handle. I flexed my hand, managing its tenderness and testing its limitations.

Rambo-up, Cass. It's only pain.

Using my right hand, I closed the door behind me and stepped into the garage. Rays of light seeped through seams around the main garage door and from cracks from the side wall to my right. As my eyes adjusted, I saw a workbench along the back wall to my left and the exterior door that opened onto the boardwalk. The far-right wall was outfitted with tools hanging on hooks. Outlines of shovels, pickaxes, a rake, and a fireman's axe were visible, but it was what stood parked in the center of the garage that most interested me—Big Bill's truck.

I walked over to the massive vehicle, amazed that it fit through the overhead garage door. Inspecting the grille, I ran my hand along the steel bumper, my fingers gliding freely over the chrome finish. I leaned around the front end to look along the surface of the driver's side. Shadows pooled in the dips and curves of the truck but failed to hide the one thing I had hoped to see. The color of its paint job. A feeling of validation and pensive frustration stirred within me.

I moved to the passenger's side and ran my hand along the front panel. The metal and high-dollar paint job felt sleek to the touch, but as expected, my fingers found a rough patch of scratched metal just above the front wheel well that extended to the passenger-side door. Shadows swam on this side of the truck as well, but there was something I had to see in the light. I pulled my cell phone from my pocket. Its dim screen activated at the movement, then grew brighter when I pressed the codes to unlock it. Riding the scratch marks like a surfer shredding a wave was a long, very distinctive line of red paint.

"Damn, I knew it!"

Keeping my voice low, I leaned close, bringing the phone closer still and examined the damage on the truck.

"No way in hell Chance let a deer run him off the road. Driver be damned, but it was this truck that did the job."

A paint transfer analysis would be needed for confirmation, but I was sure that this paint matched the blue scratch I discovered on Chance's pickup.

As I straightened my stance and turned, the gleaming whites of terrified eyes staring at me from the darkness of the garage made my heart skip a beat and my grip tighten around my weapon.

CHAPTER FIFTY-SEVEN

Paralyzed, the mouse waits for just the right moment before attempting a frantic escape from the elusive snake, whose hypnotic bend of the neck and mesmerizing stare mark the calm before a lethal strike. That was what we were to one another, a terrified woman and an armed soldier, each not knowing who would act first. But who was the serpent and who was the mouse? To each other, we were both predator and prey. One wrong move could trigger disaster for both of us.

With slow, purposeful movements, I lowered my weapon and raised my left hand in front of my face. I pressed one finger to my lips in a shushing motion, then extended my hand toward her, palm out. She flinched at my first move, then followed my hand with wary eyes. Each second was a step across a glass bridge.

With my palm raised and settled, her look changed. Her eyebrows curved upward. Her head tilted a notch to one side. As our connection furthered, I recognized her as the woman with the man I had tried to help, the man who was now dead. The picture in my mind became clearer. She was also the woman whose face I saw in the window before having been yanked from view when Chance and I came by the Bar S yesterday morning. Had she recognized me as well?

With cautious movements, she stepped forward and reached out with small, fragile hands, cupping my burned hand in hers. Leaning closer still, she studied my palm.

"*Nǐ shòushāng le.*" The woman spoke with soft breaths tinged with obvious concern, but her words were beyond my understanding. With the gentleness of a flower petal, she traced my wound with her fingertip. Despite the discomfort, I endured her caring and meticulous examination of my hand. Repeating herself, she looked at me, "*Nǐ shòushāng le.*"

The terror she had exuded was gone, replaced with a sense of purpose.

"*Zài zhèlǐ děng.*"

I shrugged.

Still don't know what the hell you are saying, I thought.

The woman released my hand, raised both palms, then pointed to the ground.

"Wait?" My voice was hushed but filled with urgency. "I can't. I am looking for my wife."

She met my words with a blank stare and a hesitant smile, mimicked my shushing gesture, and swiftly exited through the garage door before I could object.

I hurried behind her catching the door before it closed and peered around the edge. She walked across the boardwalk and entered the main house, never once looking back.

Trust among strangers is a complex thing—a moment filled with foreign words and unspoken intentions, yet a connection formed, nonetheless.

Help me or not, I thought. *I gotta move.*

I closed the door and locked it from the inside, then jogged to the back of the garage quietly exiting the same way I came in. Moving past the trash cans, I crept on quiet feet to the edge of the garage. Peering around the corner, I saw a corral with fencing that led to the barn on one side and to a series of chutes that zigzagged to a metal swing gate on the other. Beyond that, open range filled the void beyond what light could touch, wrapping itself around the perimeter of the northern section of the ranch along a wood rail fence. The yard extended from the side of the garage about fifty yards before meeting the fence line, a veritable kill zone for anyone caught out in the open.

I slipped along the side garage to the front and crouched. It was a twenty-yard dash to the corral from my position and in full view of anyone watching. I eyed the barn. Its main door was open creating a gaping entrance wide and tall enough for a semi-truck to pull through. The men who had been talking in the center of the yard now stood in the opening, their colorful clothing pronounced in front of the darkness behind them. It would have been so easy to pick each of them off with three quick shots, falling dead before they reached the ground, but that was not my mission. Not yet anyway.

Ramón's timer had been ticking the whole time. The camera feed going down had only one task—provide a window of blindness so we could access the property unseen. After that, it was up to us. I pulled my cell and glanced at the time.

9:04

Any minute now, Ramón's countdown should trigger the security system to shut down, then reboot. I was already beyond the front-line cameras, but where was Flint?

With a flip of the numbers, the time changed to the target minute. I scanned the yard and adjacent buildings for Flint, but he was nowhere to be seen. Not a second later, I heard a hum grow like a transformer overloading from a surge of power. It hung in the air, then with a brilliant electrical buzz, the hum ceased, and all the lights on the ranch went out.

My legs were moving before I processed what had just happened, pumping faster and faster as instinct had taken over. Voices rose from the dark, chattering with annoyance and impatient urgency as I covered the ground between the garage and the corral fence. My pack swashed back and forth across my back. Sweat on my brow caught the breeze from my advance and felt cool as it dripped over my cheeks.

In seconds, I had reached the fence and was up and over and closing in on the edge of the barn. Ramón's glitch caused more fuss than I expected, but it happened at just the right time. Luck, for now, was still on my side.

I worked well under the cover of darkness, sliding along the outer barn wall until I found an open passageway leading past a series of stalls.

Men shouting to get the lights back on echoed throughout the barn, but there were no animal sounds to accompany their ruckus. I peeked into a stall as I worked my way into the heart of the barn and found it empty, save the lost and forgotten remnants of compost. The smell of old hay and dried manure floated in the stale barn air, filling my nose and making me wonder how long the barn had been left unattended. Maybe it was a purposeful move by Big Bill, made to retain the appearance of a working ranch, but the old stench would not hold a candle to the experienced nose of a true West Texas rancher. I supposed the Bar S was not long on visitors, but every façade had its purpose, even for the few that might have made the trip.

Each moment the ranch remained in the dark, the better. With my rifle at the ready, I passed the halfway point down the stall corridor before it opened into what I expected was the main hall of the barn. Chatter grew louder as I approached, but one man's voice caused the hair on my neck to rise as he barked at the others.

"Tired of this shit," the man grumbled. "I gotta take a piss." His footsteps were heavy, each one pounding as he moved in my direction.

"Hurry it up! Boss says we're leaving ahead of schedule."

Mumbling to himself, the man was indignant.

"Sum bitch. They don't pay me enough to manage this shit. Everyone around me is a moron!" His voice rose, turning accusatory and meant for all to hear.

A simple *fuck you, Roy*, echoed behind him as each aggravated step brought him closer to my position.

Five men for sure inside, counting this dickhead. A couple more, possibly, plus Big Bill and the Chinaman. My mind raced over the few facts I had gathered. *Time to bring that number down by one.*

Piss-bound Roy walked right past the stall I had ducked into, not noticing I was there. I watched as he offered a gift any fox would lick its chops for as he opened a pen door two stalls away from me and walked inside. I heard the metallic zip of his fly, then a dull constant thud as his stream hit the dirt floor.

On silent feet, I swept in behind him, covered his mouth with my right hand while I wrapped my left forearm around his throat. I paused long enough to whisper one thing into his ear.

"Never get caught with your pants down, Roy."

My grip tightened around his throat like a hot dog in a vise. His arms flailed out with blind, frantic swings. Losing both his balance and control, what was left of his flow ran down his leg, dribbling over his feet. A muffled grunt and his pants falling around his urine-soaked ankles were the only sounds, both of which were lost in the concealment of the smelly horse stall. I leaned his limp body against the wood stall slats, then pulled a zip tie from my bag and bound his wrists together. There was no way in hell I was touching his ankles. Instead, I used an additional zip tie to secure him to one of the slats above his head.

"There you go, Roy. Hang tight." I grabbed a handful of dried hay from the ground and stuffed a solid helping in his mouth, insurance should he awake before I was ready and call for help.

I stood over Roy, invigorated and ready for more, then whispered affectionately to him. "That'll do, pig. That'll do." His head would pound for hours once he came around, but he was alive.

As I leaned into the passage and saw the coast was clear, a new sound filled the rafters, sending a roosting owl fluttering and swooping down in a screeching escape. Tingles ran along my skin, not from the bird's dive bombing, but from the rumble of a big rig's engine firing up and the orange pulse of trailer lighting cutting through the darkened barn. Making matters more urgent, above the loud idle, I heard someone in distress yell out, "NO!"

CHAPTER FIFTY-EIGHT

That sudden shout and simple damning word mashed together sounded terrified, but it was not Raven or Charlotte's voice. Still, someone was in trouble. Step over step, I advanced along the stalls, my position becoming less covered but my field of view more pronounced. The orange marker lights cast a glow along the frame of the trailer's long, white body. The side I could see was plain, with no writing, logos, or anything that would make this truck more memorable than others when barreling down the highway.

Without the buzz or hum of electricity pulling through the lines, lights around the ranch flickered, then failed again. Like a cockroach caught on the kitchen floor, I scurried into the nearest stall, crouched low, and aimed my rifle toward the truck.

The abrupt flash killed my night vision causing ghosting images of the truck with its orange lights to drift and swirl like a psychedelic dream across my line of sight, each one morphing into a colorful nautilus of infinite recursion.

Chatter near the truck rose then barked in agitation at the surge. A familiar voice called out, "What the hell is takin' Roy so long?" Grumbles of "I don't know," and "Not my problem," replied.

I blinked to clear the dizzying kaleidoscope from my eyes and process what I had seen during the flash—two men standing guard along the side of the trailer, each holding Type 56 Assault rifles, the Chinese equivalent to the Russian AK-47. The men were dressed in black from head to boot. One looked Mexican, the other Chinese. My glance was brief, but there was no doubt in my mind about what I saw.

Could be the same men Cody described, I thought. *Two of the three who were at the CR earlier tonight at least.*

Of all the men I had seen on the Bar S, these two were the most heavily armed, making my assumption plausible. But where was the third man? He was the Chinese SOB I wanted.

When my eyes were fully adjusted, I peered over the top rail of the stall where I was hiding. I saw silhouettes of the guards pacing back and forth. Additional men passed in and out of view, each carrying something one way, then returning empty-handed as if they were loading the trailer. I had seen them pass each other twice, but on the third time, they stopped and looked in my direction. Shadows hid their faces, but one wore a hat like the man who had met and escorted Ramón into the barn.

"Ol' Roy thinks he can skip on the job and still get paid, I guess," one man said.

The one wearing the hat stepped closer to the passage leading to the stalls, to me. He called out.

"You go on. Take all the time you need, Roy. In fact, don't bother coming back. When the boss finds out you ain't don' jackshit, you may want to run for the river. Just don't get caught. You know from watching what happens then."

Sudden shouting near the front of the barn caused the man to whirl around.

"What the hell is going on around here!" he said and marched toward the commotion. The other man fell in line behind him as he passed by.

The armed guards were just as caught off guard, and quickly moved to the head of the trailer as well. I slipped out of my hiding spot and moved to the edge of the last stall in the passage, crouching near its wooden beams. Shouting beyond the front of the truck continued to attract attention leaving the rear of the truck unattended. Staying low, I ran to the trailer, then ducked underneath and out of view. Concealed in the shadows, I was out of sight for the moment.

On elbows and knees, I crawled to the rear of the trailer. The commotion continued with shouts becoming rhythmic as if a crowd were watching a fight unfold. I pulled myself from beneath the trailer and found myself looking into the cargo area. Wooden crates lined both sides, but I could only see about a third of the way down the hold. Risking getting caught and possibly trapped inside, I climbed into the trailer, pulled my cell phone from my pocket, and activated the screen. The dull light was enough to illuminate objects close to me yet not signal someone outside that I was snooping around.

I swept the phone over the crates nearest me. Long, back strips of Chinese characters marked the exterior of every mysterious box. Moving further into the belly of the trailer, I found one crate with similar markings whose top was not secured like the others. Digging my fingers into the slit between top and box, I pulled up. Nail heads squeaked as their necks stretched from their beds of the fresh crates, but it was not their objection to being pulled free that startled me. It was a sudden intake of breath followed by a different squeak, a noise only a human could make.

As I turned to the noise, I dropped my phone and slipped my hands around my rifle and aimed. The knock of hardened thousand-dollar plastic and metal on the wooden slats was concerning and might alert someone outside the trailer that I was inside, but if I had an enemy here in the dark, I was burned already. I squinted, trying to see beyond what was possible, all the while my finger hovering near the trigger.

Through the black interior of the trailer, muffled whimpering found its way into my ears. Keeping the head of the trailer in my sights, I slowly bent down and picked up my phone. The screen had cracked, but it was still functional. I twisted it around to face the front of the trailer and stepped forward.

One step.

Darkness still prevailed, hiding the now constant whimpering.

Two steps.

Ambient light from the phone found the base of something metal. Gnarled screws stuck out at odd angles from an iron plate on the trailer floor.

Three steps.

I stopped and swiped my phone from the floor to eye level.

Dear God.

Solid bars from an iron cage more suitable for housing wild animals imprisoned three terrified faces. Each set of eyes drawn wide and staring. Each shivering with fright. Their fear spoke clearly to me. *Could he be one of them?*

I stepped closer, causing their huddled mass to flinch.

"Shhh," I lowered my weapon and knelt. "Everything is going to be okay."

From within the whimpers, a voice rose whose innocence pierced my heart.

"Mr. Callahan...is that you?"

CHAPTER FIFTY-NINE

I rose to my feet and lunged at the cage.

"Charlotte?"

I slipped my fingers around the bars and looked at the frightened faces inside. Girls. Young girls. And smack dab in the middle, with arms wrapped around the other two prisoners, was Charlotte.

"Please, get us out of here," she whispered, her voice wavering with each syllable.

I stepped back to examine the cage, looking for the locking mechanism, a release, a key, anything that could help me open the door and get the girls to safety. As I searched, two voices echoed in my mind. The first was plain and sounded just like me.

"The mission has changed, Cass. Get the girls to safety, then come back with the cavalry."

I heard the message and knew that it spoke true, but then the second voice chimed in.

"They're not your mission, Cass. Where is Raven? Where is your *wife*? Leave them."

I pressed my eyes closed. My mind sparked with flashes of exploding fireworks and bright light. *Where was*

Raven? That was the question to which I needed an answer.

Time was ticking. Both voices repeated themselves, one talking over the other like a battle of politicians in a debate. How could I choose between the girls and Raven. Innocence vs. the love of my life.

At once, the voices in my head ceased. The brilliant show of light behind my eyelids disappeared. My sense of urgency calmed. A cool, comfortable feeling swept over me as if tender fingers were running through my hair. It was not a touch to my head, but that of a small hand on my arm that chased away the voices and grounded my sudden internal turmoil.

I looked at the hand, my gaze trailing up to the sweet, young face of Charlotte. Her cheeks were blushed and stained from a deluge of tears. Her lips quivered with anticipation, then parted as if to speak. Only soft breaths followed. A look of both desperation and salvation poured out of her as we stood connected by her touch yet were separated by the restraints of the iron cage between us.

I placed my free hand on hers.

"Don't worry. I'll get you out. You and the girls try to remain calm and quiet."

Charlotte shook her head and returned to sit between the other girls. Taking a closer look at the cage, I noticed the hinges had gaps between the pins and their cylindrical housings. I grabbed the door with both hands and pulled up and down, seeing if there was any give beneath my force. Nothing. I stepped back and shined the light from my phone over the hinges and doorframe again. The cage was poorly assembled but was strong enough to do its job.

"What the hell are you doing in there?"

An inquisitive voice bellowed from the rear of the trailer.

Shit.

I pressed the phone to my chest, covering the lighted screen, then slid it down my body and into my pocket. The shouting out front continued. This fella must have either lost interest or was the kind of stand-up, get-the-job done kind of guy any employer would appreciate. However, his halfhearted interrogation and lack of action spoke volumes.

Facing the girls and certain that the man could not see this far into the trailer, I whispered to Charlotte.

"Answer him. Ask him to let you out."

Her eyes widened, unsure and confused.

"I need him in the trailer."

"Are you going to kill him?" she whispered.

"Well?" the man said.

His temperament began to change causing his voice to echo louder throughout the trailer.

"Now, Charlotte." My voice soft but firm.

Squeezing her eyes closed, Charlotte answered the man.

"Pl...please, let us out. I think there is a rat in here."

A lop and thud sounded out from the tailgate as the man crawled onto the trailer's platform.

"They'll be more than a rat that'll be interested in you three before all is said and done."

He's the guy the man in the hat was talking to, I realized, recognizing his voice.

He talked as he walked closer to the cage. Each step clomped as his boots hit the decking. I hid between the sidebars and a stack of crates, waiting for the right moment. With shallow, controlled breaths, I blended into the background, unnoticed by the man as he approached the cage.

"You pretty little things. Look at ya. I've I mind to open this door and sample the goods." He chuckled, then reached into his pocket. "With the boss beatin' on that fella outside, I think we'll have plenty of time to..." He pulled a ring of keys from his pocket, its jingling singing in the dark. "...have a quick party of our own?"

He fumbled in the dark, searching for the right key.

"Ah, there it is." His voice slurred as his anticipation for what he planned to do heightened. "Listen here." The key slid into the lock. "Stay quiet or I'll beat the shit out of ya."

When the locking mechanism clicked, the door swung open just enough for the man to slip his fingers around the iron frame and pull.

With one quick lunge, I sprang from my hiding place and rammed the man's body against the cage. The door slammed closed but his hand caught in the frame, muffling the sound of clanking iron while composing a symphony of crackling bones within his crushed fingers. Before he could scream, I smashed the butt of my rifle on the back of his head, splitting the skin and knocking him out cold. I reached out to catch him and found that he was lighter than the first man I had overpowered, but his awkward fall and sudden burst of blood from his scalp caused me to lose my grip which sent him tumbling into a stack of crates to the left of the cage. A dry thud sounded out, loud enough to worry me that someone outside the trailer had heard the noise.

"Quick!" I opened the cage door and reached my hand out to the girls. "We gotta move. Now!"

Charlotte was the first to her feet. The other two followed her lead. Once they were free of the cage, I grabbed the man under his armpits and dragged him inside. He was a crumpled mess, but damn him for what he had planned to do to the girls. I stepped out of the cage and locked the door, taking advantage of the key still dangling in the keyhole. Taking the lead in front of Charlotte, we crept to the rear of the trailer.

"I'll go first and check to see if the coast is clear. When I say so, hop down and keep quiet."

"K," Charlotte replied.

An ambient orange glow hovered above the rear of the trailer, marking its height while casting an eerie fauna that could have just as easily been the first pitstop on a road to hell. The light illuminated the faces of the girls. Charlotte looked ready to run, but her companions still looked confused and terrified. Seeing the two on their feet and moving was a good sign, but the poor things could not have been more than twelve or thirteen years old. Add ball busting to the list of things I planned to do to anyone else that stood in my way.

I eased out of the trailer, sweeping my rifle from left to right, securing our position, then moving to the edge of the trailer. The commotion in the yard had died down a bit, which allowed me to hear one distinctive voice above the rest.

"You sons a bitches had enough? Put yer goddamn guns away an' let's finish this."

Flint!

What in the hell are you doing, you crazy bastard?

I did not have time to waste. I wanted to run and help, but getting the girls to safety came first. One by one, they hopped out of the trailer, Charlotte helping the others as they came.

"Listen, run with me. Right behind me." I nodded at Charlotte. "Go!"

Like children playing a game of hide and seek, we scurried from the rear of the trailer to the passage past the horse stalls.

"Take him out, Tank," I heard one man yell as we ran. As we slipped into the stall corridor, I came to a sliding stop at the sound and echo of a single gunshot. The girls bumped into my back like Mo, Larry, and Curly in a *Three*

Stooges skit. The hairs on my neck prickled as ice water filled my veins.

Jesus, did they just shoot him?

Opening the stall door nearest me, I pulled Charlotte's arm, encouraging her to lead the others inside.

"Hide in here. I will be right back."

"You're leaving us?" Charlotte's voice squeaked. "Mr. Callahan, please don't go."

"I'm not leaving you, but I have to help Flint. Stay quiet and hide in here with the door closed. Nobody knows you are missing, so nobody will be looking for you."

"But what if something happens to you?"

I paused. Charlotte made a valid point. Her head tilted to one side as if she knew she had struck a chord.

"Nothing is going to happen to me. Trust me. Can you do that?"

Charlotte nodded reluctantly, then mustered a forced, "Uh-huh."

Summoning what strength she had left, Charlotte wrangled the girls to the rear of the stall and hid with them beneath a small tack shelf. It was a tight fit but did the job. I stepped into the passage and closed the door, then hurried on silent feet back to see what was going on outside.

Slinking around the corner to the main wall, I made the dangerous decision to creep to the edge of the large barn door. Bar S men stood just outside in a semi-circle, their backs shining in the big rig's beaming headlights. The guards with the guns stood side by side, spectators to the event in front of them. Beyond the human blockade, I saw the legs of two men. The one wearing black pants and shoes that looked more like slippers or TOMS paced back and forth. The other man stood still, his jeans like tree trunks, his boots like roots sticking out of the ground.

With one sweep of the leg, the man kicked out. A rolling wave of "Ooooos," and one "Hell yeah!" did not over-shadow the dull thud and *umph* that followed.

The line of onlookers shifted, causing a gap that allowed me to see my worst nightmare come to life. Flint lay on his back clutching his right leg. I could see blood spilling over his fingers, but it was the look on his face that concerned me so. Blood streaked across his cheeks. His nose looked broken, but the fire in his eyes burned brighter and hotter than I had ever seen.

Flint was a fighter. He was one to never give up, regardless of the circumstances. His toughness was branded onto him by years of ranch work, servitude to miles of endless land, and the wrestling, wrangling, and rearing of hundreds of heads of livestock. That, and the son of a bitch never took shit from anyone.

Rolling over to his hands and knees, he never took his eyes off the man who kicked him—the man who I could now clearly see, as he circled to Flint's weak side, as Big Fucking Bill. He reared a leg to kick again, when the man in black pants shuffled his legs and shouted.

"*Gòu le, bié wán yóuxì le.*"

Big Bill stopped. The line of onlookers jerked their heads, all staring in the same direction, all focused on the mysterious Chinese man.

I watched in horror as the Chinese man aimed a pistol at Flint. Staying on the sidelines was now off the table. I raised and steadied my rifle, let a half breath escape my lips, and pulled the trigger.

CHAPTER SIXTY

Every moment holds meaning in a gun battle, from the first pull of the trigger to the last wisp of smoke trailing out of the barrel after the final shot. Everything in between follows a precise sequence, yet if just one element skews, the game can change dramatically.

At the same time that I depressed the trigger, the gap in the line of men shifted. The blast of my rifle sent the whole yard into a flurry as my shot disrupted the execution but missed its foreign mark. Instead, the bullet clipped the left shoulder of the smoker, an unarmed man but just as guilty as the rest. Marred by blood and torn fabric, the man lurched forward, collapsing on the ground, writhing. He would live unless he decided to do something stupid. The men around him scattered, leaving him in the line of fire.

Jerking around before the echo of my shot dissipated, the Chinese man aimed at me and fired three shots. I ducked, then rolled twice, firing each time I came to my stomach, then popped to my feet and ran to the edge of the rig for cover. The two armed guards had whirled around, aimlessly letting loose the entirety of their magazines at the barn. Wood splintered in explosive bursts. The man in the hat drew his gun, hesitating as he scanned for a target. The instant he spotted me with him in my crosshairs, he let his gun fall and spun around to run, just a heartbeat before I fired. The man I had shot in the shoulder clawed his way to his knees, then rose on wobbly feet and, like a drunk fresh off last call, staggered toward the house. Flint lay flat on his stomach, head whipping around as he followed the action. Behind it all, I saw Big Bill and the Chinese man run for the house. As they fled, the Chinese man called out.

"*Shā guāng tāmen!*"

The Chinese guard responded immediately. He turned around and advanced on Flint. With expert timing, the Mexican guard released the empty magazine from his weapon and replaced it with a new one. Using controlled bursts, he continued to keep me pinned down next to the truck. I watched, dodging bullets and ricochets as the Chinese guard raised his rifle, barrel to the sky, then slid the bolt handle back to load what was meant to be Flint's fatal round. I leaned out to fire but was met with immediate resistance. One bullet whizzed past my ear like a killer housefly searching for meat.

The Chinese guard was closing in on Flint. He lowered his rifle. Flint rose to his knees and glared at the man. If he was to die, he would embrace his fate head-on. The guard's lips moved. His face contorted into a wicked grin, and then disintegrated in a smattering red mist and shredded flesh and bone.

Leaping from behind his El Camino, Ramón sprinted toward Flint with his silver-plated Benelli in hand, fresh smoke drifting from its barrel. The blast rocked the yard, causing the Mexican guard who had been engaged with me to turn and take aim. He was quick to shift gears, but I was quicker.

Stepping out from my covered position by the truck, I raised, aimed, and fired all in one fluid, expert motion. My bullet tore through the air, ripping into the Mexican guard just below his armpit. His chest exploded as the bullet severed his spine and exited at an altered trajectory through the front of his body in a spewing mass of jagged ribs and gushing red.

Ramón made it to Flint and helped him to his feet. Together, they retreated to safety behind the El Camino.

I swept my weapon side to side while running to meet them. Rounding the front of the car, I slid to a stop behind the driver's side door. Ramón kept watch near the tailgate. Flint rested with his back leaning against the rear wheel. When my dust settled, we locked eyes.

"Plan workin' out like ya figured, Cass?" Flint said with a grumble.

"Yeah, right." I looked over at Ramón. "Thought you were just killing the cameras."

"Cameras, lights, they're all connected, I guess. Call it a bonus."

Unobscured light from the big rig's headlight filled the yard. Its glow encapsulated the El Camino, allowing me to see as if we were under a full moon. I looked at Flint's injuries. His face, his leg, both bathed in a mix of crusting and fresh blood.

"You don't look too good," I said.

"Ain't nothin'. Had worse done ta me years back in Mexico. Didn't work out so well for the other guys then. Reckon that'll be the same tonight."

I lifted my head to look at the house through the car windows.

"You've got great timing, Ramón. Where you been hiding out?"

Ramón crouched behind the car and looked at me.

"Like before, I had to play the part, Cass. After they told me the job, they said I had time to kill, so I went back to the car and waited. With the armed guards and that crazy Chinese *pendejo* carrying on, I wasn't going anywhere until I had to."

Ramón shifted his weight to one side and peered around the car before continuing.

"Then Flint shows up, fists flying with the big guy. Everyone crowded around, turning it into an all-out tag team event—Bar S vs. Flint. He got the best of most of 'em, but the big guy played dirty, coming at Flint from behind with a solid crack to the face. That knocked him down. There were too many weapons for me to jump in the middle of it.

"When the Chinese guy in black pajamas turned his gun on Flint and shot him in the leg, I reached for my shotgun and slid out of the car. With the crowd moving and Flint caught between the big guy and the Chinese *cabrón*, I didn't have a clear shot, but damn, for a second, I didn't think I'd need one." Ramón patted Flint on the shoulder. "This *loco de mierda* looked up at everyone, cursing them to finish the fight like men. That's when everything escalated, and you showed up, guns blazing."

Flint's breath was heavy. He hurt, but was not going to let anyone, let alone me know it nor let it stop him.

"Raven," Flint started to say.

"Don't know yet where she is but I did find Charlotte and two other girls. They're hiding out in the barn. We need to get them out of here."

"No. Shut up an' listen, Cass. Raven is in the house. Before I left the security shack, I heard someone over the radio bitchin' that the guard he clobbered," Flint thumbed at Ramón, "hadn't shown up fer duty inside. Before runnin' fer the house, I tied him up with the keyboard cord an' stuffed a half-eaten bologna sandwich in his mouth in case the sumbitch woke up and tried to yell fer help. I got to the house with no problem and got a few good looks inside before I was spotted. Course, the dumbass with the hat bought my story 'bout bein' extra help an' let me be. Wasn't 'til I ran into that big fucker from the other night that let the cat outta the bag."

"How do you know she's inside?"

I looked at that big SOB square in the face an' told him I was goin' in after her. Had my gun tucked in my britches, and went to pull when that slanted-eyed, no good..."

"Skip that and tell me, Flint. Where in the house is Raven?"

Flint huffed.

"Fine. I read it in the man's eyes. Ya ever see the look on a horse's face just as they're gettin' rounded up fer slaughter? They know what's in store for 'em. The truth of their fate is in their eyes. That's how I know. I saw how Big Bill looked at me when I said it."

The yard had become quiet. Too quiet.

"Flint, I know you want to come with us to find Raven, but I need you to do something else."

"Horseshit, Cass. She's the only reason I'm here."

"And the best thing you can do right now to help her is to not get yourself killed. Charlotte is holed up in the barn in one of the stalls with two young girls. Prisoners I found in a goddamn cage in the trailer. I need you to get to them and keep them safe. Feel free to bust any balls that get between you and them. She'll recognize you. She'll go with you. Get them off the ranch if you can but stay out of sight."

Flint's jaw hardened.

"Do that for Raven."

Flint stared straight ahead. I could see that the bucking horse in his mind was more tumultuous than ever. With a grunt, he bent both legs, stretching the stiffness from being on the ground and testing his injury's resolve.

"When this is all over, you an' me are gonna go on a whoopti-do, Cass."

I looked at him, confused. Ramón grinned, bobbing his head as if he understood what Flint had said. Before I could question Flint, he pulled himself to his feet and shuffled to the front of the El Camino. Crouched in a racer's stance, Flint glanced over his shoulder.

"Take yer own advice, Cass."

I looked on.

"Don't get killed."

With a forward lunge, Flint ran to the barn, his limp pronounced but his speed unfaltering. I watched until he disappeared into the shadow of the doorway, then turned back to face Ramón.

"Whoopti-do? What the hell is that?" I asked.

"*Ese*, I could tell you, but..."

Ramón laughed to himself, making me wonder if he was reminiscing about having been a part of this mysterious *thing* in the past and knowing what I was in for, or what.

"Great."

Shifting gears, I scooted closer to Ramón.

"New plan," I said. "You take the side door by the garage. I'm storming right through the front."

"That's crazy, Cass." Ramón squinted his eyes and curled his lips into a menacing smirk. "But I like it."

"We know they are armed and that they have Raven somewhere inside," I continued. "But I'm not waiting around or negotiating with anyone. Not tonight. There are two other guys hiding somewhere, but they look out of place. Maybe business associates. Definitely not hired guns. You have a problem with getting a little dirtier than expected, stay here and have the car ready to roll."

"Callahan, it ain't even a question. I'm going in."

I nodded, then positioned myself at the front of the El Camino.

"On three," I said.

I dug my feet into the dirt, feeling my leg muscles twitch. It had been minutes since I had felt the burn on my hand, but now, in the eye of the storm, my heartbeat pulsed through my palm.

I liked how our numbers stacked up against theirs and that even with the truck's beams illuminating part of the yard, there were plenty of shadowy pockets in which to hide. All in all, I felt good about what we were about to do.

"I'm coming, Little Bird."

One, two...All that changed when the power returned to full capacity and the lights on the Bar S turned on.

CHAPTER SIXTY-ONE

Artificial light cascaded all around the property pulling us out of the dark and into what felt like The Strip in Las Vegas. I had to squint to adjust to the sudden brightness.

"Three!" Ramón's voice yelled.

With reckless abandon, he charged across the yard toward the garage door entrance, his silver-plated Benelli rocking back and forth in his grip. It was a good thirty yards away, but under the spotlights seemed more like one hundred. He was nearing halfway by the time I registered that he had charged.

Go. Go. GO!

I heard myself screaming inside my head to get moving. Leaping from behind the hood of the El Camino, I made a mad dash for the front door. As I advanced, I heard shots ring out and saw dirt fly in Ramón's wake, missing each step by inches. His head start, albeit dangerous as hell, was the distraction I needed to make it to the front porch without drawing fire. Shots continued as I sprinted ahead.

Taking a quick glance at Ramón just before I hit the

porch, I saw he had safely made it around the edge of the house. The front door grew larger in front of me with each pounding step, but I did not stop. Instead, I accelerated, summoning everything I had in the tank, and soared over the porch. In one thunderous crash of splintering wood, I barreled through the door, ripping it from its hinges.

Landing in a small foyer, I swept my rifle left and right. All was clear except for the blank, taxidermized eyes that stared down at me from their mounts on the wall. Deer, mountain goats, a bobcat, and even a rattlesnake poised to strike, it looked like Ace Ventura's worst nightmare.

The foyer led in two directions on opposite sides of a rear window. To my right, there was a sitting room with an old, red felt-covered couch positioned at an angle so all who were seated could have a clear line of sight of the entrance. A wrought iron coffee table stood in front of the couch with back issues of True West Magazine, Time, and a copy of The San Antonio Express News. The paper was opened, then creased like a triangle and left dangling over the edge of the table. I made a quick tactical sweep of the room ending up behind the couch. From my position I could not only see toward the front door, but past it down a hall that ran the length of the house.

A thought struck me funny in that the *feng shui* of this house was all wrong—exterior doors opening directly to face other doors, windows aligned across from windows, creating a straight path for energy to rush through and escape. In feng shui, such direct alignments are said to disrupt the natural flow of qi, allowing prosperity and harmony to slip away as easily as the wind through an open window. This architectural anomaly meant jack to me, but to the Chinese living at the Bar S, it could have made them quite uncomfortable. Maybe that was how I came to enter their picture. Their balance and fortune were fucked.

I glanced at the paper on the table as I made my way back toward the foyer, reading a headline that had been underlined in black marker. *Chinese detained at the border in Eagle Pass...Who's Got Next?*

"Keeping tabs on current events, or keeping track of comrades in arms?" I whispered to myself.

Passing through the foyer, I headed into the heart of the house. With Ramón sweeping the opposite side, I had expected that he would be in a position where I could see him by now. Where the hell was he? Each step brought me nearer the next door, mirrored by another door. It was like a horrific game show where I had to pick the winning room. Choose wrong and it could mark the end for all of us.

Pressing my back to the wall, I opted first for the room whose door was ajar. Using my foot, I nudged it farther open. Leading with the barrel of my AR-15, I entered the room, sweeping and clearing it within seconds. The room was a small guest room, neatly organized with a hand-woven Mexican quilt draped across the bed, a cedar chest at its foot, and a large oil painting hung on the wall depicting a scene from a traditional Spanish bullfight.

With a sword poised to strike in one hand, El Matador taunted a bull with a red *muleta* that he held in the other, daring it to charge. Blood dripped from the bull's shoulders where colorful banderillas had been stuck by eager banderilleros.

I stepped back to the door, my nose snorting breaths of anticipation just as the bull, injured as it was, prepared to charge. Matadors may have been masters of their arena, but even they met the same fate of the bull from time to time.

I stared at the door across from me and prepared

myself to enter yet another unknown arena, when a familiar voice echoed softly from down the hall.

The words melted my heart and enraged my being as their sounds were both tender and tormented.

"Cass, don't come any closer."

I peered around the doorframe, looking down the hall to where the voice had originated. Standing in the middle of the passage with arms and legs trembling, eyes pleading, and a single line of blood running down her cheek from a gash on her head, was Raven. Rising into view behind her was the Chinese man in black. He held a gun that was pressed into the nape of Raven's neck.

CHAPTER SIXTY-TWO

"You do not know when to give up, Mr. Cass. I give you plenty of chances, more than some of my own, I think."

Raven's head buckled as the Chinese man pressed the barrel of his gun deeper into her skin. It was...*him*. Standing before me, breathing what I hoped were his last breaths, was the man I had fought at the park the night our unexpected visitor showed up at camp. *Small fucking world*. He was the man whose face I saw in the mirror of the truck when I stopped to help the stranded travelers, the man who walked so nonchalant with Big Bill and his henchmen into Rancho Arroyo Steakhouse for a normal meal. Nothing was normal for guys like him. They could not *be* normal. I glared at him, wanting to rip his arm off and beat his beady little eyes off his smug face. The pit of my stomach burned as I stood there, under the gun and unable to pull Raven to safety.

"Put down your weapon, Mr. Cass."

I locked eyes with Raven. Fear, love, forgiveness, worry, confusion—a juggernaut of emotion swirled between us.

"It's going to be all right, Rave."

I knelt with both Raven and the Chinese man in my sights and set my AR-15 on the floor in front of me.

"Slide it away. Use your feet." I cringed at the sound of his voice but did what I was told. "And the gun in your belt, as well. You Americans are not too good at hiding your weapons. Always predictable."

I was fast on the draw, but too many variables kept me from making a clean shot at the man's head over Raven's shoulder. I reached behind my back, fingers curling around the handle of my Glock 17, its cold steel urging me to pull the trigger. Instead, I tossed the gun into the seat of an armchair near a small nightstand that overlooked the Bar S through a window. I could picture Roy Sinclair of the Double SS sitting there once, sipping coffee and silently criticizing everything happening in the yard. That son of a bitch was never satisfied.

As I stood, my backpack shifted and clinked.

"More surprises, I see," the Chinese man said, smiling. "Take it off."

One arm at a time, I slipped my backpack from my back and set it down at my feet. I saw the top zipper was parted enough to slip two fingers through to the inside, but how could I chance any move that would get Raven killed. There was only one option in my pack that would ruin the day for all of us, but I wasn't ready to take things that far, yet.

"There. Now, let her go."

"Oh, Mr. Cass. So sorry for your confusion. Nobody is going to be let go."

At that moment, Big Bill entered the room. He dragged Ramón by the collar behind him.

"Found this beaner poking his nose, and a pretty mean looking shotgun, into the kitchen. Guess he's more interested in getting killed than driving for us, Mr. Li."

There it was. Finally. A name I could tattoo on the forehead of this Chinese motherfucker. *Leah. Lee. Li.* Hearing it caused a recurrence of the name to spin in my mind like a skipping record. There was something familiar about the name, like knowing the lyrics to a song but being unable to remember its title.

Leigh, Lee, Li.

Like an electric shock, sudden and overwhelming, a rush of thoughts, names, and places surged through my mind. Random bits of meaningless information, once scattered and forgotten, now spun together, swirling like stars streaking by at warp speed.

Bruce Lee, Jet Li, Lee Trevino, Stan Lee, Lee Goldberg, General Lee, nothing fit. Faster and faster, the name echoed through my ears. *Master Lee*—my first Taekwondo instructor, *Uncle Lee's Cafe*—best Asian food on the west side of Houston, *Lee's Liquor*—an establishment I busted for selling alcohol to minors, whose nephew, *Frank Lee,* represented him in court and found a way to get his uncle off with a slap on the wrist. God, I hated lawyers!

Like a car crashing into a brick wall, the gears in my head stopped spinning, leaving only one name remaining to float in the darkness behind my eyes.

Lee, or is it *Li*...as in Horowitz, *Li,* and Calderón?

Son of a bitch, the damn law firm! Were they all in it from the start? How far did this conspiracy go, and what more were they hiding? Planning?

Big Bill let go of Ramón. Unconscious, his head banged against the solid wood floor with a dull thud.

"What do you want to do with these two?" Big Bill asked of Li.

A sadistic smile drew from the corners of Li's lips.

"This one," he said, jamming his gun ahead and causing Raven's neck to buckle. "I will hold on to her. She is too old to be offered for sale, but she is beautiful."

Big Bill looked at me and smirked.

"How's that make you feel, Callahan? Guess you should have kept to your own business instead of getting into ours."

"What goes on around here *is* my business, Bill."

Big Bill stepped around Li and Raven, squaring off with me directly. His frame was wide and solid, as was his height over mine.

"Seems to me, our people have already made it clear what would happen if the county continued down this path, or didn't your good friend, the sheriff, tell you?" Big Bill paused, raised a finger and his eyebrows as if an idea had just struck him. "Wait a minute. Didn't I hear that he had some sort of accident? Hit a deer or something? Be a real shame for him to die on account of reckless driving."

My blood boiled.

"Say what you want, Bill. I know you ran him off the road just like I know y'all had that Chinese man killed."

Big Bill's face drooped with sarcastic grief.

"Oh yeah? The cook. That's right. Sure was a shame about what happened to Kang. His wife was pretty beaten up by it, too. Bet you're wishing you could have detained them when you had the chance." Big Bill stepped close enough to me that I could smell and feel the heat from his breath on my face. "No, you let them go without a fight. And now, here you are, caught trespassing again with a loaded weapon and intent to kill written all over your face. Bet if I looked outside we'd see some of your helpless victims already."

His wild descriptions of what lay in the yard made me smile at his ridiculousness.

"Helpless victims? You mean the ones holding the automatic weapons?"

Big Bill smiled back at me, but it was not a friendly look. I saw his neck muscles tense. His jawline stretched the skin around his face as he twisted the smile into a clenched jaw. Between freshly gritted teeth, Big Bill spoke with a hiss.

"I'm going to enjoy this."

"Ai-ya!"

The high-pitched scream sliced through the tension in the room with a razor-sharpness equal to that of the knife plunging into Mr. Li's back. Big Bill whirled around. Li's eyes bulged wide as he arched his spine. His arms fluttered, losing their grip on Raven, but not his gun.

The flash was instant. The blast was deafening, but my own screams overpowered its rapport, reaching pinnacles of terror and rage unlike any I had ever known as I watched Raven fall.

CHAPTER SIXTY-THREE

Blood sprayed from Mr. Li, showering the face of the Chinese woman as she removed the knife from his back and recoiled for a second strike. Bursts of angry Chinese shouts, a mix of pain and rage, male and female, became the soundtrack for the next few moments. Raven rolled on the floor, covering both ears with her hands. I bolted ahead, but the brick wall that was Big Bill turned around and blocked my path. Big mistake. Even the mighty fall under pressure, and I was a goddamn jackhammer ready to explode.

I charged ahead, lowering my shoulder into Big Bill's ribs with the force of a linebacker creaming a QB. He absorbed most of the hit, grabbed my waist on contact, then lifted me off the ground and twisted, throwing me against the rear wall of the room. I crashed into ancient paneling, cracking the wood with my hurling body. I slid down the wall, catching splinters on the way to the floor. Big Bill was two steps closer to me by the time I sprang to my feet, which gave me no time except to dodge his powerful right hook. His fist breezed over my head, smashing a hole in the wall where my face had just been. Pulling his fist back, blood caked his knuckles, but it looked as if he felt nothing.

The yelling and screaming continued as the Chinese woman stabbed down with the knife again. Its blade glinted in the light, hungry for slicing and dicing, indifferent to whether it cut through live flesh or processed meat. Li, anguished from the surprise attack, twisted his body before the woman could bury the blade a second time. The razor-sharp edge, offering only a taste of blood, merely nicked his forearm. Li let out a vengeful yell, then lunged at the woman causing her to trip over Ramón's crumpled body and fall. When she hit the floor, the knife flew out of her grasp, clanking and sliding on the hardwood floor coming to rest half a room away.

Enraged and in agony, Li stumbled forward, his hands reaching for his dropped gun.

Big Bill lunged at me again. I blocked his first punch with my left forearm and countered with a right hook that struck the side of his face. I had aimed for a debilitating nose shot, hoping to disorient him long enough to circle around and grab a weapon. But despite the solid hit, my fist only seemed to enrage him further. Snorting like a mad bull, his eyes flared as he stretched his arms wide and jumped, his tree trunk legs and long reach giving me little time to react. I grabbed a floor lamp, minding its own business in the corner of the room where I was being herded, and swung it like Jon Snow fighting a White Walker. The lamp's shaft bent around his shoulders on impact, but it bought me the split second I needed to escape his trap.

As I jumped, then tucked and rolled out of the corner, I saw Li pick up his pistol. Raven remained on the floor, now motionless, her hands no longer covering her ears.

Oh god. Please. PLEASE!

I surged ahead as Li turned the gun on the Chinese woman, ramming him from behind. My face and shoulder were buried in the small of his back as I lifted his light-weight frame off the ground. Fresh blood smeared my cheek and pressed beneath my nose like Vick's vapor rub. The metallic tang of his blood filled my head, where I could taste its coppery filth in the back of my throat.

Li screamed, sounding like a high-pitched Beijing opera performer. Blasts erupted one after the other from his gun. Ceiling shrapnel rained from above as Li's attempted murder spared the woman but killed the house. Our momentum carried us into the hallway beyond unconscious Ramón and the blood-spattered and frightened Chinese woman, ending with a violent crash into the kitchen when our struggle caused me to slip on the linoleum floor.

Rolling, I wrapped my legs around his torso from behind and slipped my left hand over his mouth. Blisters on my palm burst. Serum lathered my hand and smeared on Li's lips and chin. Wriggling in a slithering mass of blood and bodily fluid, Li was able to slip free of my legs. Before escaping completely, I grabbed his elbow with my right hand and pulled down hard. Losing his footing, Li face planted on the floor next to me. With a slashing move of my body, and still grasping his elbow, I twisted his arm around his back and lifted with enough force to break his arm and separate his shoulder from its socket. The snap of his arm was distinct, but his shoulder slipped quite easily out of place, reminding me that it was the second time I had injured Li in this way. Screams continued, but their tone changed from rage to mercy.

I backed off in time to see Big Bill walking down the hall as if nothing urgent was on his mind. He had no reason to show fear, especially now that he was holding my AR-15 in his hands.

"You're one irritating son of a bitch," Big Bill said. "Like a cockroach that just won't drown no matter how many times you flush it down the toilet."

He pulled the receiver back, then let go, ushering a fresh round into the chamber. It was not a necessary action, as he expelled a perfectly good round from the rifle, but I supposed it was his dramatic way of showing me he had the upper hand.

"The thing about cockroaches is that you have to stomp the crap out of them if you want to be rid of them. They crunch pretty damn easily under a boot heel."

"How's that workin' out for you?" I asked. "Pretty man like yourself isn't one to wear boots all that much. I'm right about that, anyway."

Big Bill laughed as if we were old friends, then pointed the barrel of the AR at me.

"I'll give you that one. I hate the boots. And the cowboy façade we have to put up? It's like my Chinese employers watched too many John Wayne movies. The money is good, but damn, I hate it out here. Give me a condo in Manhattan any day over the nothingness and foul smell of West Texas."

"Funny how greed overshadows what a man truly desires. Guess that's why I kept pursuing you. I got lost in the hunt, and now I'm paying the price."

"Damn right, you are. But don't worry."

Big Bill stepped into the kitchen—barrel fully extended, grin wiped from his face, eyes deep and hollow. A voice, soft yet melodious, like a songbird seeking its mate, called out from the shadowed darkness in the hall behind him.

"Cass..."

That sweet fluting vanished in the loud roar of a diesel

truck engine followed by its bellowing horn. Big Bill and I both looked to the kitchen window, then in sync, raised our hands over our eyes to block the surge of oncoming lights.

Oh, shit!

CHAPTER SIXTY-FOUR

The massive nose of the semi-truck barreled into the side of the house, crashing through exterior wood slats, snapping studs like toothpicks, and disintegrating the kitchen window in a rumbling chorus of grinding gears and chewing metal.

As the rig buried itself in the house, I leaped out of its path, dodging the displaced kitchen sink as it hurtled past. Dust and steam filled the air as the truck came to rest where Big Bill and I had been standing. Debris rained down, bouncing off the truck before scattering across the floor. The fizzing sound of engine fluid hitting hot metal and the hiss of air seeping from the brakes added to the cacophony of destruction. The sharp, hot smell of oil tickled my nose.

Finding my footing, I pulled myself up and surveyed the devastation in front of me. The old house was no match for the truck. I looked to the cab, but the windows, riddled with cracks and dust, kept me from seeing inside. But what I saw outside of the truck made my stomach lurch.

Caught under the front wheel like Robert Shaw

dangling in the jaws of a great white, Li's bloody torso jutted out. One arm flailed limply to the side, while his ruined arm twisted back at an unnatural angle behind his head. His eyes bulged, the left one bursting free from its socket. The truck's left turn signal flickered on and off, flashing a red glow over the body.

With a clank of old metal and a yawn of hinges rotating, the driver's door opened, and Flint slid out of the cab. Grimacing, he balanced on one leg against the rig. The other had a rag tied over his wound and was soaked from thigh to shin with red.

"Where are Charlotte and the girls?" I said.

"Safe. Tucked away like ya had 'em."

"How's the leg?"

"I'll live." Flint turned to look at what was left of Li. "Damn. Now that's some roadkill I ain't cleanin' up."

Debris continued to fall around the truck. Dust floated in the air like fresh ash from an erupting volcano.

"Come on, fight's not over yet. Check around the other side for Big Bill. I gotta get to Raven."

Flint moved toward the front of the truck as I slipped through the side door between the house and the garage. The door was gone, torn off its hinges when the truck crashed into the house. All that remained was an open, jagged frame. I sprinted to the front of the house, skirting the edge of the eighteen-wheeler sticking out of the kitchen. My shadow stretched out before me, chased by the harsh spotlights glaring down on the yard.

As I rounded the trailer, I came face to face with the three casually dressed men I had seen earlier. The one I had shot in the shoulder sagged between the other two as they supported him. I skidded to a sudden stop and their eyes bulged like those of an animal caught in the headlights of an oncoming car. The injured man's face was white as a ghost while the others wore a mix of confusion and fear.

"Stay put, fellas," I said. "And get some pressure on that wound of his. We have a lot to talk about."

I left them as quickly as I had met them and headed for the front of the house. But before I could reach the entrance, the door creaked open on its own. Raven stepped outside, followed by Big Bill holding my Glock 17 in his hand. His face was bloodied, and he walked with a limp. The front of his shirt was torn open, revealing a long scratch that looked like a lion's claw had raked across his chest.

"You can't kill me, Cass. That's not how this story's going to end."

Raven looked exhausted. Her face was pale and streaked with tears and anguish.

Ignoring Bill's remarks, I spoke directly to Raven.

"Everything is going to be okay, Little Bird."

Our eyes met. I mustered a smile, a simple gesture to help reassure her that what I said, I meant. Her lips flickered at the corners of her mouth but there was a shimmer in her eyes that spoke to me. It both excited and frightened me.

"Go on." Bill chortled. "Keep telling her that."

Switching my gaze to Big Bill, and with Raven in my peripherals, I saw both my enemy and my lover in one large, disturbing picture. Blood dripped from Bill's chin. He waved the gun back and forth, first pointing at Raven, then at me.

"The way I see it, there's only one way out of this," Big Bill said. "And you're not going it like it."

Raven slowly slid one hand into the waistline of her pants.

"I mean, this is Texas, right? A man has the right to defend his property at all costs, especially against a violent trespasser such as yourself."

I watched Big Bill, but also saw Raven remove her hand, then cup them together near her stomach.

"It's over, Bill," I said.

In the distance, I heard the faint wail of sirens screeching out over the open West Texas terrain.

"For you." Bill pointed the gun at me. "For her." He aimed the gun at Raven. "You were never going to win this one, Callahan. The second our people bought the ranch and moved in, you were out of the game. My employers have some big plans around here. Hell, it's a shame you're not going to be around to see it."

Big Bill pointed the gun back at me.

"It's going to be huge. Bigger than the both of you could ever imagine."

I shifted my gaze back to Raven. Even now, in the ragged state she was in, she was more beautiful than ever. I could not have loved her more.

"Rave," I said. "I'm sorry. But there is nothing in this world bigger than us."

Without a second thought, I charged Big Bill. The first blast of my Glock in his hands sliced through my bicep, knocking me off center. That slight shift saved my life as I felt the next blast zing past my ear like a swarm of wasps.

Raven turned into Bill, grabbing his arm with the gun with her left hand. She rammed her head into his chest and wrapped her right arm around his waist, but he was too big and too strong to be deterred by her attack. She struggled on, then as sudden as a flash of lightning, she stopped fighting him. He pulled free with very little resistance, then tossed her into his line of fire.

Raven's body flailed toward me. Nearly losing her balance, she caught her footing and was able to bound two steps further away from Big Bill. With outstretched arms, she grabbed hold of me, the force of our collision dragging us both to the ground. She landed on top of me, and I instinctively wrapped my arms around her waist, rolling to shield her from whatever was coming next.

My arm throbbed. I could feel the warmth of fresh blood seeping from the hole in my arm, the sting of my burned hand, the pain in my chest from an aching heart cursed by the recent decisions I had made and the words I could never take back. It was not enough to say I was sorry. What more was there to do? Entangled in each other's arms, I pulled my head back, locking eyes with her one final time, bracing myself for the final blasts of Big Bill's gun. My gun.

Every single memory flashed by in an instant.

Behind us, Big Bill laughed.

Beneath me, Raven's lips curled into a wide grin—an expression so out of place in this deadly moment that it froze me in confusion. Her hands slid up my chest, her eyes sparkling with something unexpected. She wriggled free from my grip, her gaze shifting to her right hand. In the harsh spotlights of the Bar S, with Big Bill's triumphant laughter echoing around us, a jolt of excitement surged through me. Dangling from her fingers was the pin to my M67 fragmentation grenade.

CHAPTER SIXTY-FIVE

B *oom!*

CHAPTER SIXTY-SIX

I lay on top of Raven for what felt like hours following the blast. Shrapnel—some solid, some wet—rained down on us, but I could not pull myself away from her. Not in that moment. Not ever again. When the ringing in my ears subsided, what had been the faint wail of sirens grew louder, closer. Behind us, wood crackled and crashed as the blast had damaged part of the porch. I would have stayed in her arms forever had it not been for Flint's voice cutting through the haze.

"Son of a bitch! Cass. Raven." Shuffling footsteps drew near. "Y'all okay?"

Raven placed a palm on my dirty face, her fingertips stroking my cheek. Her eyes, glowing and pure, met mine before she leaned forward and kissed the end of my nose.

"We're okay," she whispered.

Flint slumped to the ground beside us, helping us both sit up. Like pals camped around a firepit, we each surveyed the destruction around the Bar S. When our eyes met again, Flint cocked his head.

"One of y'all mind tellin' me what happened?"

I pulled Raven close as we both looked at Flint.

Flashing blue and red lights flickered across our faces, cast from two familiar Brewster County Sheriff's patrol cars pulling up to the scene.

"You know our Raven," I said, smiling. "She packs a punch and is always full of surprises."

Flint cracked an amused grin and reached out, placing a palm on each of our shoulders.

"Yer goddamn right about that."

EPILOGUE ONE

A hint of medicinal disinfectant lingered in the clean air of Chance's hospital room. Bedside monitors tracked and recorded his vital signs. An IV stand with clear bags hanging from hooks with tubes running through an infusion pump rhythmically distributed a controlled drip into his arm. A small, red glow surrounded his finger indicating his pulse oximeter was doing its job. Chance lay back, his bed inclined to a standard Fowler's position. He was alive and recovering quite well from his accident and surgical procedures. The only thing that seemed to bother him was the flavor and consistency of the hospital gelatin his nurse had delivered.

I sat in a solid wooden chair next to his bed, my hand and arm wrapped and set in a sling across my chest and looked into the eyes of my friend.

"They expect me to eat this goop," he said, stirring the orange gelatin with a kid-sized wooden spoon.

"It's fitting for a man your age, don't you think?" I said, smiling, though an underscore of discomfort prodded at me.

"Watch yerself, Cass. I may be laid up in bed, but I can still whip yer ass."

Chance's face turned serious. The air conditioning hissed overhead as we sat, eyes locked in a high noon stare-off. Wheels of a gurney in the hall squeaked in rhythm, rising and falling in volume as it passed by. My pulse throbbed through the gunshot wound in my arm, but I was not about to concede. The tumbleweed that toppled the fence came when a subtle twitch in his mustache broke the barrier between us, causing me to look away and hold back a laugh. As certain as a sunrise, Chance's mouth curled into his trademark Cheshire smile.

"Too easy, *mi amigo*." Chance shifted in bed and changed his tone yet again. "Tell me, Cass, how are *you*?"

Here I was, sitting with a man recovering from a horrific crash, and he wanted to know how I was doing? What could I say that he would accept as truth? The truth was, I was nervous as hell. I had something to tell him, but for whatever reason, the words would not cooperate.

When I did not reply, Chance looked away, then spoke as if I were standing on the opposite side of the room.

"Yer a lucky man, Cass. Yer surrounded by people who care about ya. Who want ta see ya succeed. Times have been tough recently. Hell, you know that better than anyone, but here's the good news, things are gettin' better every day." Chance refocused on me. "The way ya handled things at the Bar S, I wish I could go back and see things through yer eyes from the start, but I, like you"—Chance pointed his glowing finger at me—"we're both bound to duty, limited in the actions we can take by the county and state. It's a damn roadblock at times. Yer gut says one thing, the law says another. As yer friend, I can forgive ya for ignorin' orders. As the sheriff, it puts me in a tough spot, even though I have to admit that you were right all along, Cass."

I took a deep breath, then leaned forward, closer to my friend.

"The last thing I want is to muddy the waters between us, Chance."

I reached around and pulled an unmarked envelope out of my rear pocket and handed it to him. Without opening it, Chance tossed it at the foot of his bed.

"That what I think it is?"

I nodded. Chance pursed his lips, then glanced at the envelope teetering on a fold in the bedsheet.

"You need to know a bit more, Chance. I..."

Chance raised a hand, stopping me.

"I already know, Cass. Ya think just because I'm stuck in this bed, I don't keep tabs on the county? On my *people*?"

I sat back, slumping in my chair.

"POS Special Agent in Charge, Sharp. The son of a bitch couldn't wait to let me tell you myself."

Chance nodded.

"TITON is an elite group, Cass. Not more than ya can handle, but it's not like what we're doin' out here in the sticks. They walk a fine line between the letter of the law an' the code of the old west." Chance paused, then offered me his hand. "I expect you'll be around the office from time to time. Gonna miss openin' the new building next fall, but yer always welcome."

We shook and held tight as friends do when parting ways.

"And I expect you out at the CR, otherwise we'll both have Raven to answer to."

We parted hands and I stood next to his bed.

"This is not the end for us, *amigo*. Ya can always count on me ta watch yer six."

The door to Chance's room swung open, and a young nurse entered with a tray of medications and a glint in her eye suggesting that Chance may very well be her favorite patient. She crossed through the room, stopping next to his bedrail.

"Never off duty?" I asked, glancing back as I walked away.

"Never off duty."

Chance turned his gaze to the nurse, unfurled his smile, then looked back at me and winked.

EPILOGUE TWO

R 170 looked different as I drove a new model, agate black metallic Ford F-150 XLT 4x4 Super Crew along the lonely West Texas highway to the CR. It felt strange behind the wheel. I missed my jet-black Explorer, but at the same time, the change may have been just what I needed. The tires hummed on the black-top, each mile bringing me closer to home. Closer to Raven and Miguel. I needed to see them both.

In the days following the raid of the Bar S, Flint had refused my offer of time off from work to rest his leg. He resorted to his usual, "I've got shit ta do" statement, so I did not put up a fight. The 6M crew carried on with their ranching duties as if nothing out of the ordinary had happened. Word around the bunch was that their stay on the CR might last a little longer than expected. No one seemed out of sorts by the news. Cody was recovering as well and had been ordered to remain in the barracks until further notice to heal up, but he was too much like Flint, joining the crew on the range anyway and without complaint. Deep down, I think Flint expected that.

Raven saddled up as well, though I could sense she

had not yet processed everything that had happened at the CR and the Bar S. She would in her own time. She had grown tough since moving out west. It was an unexpected outcome, but I welcomed her transformation. She was a Callahan after all.

The three casually dressed men at the Bar S turned out to be couriers for Horowitz, Lee, and Calderón, who surprisingly became unreachable following the incident. Funny how the tables turned. Not every Californian wants to stay in Texas after all. The law firm's absence left the three couriers high and dry, though I'm sure that they would hold onto the story of what happened at the Bar S for years to come. Each would have twelve to eighteen months to think about how they would retell their story and dream about fresh margaritas, cosmopolitans, or whatever the posh drink of the hour was once they returned to city life.

Ramón was a fighter. He came out of the Bar S raid with only a few scrapes and one large lump on the head. He came out to the CR a few days after everything settled down to tell me he was heading back into Mexico for a while but to remember that he had eyes and ears everywhere.

"You need me, *ese*, I'll know," he said before driving away in his freshly polished and sparkling El Camino.

The gradual rise and fall of the road felt soothing. The distant mountains called to me, inviting me to explore their mysterious boundaries. Tempting as it was, I dismissed the feeling, content with where I was and the direction my life was heading. I had escaped the clutches of the darkness rising within me and was not ready, or willing, to subject myself to another journey into the unknown.

A chime from the truck's speakers signaled an incoming text, followed by a voice prompt to read or listen to the message. I pressed the accept/listen button on my digital display and a shockingly lifelike female voice graced the airwaves inside the cab.

"Text from Dr. Frannie Tasker-Lopez: '*Cass, you sure know how to keep me busy. I've finished my report on the half-sized Chinese fella and am submitting it to county this afternoon. Thought you'd like to see what I found underneath the blood and gore you so kindly sent my way. Tell Raven I said hi.*' Would you like to respond?"

"Sure," I said.

"Would you like to respond?"

"I said, sure."

"Would you like to respond?"

"Shit, truck. You and I are going to have to get used to one another if we're going to get along."

I pressed a button on the display to end the back and forth between me and the truck's AI, then pulled my phone from its cradle on the dash to look at the image attached to the text. The ashen gray color of Li's exposed torso had been scrubbed clean, accentuating the decay in his skin while highlighting a brilliant tattoo that covered the left quadrant of his chest.

A red-inked bird hovered above bamboo poles entwined with razor wire, its wings wide and feathers detailed with precision. The crimson ink blazed against the cool greens and grays. Its sharp beak curved down, fiery eyes glaring. In its talons, the limp body of a serpent dangled—a creature with dragon-like features: a hairy chin, large nostrils, short horns, bulging eyes, and a lolling tongue.

I lifted my foot from the gas, coasting the truck and steering to straddle the solid white stripe dividing the shoulder from the main road.

My first thought was that I had seen a similar tattoo before.

The truck slowed further.

I brought the phone nearer my face.

The tires edged over the sleeper lines, rumbling beneath and vibrating into my seat.

I know this tattoo, but it has to be a coincidence.

The tune to "Bad Boys" by Inner Circle rang out from the phone, startling me. Then the truck's AI voice spoke out.

"Call from Ray Tucker. Answer or ignore."

"Answer, answer, answer," I shouted.

The truck came to a complete stop on the shoulder when Ray's voice came over the line.

"Cass. How the hell are you?"

"I'm good, Ray."

"You're a bad fucking liar, Callahan, but whatever. I'll take you at your word. How's Raven?"

"Oh, you know. Nothing like blowing up the bad guys to get your mojo flowing."

"She's a tough cookie. I'm sure she's fine." Ray paused, then added, "Finally heard back from Duds."

"Who?"

My eyes remained fixed on the picture of Li's tattoo while Ray spoke.

"Dudley Peters. Duds. The guy I met at Cooter Brown's Place. Come on, Cass. The pictures of those Chinese fuckers."

"Right, right."

"You still want 'em?"

"Yeah. Send them now if you can."

"Hold yer horses." Ray's voice trailed away. A moment later, I received a text from him. The truck's AI did not interrupt the call to announce its arrival. "Let me know if they went through."

"Opening them now."

I fumbled my fingers over the buttons, clicking on the

text to access and view the pictures one at a time. The first was a group shot of the three Chinese caught at the Port of Houston. Swiping my finger to the left, I looked at the next few pics. Each was an individual photo of the men, resembling mug shots. Nothing looked extraordinary. I swiped again, then froze in place, my finger pointing in the air just above my phone's screen.

"Cass? Still there?"

"Shit."

My voice was but a whisper, but Ray heard.

"What is it, Cass?"

I toggled the phone to my photos app, then quickly scrolled back through the pictures.

"Hey, am I talkin' to myself or what?"

"Hang tight, Ray."

There, framed in black and illuminated by a camera's flash, was the picture I had hoped to find.

"Same tat," I said.

"So what? People get similar tats all the time. Remember the greaser we..."

"It's not just similar, Ray. It's exact."

Ray's voice dropped, more focused now. "Keep talking."

"Your guy from the Port, the guy I told you about in Big Bend." I paused to consider my thoughts, then felt a twist in my gut. "Li at the Bar S."

"Yeah?"

"Ray, we've got a connection here. The guy in Big Bend had a device of some kind. A device that someone would kill for. Turns out that killer was a Chinese guy named Li. What makes this thicker is Li was one of the assholes at the Bar S. He's dead now, but he was neck deep in human trafficking, and some kind of tech business if the contents of the trailer we seized says anything at all about him. Your guys at the port are what's throwing me, but here's the thing—if I were planning something big, I'd create a small, elite group to carry out the mission. I may be wrong, but I'd bet the farm that these tattoos tell us more about who they are and where they come from."

"China, Cass. Did you miss that part?"

"You know how many organizations over there want to see the United States fail, their government included? You realize that right across the border, we've already discovered numerous groups of Chinese working with the cartels to traffic drugs, humans, and weapons across the border. Shit, Ray. Maybe you listened to a drunk sharing war stories, and I might've been camping in the wrong place at the wrong time, but I think we both stumbled onto something huge."

As I talked to Ray, the phone buzzed with an incoming call. I held the phone so I could see the screen.

Raven.

"Ray, I've got to take this."

"Just like that, huh? Wham. Bam. Thank you, Ray?"

"Hey, I'll call you in the morning when I hit the road."

The phone buzzed again.

"The morning? Where the hell are you going now?"

"Grab some beer and clear a space on your couch. I'm coming to Houston, Ray."

IF YOU LIKED THIS, YOU MAY ENJOY:
ROWDY: WILD AND MEAN, SHARP AND KEEN

Blood, bullets, and tears bring Rowdy's world to a showdown...

Thrust to the mercy of the Mississippi river, thirteen-year-old Rowdy floats safely away as he watches the smoke rise from his burning farmhouse. His father, dead. His brother, dead. Both gunned down in front of him by a murderous gang of bandits.

Now alone in the world, Rowdy's perilous journey of survival begins, challenging and shaping him into the young man his father would want him to become. Pulled from the waters, he is given a chance by a lone river Captain and his mate. Working the trade routes between St. Louis and New Orleans, he learns to navigate safe passage. Rowdy grows strong working the river, but he must use his wit as well as his strength to confront a bullying crewman and survive a surprise attack by river pirates.

Facing life and death decisions, Rowdy's only option is to run. Survival is what Rowdy has come to know all too well. As his escape across the plains towards Lincoln, New Mexico, nearly claims his life, through a stranger's help, Rowdy recovers but is faced with questions about his rescuer's motives.

Blood, bullets, and tears bring Rowdy's world to a showdown. Fighting for what is right is his code, living life for others becomes his way, and staring danger in the face is what he must do if he can truly be Wild and Mean, Sharp and Keen.

AVAILABLE NOW

ABOUT THE AUTHOR

Chris Mullen is an accomplished and award-winning author, recognized for his captivating storytelling and literary talent. Hailing from Richmond, Texas, he is a proud graduate of Texas A&M University.

With a career spanning twenty-three years in education, Chris has been a dedicated teacher in both Kindergarten and PreK, cultivating his passion for storytelling and nurturing young minds. In 2019, he received the prestigious Connie Wootton Excellence in Teaching Award—a testament to his commitment to education and his profound impact on students' lives, bestowed upon him by the Southwest Association of Episcopal Schools (SAES). It was during this time that the idea for his young adult western adventure series, Rowdy, was born.

When he's not weaving stories, you can find Chris honing his craft in local coffee shops, pizza places, or even the neighborhood grocery store.

www.chrismullenwrites.com